Boundless HEARTS

D.D. LORENZO

Boundless Hearts
by

D.D. Lorenzo
Original Copyright 2020
2023 Edition
Formerly Titled: C-26
ISBN Paperback: 978-1-960755-02-5

Cover art: Samantha Cole and D.D. Lorenzo
Editing: www.abookaday.net—Alyssa Nazzarro
Proofreader: www.abookaday.net—Renita McKinney

All rights reserved. No part of this book may be reproduced or transmitted in any form or by any means, electronic or mechanical, including photocopying, recording, or by any informational storage and retrieval system, without the written permission of the copyright owner.

This book is a work of fiction. Names, characters, places, and incidents either are the product of the author's imagination or are used fictitiously, and any semblance to persons, living or dead, events, or locales is entirely coincidental.

This book was formerly titled C-26
Boundless Hearts is available in e-book and print from most online retailers.
2023 Edition License

If you would like to share this book with another person, please purchase an additional copy for each recipient. Piracy of intellectual property is a crime and is punishable by law. If you are reading this book and did not purchase it, or it was not purchased for your use only, then please return it to the appropriate retailer and purchase your own copy. Thank you for respecting the hard work of this author.

PRAISE FOR D.D. LORENZO

Praise for D.D. Lorenzo

"D.D. Lorenzo brings heart and heartache to BOUNDLESS HEARTS, a beautifully written tale of timeless love. After you're done catching your breath and wiping your eyes, you'll believe these characters, and all their incarnations, were truly meant to be."

~*Meredith Wild, #1 New York Times Bestselling Author, Waterhouse Press CEO*

"BOUNDLESS HEARTS is a hauntingly beautiful story of love and sacrifice that surpasses the constraints of time."

~*Aleatha Romig, New York Times Bestselling Author*

"*Phenomenal, breathtaking, awe-inspiring* are only a few of the many ways to describe BOUNDLESS HEARTS! D.D. Lorenzo has written an emotional story that spans lifetimes and the love that transcends them. For anyone who believes in love and soulmates, I highly recommend reading BOUNDLESS HEARTS. True love never dies—you take it with you."

~*Samantha Cole, USA Today Bestselling Author*

"BOUNDLESS HEARTS by D.D. Lorenzo is a surprising twist on a modern-day romance, full of heart and soul that passes through ages. Not your typical romance, BOUNDLESS HEARTS is much more. The author pulls you in from the first chapter and carries you along, feeding your need to find out the ageless connection of love."

~*Maryann Jordan, USA Today and International Bestselling Author*

"This book completely and utterly gutted me. D.D.'s writing is beautiful and tragic, and Skylar's journey is one that women everywhere will understand and fear to the depths of their hearts. But it's a book women need to read to find the courage to go on and hope for love again."

~*JM Madden, USA Today and New York Times Bestselling Author*

PRAISE FOR D.D. LORENZO

"By the time I made it through the prologue, tears were in my eyes. Gut-wrenching, heartbreaking, and soul-cleaving, the love Izzy and Abigail shared makes you believe love can transcend mere mortal bonds. I was sold at the end of the prologue. As for the rest of the story, it packs a punch. Your emotions are not safe, and they will be put through the wringer. If you're strong enough to begin this journey, you'll believe in the timeless nature of love. DeeDee Lorenzo crafts a beautiful story that is wonderful, captivating, and worth getting lost in. But know that every worthy love comes with a price."
~*Ellie Masters, USA Today Bestselling Author*

"BOUNDLESS HEARTS is a moving love story that grabbed my heart from page one and never let go. Different from any other romance novel I've ever read, this couple's incredible journey is real, uplifting, and heartbreaking, all at the same time. Ms. Lorenzo draws the reader in with her words, painting a vivid picture of not only the story's scenery and characters, but also their deep and genuine emotions. It's been a long time since a book made me cry, but this one absolutely moved me to tears. I highly recommend it to anyone who loves stories about love and unbreakable soulmates."

~*Anna Blakely, Amazon Bestselling Author*

DEDICATION

To the one who stole my heart
and
The one who gave it back

THE SEARCH

My heart, my center
My one
In a universe of stars and wonders
I looked for you
In the midst of space and time
I saw you
In a world of blood and bone
I kissed you
In the infinite scale of eternity
I loved you
In the lost and lonely darkness
I will always find you

PROLOGUE

April 15, 1912

"Don't be afraid, Abby. Just look at me."

There was no madness in Isidore Eisenberg's eyes, despite the chaotic circumstances. His tone was calming, something his wife desperately needed. She was shaking, the motion rattling her body all the way to the bone. Abigail didn't know if it was from fear, the cold, or a combination of the two, but her husband's sweet words tucked around her like a warm blanket. It was the only comfort she could feel.

"Do you think it will take a long time, or that there will be much pain?" Though Abby asked the questions, she wasn't confident she genuinely wanted the answer. It would take however long it would take; there was nothing more they could do. The outcome of their circumstances was bleak, at best.

As the couple lay side by side in the darkness, Abby tried to think of something on the bright side. She could only think of one good thing about their current situation, that they were together. She wasn't a brave woman. Though she hated knowing her sweet husband, Izzy, shared her fate, there was a part of her that was grateful she wouldn't have to face the horror of death alone. She looked into her loving Isidore's eyes, knowing full well he read her thoughts.

"Now, Abby," he said as his hand brushed her cheek, "don't worry, my love. This situation is something we can't control. We must look forward. Our time after today will be an eternity, dearest. What we're going through—what is happening right now—is a temporary inconvenience. We've always known death was a certainty, we simply never knew when it would come. And isn't this exactly what we'd hoped for? To be in each other's arms until the end of time?"

Abby nodded. Her husband always spoke the truth, and today was no different. From the day she'd married him, Abby had told him he was her life, her breath, and her destination. On that beautiful June day, she'd also promised to stay by his side for the remainder of her existence. By the end of today, her promise would be fulfilled.

An eerie whine was followed by a loud bang, causing the iron bed to shift. Muffled screams in the distance carried through vacant staterooms and hallways and found their way to the couple in cabin C-26. The sounds were frightening, immediately bringing to mind how quickly their impending fate would come to pass. Fear flooded Abby's veins with adrenaline. Her body jolted, every limb reacting to what she knew was in store. Death.

Though she quickly tried to hide her reaction and regain her composure, Isidore noticed. He knew her so well. Sadness veiled his gaze, a look Abby couldn't remember seeing in all their years together. But a solution for this disaster wasn't within her husband's control, nor was any of it of his making, for if Izzy could have changed their circumstances, she had no doubt he most certainly would have. He squeezed her hand, lassoing her torturous thoughts to capture her attention.

"Abigail, do you remember our second date?" His voice was hoarse, and his teeth chattered, yet he put on a smile for his beloved wife.

"Of course I do, but our first date stands out equally as well. Don't you remember? Our first date was a disaster."

"Yes. It was a pitiful excuse for a picnic," Izzy laughed. "My gallant attempt to chase the ants off of your skirt caused quite a ruckus—and captured the notice of everyone in the park!"

"Of course, it did! As the bugs fell off my skirt, they scrambled up my legs, and you went under my shift after them. It was scandalous! Imagine if you'd seen a young man putting his head up our daughter's skirt. I can't even fathom it!"

A broad smile hooked the corners of his mouth. His lips were perfect. They were plump, but not like a woman's. They were entirely masculine. Whereas some of the women Abby knew tried to keep their husband's advances to a minimum, she'd welcomed every kiss her Izzy had shared with her these past thirty years. Abby hadn't known much about life and men when they first married because she'd been but a girl. Still, from that very first night spent in Izzy's arms, he'd played her body as expertly as a finely tuned instrument, bringing it to life.

Their life together had been magical. The two enjoyed everything about each other. Abby especially loved her husband's touch. His simple, tender acts warmed her heart, and sex was a pleasure, despite her mother's instructions that she wouldn't enjoy that particular wifely duty. Her alone time spent making love with Izzy had never been a chore. Even at this age, and for as long as they'd been together, they'd done so often, sometimes more than once a day.

Though, for some, that might seem scandalous, Abigail relished the feeling of her husband inside her. The skin-on-skin connection was something she'd come to cherish. Remembrance of those times made her realize that stolen moments such as those would be no more, and the thought made her suddenly feel lonely.

Melancholy breezed through her mind. Elsewhere in the world, this night would play out very differently for a vast number of couples. Those lucky people would have hopes and dreams intermingled with rapture, where, instead, theirs would be, quite literally, drowned in grief. Where others in the world would enjoy touches and kisses holding promise, Abby and Izzy's would end with a final goodbye.

A shiver possessed Isidore. His arm shook as he tried in vain to control the reaction and hold Abigail close. She shifted, turning on her side to ease his discomfort. Pain and stiffness resulting from the frigid atmosphere only allowed her to move an inch at a time. She refused to let it deter her, and she moved, albeit slowly, to allow herself what little comfort she might find. When she had finally settled, they were so close that barely a breath separated them. Abby was drained from the small effort, and Isidore trembled from the cold. The lids of his beautiful, brown eyes fluttered, his dark lashes lingering on his face too long, freezing against the skin above his cheekbones. Abby knew that if she didn't keep him talking, he would fall into a deep sleep, never to awaken.

She spoke to him, not willing to let him go just yet. All that Abby needed was to hear his voice, even if it would be for the last time. She snuggled close, gently nudging him.

Her voice was barely audible as the freezing temperatures strained her vocal cords.

"Izzy, why did you ask if I remembered our second date?"

His eyes slowly opened. Even though he was exhausted, her sweet husband responded to the sound of her voice. He'd done the same when they were at home. He always had. Abby was never an inconvenience to Isidore, and, for that, she was grateful. Unlike their counterparts, her husband never behaved as if she were an obligation he had to tolerate. Every single day of their married lives, Isidore gave his wife the best of himself, never what was left of his time at the end of the day.

"Our second date?" Izzy paused, his memory was taxed, and his gaze thoughtfully traversed the blank space above them. Slowly he recalled asking the question just a few moments before. Abby traced over his forehead with a gloved hand, a gesture she'd repeated many times before, allowing her thumb to trail across his skin, lingering on the furrowed lines of his brow. "Ah, yes," he croaked. "I remember now." His concentration had given him another few moments of clarity, and he looked deeply into his Abby's eyes.

"By the time of our second date, my fate was sealed. You claimed me."

"Me?" Abby's question was laced with surprise. "What did I do?" She coughed as her trembling hand moved down his face and palmed his cheek. Izzy pulled her closer and held her tighter, the action causing a pained expression on his face. His eyes, however, reflected nothing but tenderness.

"It was your eyes, Abigail. They enslaved me. On our first date, they drew me in—those beautiful baby blues." He cleared his throat, his gaze turning a bit more serious.

"However, it wasn't until our second date that my poor heart bore the brunt of their impact upon me. Your gaze branded my soul. I knew by the end of that evening I never wanted to spend another day of my life without the pleasure of looking into them every night. It was that day I decided we would wed. I was determined to do whatever was necessary to make you agree to marry me."

Abigail's heart broke beneath the sincerity of his words. "Oh, Izzy!" A sob clutched her throat. The impact of their circumstances made her want to cry, but it seemed that even tears were denied her in the Arctic atmosphere. "It seems so cruel we've been robbed of our future together. I'm jealous of those that will survive this. It's maddening to think we planned our lives so meticulously, and now our careful preparations to enjoy the rest of our days won't come to fruition. I don't want this to be the end. Despite your high opinion of me, I am, admittedly, a selfish woman. I want more time with you."

Izzy gave his wife a tender smile. "As do I, my dearest, but we are not the controllers of our fate. One day at a time is how we measure our happiness, and even that we aren't promised."

Suddenly, the ship lurched, nearly catapulting them from their bed. A cruel, pain-filled shudder attacked Isidore as a piece of their luggage skimmed quickly across the rising water and slammed into his back. Abby opened her mouth to scream, but no sound escaped as Izzy's head snapped back from the impact. She quickly gained her composure, knowing their time was limited. She was terrified he'd been knocked unconscious, and what few, precious moments they had left, might have been stolen away by the collision.

"Izzy!" Abby's voice was panicked and hoarse, her cry a mere croak. "Izzy, please don't go! I need you."

Though the action was delayed, Isidore gradually opened his eyes. Relief flooded Abby as she gazed into the warm brown orbs that had anchored her through her entire adult life, and, though weak, she offered him a smile. Tucking her arm around his waist, it instantly locked into place due to the bitter cold.

"I'm not going anywhere without you, Abby. Hold onto me. Look into my eyes. Let the fear fade away."

Always the obedient wife, Abby did as her husband requested, anchoring herself in the love reflected in the warm, brown pools. It was the only heat between them. The piercing and penetrating cold had caused the blood to drain from his handsome face, leaving only a frosty remnant of his natural, healthy color. There were things to say, tender thoughts that needed to be voiced, and only this moment to express them.

"My sweet, sweet man. I'll say the same words to you now that I said the day we married. You are and have been, my life, Isidore Eisenberg. As I think upon our journey together, I have not one moment of regret. With my last breath, I want you to know that I am, still, desperately in love with you."

Her confession warmed his heart, and Izzy knew that they had, at best, moments to say their final words to each other. "I'm so sorry, my dearest love. This trip was supposed to be an adventure, not our end, but it's only one of the many destinations you and I have shared. It seems our next journey will, hopefully, be to heaven. I won't grieve, because at least there we'll be together."

Tears wouldn't come, but the effort stung the corners of Abby's eyes. A sudden movement made her flinch as a sloppy, frigid wave splashed atop her woolen coat. It triggered a layering effect starting with outerwear and then causing the skirt beneath it to quickly saturate with wetness. The heavy material slapped against her skin, so cold that it burned. The seawater was littered with chunks of ice, the pieces now quickly closing in on them as it rose above the top of the mattress. Abby trembled, terror clobbering her with the same ferocious impact as their ship when it hit the iceberg.

The room pitched at a near ninety-degree angle, and the bed catapulted into the wall at their feet. Again, Abby tried to scream, but dread clutched her throat, squeezing away all sound. She was terrified she would be torn apart from her husband and launched into open space. Sensing her fear, Isidore grabbed her with whatever strength he had, seizing any precious moments they might have left. In a flash, the water was around their necks, then chins, rising quickly to just beneath their mouths.

"Abby. Look at me."

Panicked, Abby looked one last time into the eyes of the man who had always made her feel safe and loved. Her quickened breaths burned her throat and chest, fueled by fear. They had seconds, at best, to share one last breath. Isidore had managed to squeeze out a final tear, and with blue lips and chattering teeth, pressed his lips one final time to the woman who would forever own his heart.

"Don't be afraid, my love. We'll be together again. Look for me. I promise; I will always find my way back to you."

CHAPTER 1

Present Day
BWI Airport, Baltimore

"Dear sweet baby Jesus! Do you think any of these people know to cough into their elbow instead of sharing their cooties with the rest of us?" Skylar Harrison mused aloud as she ground her teeth. She had little patience for stupidity. A self-professed germaphobe, her skin crawled every time someone sneezed in her direction.

"I know, right?" Skylar's friend and editor, Vincent Mannon, snapped back a retort as he sighed. He sat in the seat right beside her, sharing Sky's silent hope that their next stop on this business trip wouldn't be to one of those express medical centers for some antibiotics.

Sky huffed and nodded her agreement. She hated business trips, but they were a necessary evil for a journalist, and her work had taken her all over the world. She'd accomplished much, delving into the heart of her stories and describing them in such detail that many publications clamored for her work. *Time* magazine had featured her latest piece. Vince was convinced a Pulitzer was in her future, having witnessed the effect Skylar's stories had on her readers. He encouraged her to continue writing in-depth articles, but Skylar was now working on her third book as Eden Skye. Her goal was for her novel to hit the trifecta of bestseller lists, *USA Today*, the *New York Times*, and the *Wall Street Journal*.

Using her real name and reputation, she could quickly have done so. Instead, she'd adopted a pen name and was publishing her books independently. Once she accomplished what she'd set out to do, she planned to use her experiences in a series of articles. The world of self-publishing had upset the control traditional publishing houses once held. Amazon had opened a new world to those with vivid imaginations, and she planned to chronicle every detail of her experience and report what she found on her venture.

"I'll be right back." Vince left his backpack on the ground, giving Skylar a smirk as he approached the Cinnabon counter. A few minutes later, he returned, the proud owner of one of the giant, sticky pastries.

This wasn't anything new. Vince had a wicked sweet tooth and indulged it whenever they traveled. The airport kiosks were the perfect excuse for a treat, tempting and teasing even the most adamant dieter with savory sights and smells. Skylar followed Vince with her eyes, her judgmental expression having no effect on him as he returned to his seat with the sugary confection in hand.

"Don't you have diabetes?" She gave him a disapproving look.

"I do, but I take insulin." He shrugged. "Don't judge me."

"I'm not." Her statement was weak and flat.

"Yes, you are. It's not like I do this every day. Besides, I didn't eat breakfast," Vince scolded in a hushed voice. When anyone, especially Skylar, pointed out health concerns related to his glucose level, he became irritated. As far as he was concerned, his blood sugar numbers weren't anyone's business but his own. Besides, life was too short not to indulge in tasty food.

Just to spite her, he held the sticky roll in the air and moved it slowly toward his mouth, making a full display of taking that first, sweet bite. He then closed his eyes, enraptured as the sweet taste hit his tongue. When he opened them again, he smiled devilishly at her as he chewed.

Skylar rolled her eyes, turning away. It was too early to be goaded into a discussion about the benefits of a healthy diet. Instead, she reached down, unzipped the top of her laptop bag, and rummaged around for a pencil. Vince had his obsession with sweet things, and she had a thing for mechanical pencils. She loved them and purchased a pack nearly every time she went to stores like Target and Walmart. Pencils were forgiving. Their erasers permitted a person to make mistakes. What she didn't like were pens. Everything about them was too final. If she made a mistake with a pen, her OCD dictated she rip out the page and start all over again. No one had time for that nonsense, and that was what made pencils the number one choice of perfectionists everywhere.

"What are you writing?" Vince peered over Skylar's shoulder, making her pull her work a little closer to her chest.

"Nothing, nosey. Just looking at your edits."

"The edits are done." His tone was flat. "Move on to the next book." The hair on the back of Skylar's neck bristled. She didn't take orders, especially from someone on her payroll. There was a way to voice his opinion nicely, but Vince rarely did so.

"That isn't me, and you know it. I always re-edit when I get my stuff back." The monotone statement was one she'd delivered many times over. How long would it take for people to understand the luxury of being an indie author? Control. Skylar would always have the final say on her work as long as she published independently.

"I get what you're saying, but you have to ask yourself if it's the best way to use your time. That's why you pay an editor."

She rolled her eyes, partially because she knew Vince was right and, also, because she knew she should let the story go and move on to the next in the series. There was a vast difference between writing an exposé and writing fiction. The characters' lives she created were entirely at the whim of her imagination. There was only one problem, she became attached to her characters as she developed them. As she grew their personalities, they became as real to her as the man sitting beside her. It was hard to let them go once they were published. Not so with a piece for a magazine. Those were facts. This was fiction.

She ignored him, reaching into her bag once again to find a notebook. Vince's expression held a question. "I'm fleshing out the next story. I'm not exactly sure where I want to take it."

"So just get your thoughts down on paper and let me do the rest. Use your imagination, and I'll polish the words. You can't drag your feet, Sky. There's too much competition."

Though he spoke while chewing a mouthful of food, her disapproving look wasn't lost on him. He put his hand in front of his mouth to be polite and kept right on talking. Thankfully, only two more bites, and he'd be finished.

"This is really delicious. You should try one." He mumbled the words, pausing a moment to swallow. As he brought a napkin to his lips, he wiped away the flicked remnants of white icing that remained.

"Excuse me."

Skylar and Vince simultaneously looked up. The man sitting directly across from them broke in on their conversation. He had his laptop in front of him while he worked at one of the airport computer stations. Apparently, he'd been listening as they talked.

"I couldn't help but overhear you talking about edits and rewrites. Are you an author?"

His expression was sincere, his eyes gentle. Skylar was instantly drawn to the rich, velvety sound of his words. Some men were famous for their voices being their most prominent feature. This guy could have capitalized on that attribute.

"I'm an editor. She's an author," Vince replied. As expected, her editor's welcoming delivery and friendly mannerisms drew the stranger in.

"I'm sitting here working on a story. Do you mind if I ask you a few questions?" He gestured to his laptop, then returned his attention to Vince.

As expected, Vince saw the potential for a new client and didn't hesitate to engage. "Not at all. What can I help you with?"

As the two men continued their conversation, Sky tuned out from the world, turning back to her notebook. She had no trouble ignoring people around her and could completely disengage when necessary. It was a skill she'd mastered at an early age. She was an only child and a bookworm like her mother. Her early love of reading had taught her how to make observations and write the details within the scene. She was then able to transport herself into the stories she both read and wrote. Everything around her faded away in the distance as she immersed herself in a book. She'd traveled the world, fallen in love, and experienced heartbreak, all in her imagination. Her reader base for the new pen name was a faithful one. Although she'd created the persona of Eden Skye, she found she liked being Eden. It freed her to write romance the way she felt it should be. Sky took her obligation to the readers seriously because they fell in love with the people and places in the worlds she created, just the same as she did.

"Sky, are you going to answer him?" Nudging her with his elbow, Vince interrupted her thoughts.

"Huh?" She looked between the two men, confusion clouding her eyes as heat flushed her face. A prickling sensation raced up the back of her neck, the evidence of her embarrassment at having ignored them.

"Sorry. I wasn't paying attention. What was the question?"

"What kind of books do you write?" Again, the man's tone caught her attention, caressing her ears with much the same velvety effect as James Earl Jones, Alan Rickman, or Patrick Stewart. She loved voices, especially rich, deep ones. Skylar would eagerly listen to any of them read the daily newspaper and never lose interest.

She looked up at him, a smile filling her lips. "Romance. Contemporary romantic suspense, to be more specific."

"Ahhh. Romance." He exaggerated the phrase and bobbed his head, acknowledging her chosen writing genre with a crooked smile.

His expression wasn't lost on her, his was the response of many people when telling them she was a romance writer. She detected a hint of disapproval or condescension in his voice. Instantly, she felt the need to document his reaction with all the others she experienced for the exposé she had planned. Though he would never note the difference, her thinking morphed from romance writer to investigative reporter. It would only take a matter of minutes to tell if he was genuinely interested in her as a person or humoring her because he didn't take her work seriously. She took mental notes whenever the subject arose. What she'd discovered so far was that those on the outside of the romance genre dismissed love stories as nonsense. He would be shocked to know how many indie romance writers had healthy bank accounts.

She inclined her head as blood simmered in her veins. "Yes. Romance." The answer was defensive and clipped. It seemed she was always defending the choice to write love stories. She'd met people like him before. Judgmental. Quibbling about the content of romance novels. Everyone had an opinion. If the story was too sweet, it was judged as not realistic. Too erotic, and it was "mommy porn." She hadn't invented the chip on her shoulder; it was put there by the patronizing attitude of people who didn't even read the genre.

Really, what was the harm in escaping to love and passion within the pages of a book? She believed there was none at all and dismissed those with negative attitudes for something they knew nothing about.

Having been put in a position like this before, Sky stood her ground, trying hard not to be rude. It was more like digging deep, planting her feet in the statistics of how many romance books were sold each year. She prepared to state her position that, romance genre or otherwise, a writer was a writer regardless of content. "It seems I'm a hopeless romantic and write stories that, as a whole, generate over one billion dollars in sales per year." A disdainful smile was all she could muster for this asshole. She couldn't help but feel a little smug defending her career decision with facts. "So, you see? There's quite a market for love stories."

His eyes never left hers. She'd said her piece and readied herself for what would come next. Would he be an arrogant dickhead, or would he open his mind to something that was a little outside his wheelhouse?

She studied him, the moments ticking away as she readied herself to defend her position and that of the romance writing community. What she hadn't expected was the warmth she found in his gaze, and the longer they sat there, the more she found herself trying to resist the magnetism of the sweet, chocolate-colored pools.

CHAPTER 2

*G*rinning, he cocked his head. "What's your name?"

His deep baritone slightly short-circuited Skylar's concentration. He was a mystery that she planned to unravel. She chastised herself for forgetting her discipline as a reporter. She was supposed to stay impartial and not lose focus when investigating a story. His voice was at fault. It caught her unaware. She hadn't anticipated that something so inherently masculine would wrap around her like a fur coat and pull her in. She hadn't dated in a long time and, other than Vince, she didn't have too many conversations with men. Like a dry sponge, she soaked in the sound. The melodic tone sank into her muscles and bones.

Unfortunately for her, she didn't recover quickly enough for her liking, and her distraction cost her. The tight grip she'd had on her notebook relaxed. As her hand fell open, loose sheets of notes she'd tucked in between the pages tumbled to the floor, scattering everywhere on their way down.

"Shit." Immediately flustered, she cursed herself for the

faux pas. She tried to snatch the falling jumble of creased loose-leaf paper and Post-it notes, attempting damage control. It was too late. While she grabbed at some of the fallen items, she experienced the domino effect. Her arm bumped into her laptop bag. That, too, tumbled, spilling even more of her things to the floor.

If there had been a hole nearby, Skylar would have crawled into it. She looked anything but ladylike as she tried to catch the contents. Half the bag emptied, and she wasn't quick enough to save the other half. She was embarrassed. Her laptop, flash drives, pencils, and various other contents went everywhere. But fate wasn't done with her yet. To add insult to injury, she knocked her fresh cup of coffee, sending the venti to the floor, the plastic lid popping off when it hit. It splashed everywhere, wetting the papers that had preceded it. She was mortified. Now, not only was the research and working copy of her manuscript on the floor but they were drenched. All this time Vince watched as the disaster unfolded. His eyes went wide. All she needed were some clowns and elephants to go with the circus.

"Shit, shit, shit!" Fumbling through her pockets, she grabbed the small pack of Kleenex that was hidden within. With only a slight handful to help her, she grabbed the laptop, dabbing at any liquid that could seep through to the keyboard.

It took a moment for her editor to regroup and, when he did, he popped out of his chair. "I'll grab some napkins." The urgency in his voice meant he sensed her distress. He ran off, but Skylar didn't see him. She was too busy expending her efforts to save the electronics before they fell victim to the coffee. All she could picture in her head was destruction. One soaked keyboard meant the laptop was shot.

"Here. Let me help."

Skylar responded to the outstretched hands, though she wasn't sure who possessed them. She shoved a handful of dripping paper into open palms. The hands were much larger than her petite ones, the fingertips thick and calloused. She grabbed her Kindle and an extended battery pack, as well as four or five flash drives, and handed them to the Good Samaritan. Through her peripheral vision, she saw they were being placed on the seat next to where she'd been sitting before she looked like a failed juggling act.

She reached for the leather bag, quickly shoving in the items that had fallen, but hadn't been hit by the coffee. She was flustered when she quickly stood. It was definitely the wrong move. The sudden motion triggered off a flash of vertigo and she lost her balance.

"Whoa!" She wobbled as she tried to catch herself, reaching out for anything that would stop the spinning, when someone caught her arm before she fell to the floor. The jerky motion nearly sent her spiraling again when she crashed into a hard body before she had a chance to go all the way down. The collision ignited sparks that jolted her so unexpectedly her eyes grew wider than silver dollar size. *What the hell was that?*

Slowly, Sky regained her footing, her balance normalizing enough to stand. She looked up to thank the person who'd stopped the world from spinning when they had so quickly run to her aid. Brown met blue. As she looked into his eyes, the buzzing continued, the hum of electricity growing stronger as she was drawn into their warmth. Fireflies fluttered low in her belly. She struggled to breathe, her chest tightening as she stood captured by his gaze. The feeling was exciting, but it frightened her.

Sky moved back to identify the intercessor who'd placed himself between her and the floor. *Oh, God! Mister*

Anti-romance. He seemed to be in as much shock as she. As much as she wanted to turn away from him so she could shut down the power grid connecting them, she couldn't. A lock clicked between his eyes and hers. His pupils dilated, the gold flecks within like sparklers on the Fourth of July, in response to their contact. Though Skylar couldn't see her reflection, she was confident her own had responded in much the same way.

"Thank you," was all the response she could muster. Through reason scratched her thoughts with the idea of turning and walking away, a strange, invisible tether lassoed them. Two people knotted at the moment of contact. Sky could tell by looking into his eyes he'd felt the link and, suddenly, he didn't feel like a stranger at all.

She was more confused now than ever in her life. He smiled, studying her. His lips were full, and she couldn't shake the feeling she wanted to kiss them. The thought appeared out of nowhere, wholly unbidden and unwanted. Instantly, her gaze faltered. From one second to the next, her line of sight had dropped from his mouth to the floor. She found herself staring at the faded, grey carpet, unable to describe what was happening. Drained, she tried to think of anything other than what had just occurred.

"You're welcome."

His voice was as sinful as chocolate, and her cheeks as red as cherries. She couldn't look at him. She had no doubt his response was sincere, but too many things happening in such a short span of time had sent her into a panic—and she never panicked. Even if he'd been a temporary knight in shining armor, she was no damsel in distress. *But he did help to rescue the computer.*

As the small crowd around her zeroed in on the mishap, Sky forced herself to take in a lungful of oxygen even though she struggled to breathe. She didn't like being the center of attention, especially when air seemed to be in short supply. Helplessness didn't look good on her.

Grasping at mental straws, she made an attempt to regain her composure. She needed to calm the hell down and get ahold of herself. Had to pretend it was no big deal. It was critical she quickly adopt an indifferent air. Call up the few remaining, sentry-like brain cells she possessed and turn them into seasoned soldiers. At least maybe then she could protect what was left of her dignity. She inhaled slowly, taking in a deep, calming breath.

And another.

And still another.

Deliberately, she lifted her chin. The handsome man's gaze hadn't wavered. He was still looking at her, and that strange, fluttery feeling reemerged.

Feeling like an awkward teenager, Sky's stomach flipped. She looked away, feeling like a scared rabbit. Slowly she grounded herself, waltzing words in a melody of thought.

He's judgmental.

He's arrogant.

He's just a guy.

"Are you okay?" The stranger's voice skipped up half a beat as he hitched words to a smile, turning her insides to Jell-O.

"I'm good, thanks." She shrugged, wrapping an arm around her waist to get ahold of herself. It didn't take but a moment to shift the focus of attention away from her. As she collected her things, the people who'd been watching moved on, their attention drifting back to their laptops, books, and phones. She went back to her place, which now felt like the hot seat since Vince and the man changed seats. Now she was sitting directly across from Vince while only one seat separated her from her helpful stranger. She looked from left to right and, when she was confident she was no longer the object of everyone's attention, she attempted a casual conversation so as not to appear rude.

"Now that we've seen my method of researching for a novel, it's your turn. You and Vince were talking about editing." She leaned in his direction, pretending to peer over the empty seat at his laptop to see what was on the screen. "What kind of book are you writing?"

"Me?" He acted surprised as he looked at the content on his screen. "The great American novel, I guess. Isn't everybody?" The sound of his hearty laugh filtered through her, causing a pleasant sensation.

"Sounds like a best seller." She tucked away her earlier assessment of the man. Maybe she'd misjudged him. He seemed kind of . . . normal.

"Right. I've been writing this story on and off for years. I'll probably never publish it. It's just something I like to do."

She relaxed her shoulders, enjoying yet another mild jolt of electricity that his voice elicited. He didn't seem like an arrogant asshole at all. In fact, his smile made her curious. There was a bit of an edge to it. She couldn't decide if he was just playful or a wild boy.

As she sat back in her seat, he gave her a brief description of his novel. She wasn't listening. Instead, she studied his face—for research, of course. His cheekbones were high and noble, his jaw, square and strong. And then there was his voice. Whether he was a good writer or not, she couldn't tell, but with a voice like that he should have been a singer.

"You never know." Sky smiled. "Yours could be the next literary mega-hit. I mean, c'mon, look what happened to the lady who wrote *Fifty Shades of Grey.*"

On a huff, his eyes closed, and his chin dropped. A

minute later, he peered up, directing his attention to the screen of his laptop with a slight wave of his hand.

"What I'm writing has absolutely nothing in common with those kinds of books. Nothing at all. This is literature. Not erotica. It's complex. A period piece. A tale of discovery and grit. There's no kink in my story—or fluff."

Sky bent her resolve, giving him a narrow glance with a playful but deadly message.

"I think Ms. E.L. James might object to her multi-million-dollar babies being referred to as fluff. The only thing fluffy about the figures in her account are the clouds she floats on when she goes to the bank." Light sarcasm tickled her tone. "I guess I should add that the book we're talking about sold over one hundred and twenty-five million copies. And that was just the first book. It's part of a trilogy."

He gave her a knowing look, his smile never leaving his face. "Have I offended you? I'm not trying to. I'm just stating the differences between a romance novel and serious literature. You can't compare *War and Peace* with *Fifty Shades of Grey*."

"I can if the sales are there." Her comeback was lightning-fast. *"Lord of the Flies"* sold a little more than twenty-five million. *To Kill a Mockingbird*, a bit more than forty million. And let's not forget the darling of romance, *Gone with the Wind*. That little gem—thirty million." She quirked a spunky brow. "You, sir, should know your facts and figures before you dismiss something of which you, clearly, have no understanding."

An impish grin wrinkled her forehead. She didn't mind defending her craft. Her bank account was nowhere near as healthy as E.L. James's, but she couldn't complain. Writing romance had proven to be a good career move for her, and no one could say she didn't have peer loyalty. Was he up for the challenge of a debate? Because she could play that game all night. She'd done her research.

The rumbled laugh was robust and thick. Deep and smooth, that luxurious kind of sound came from deep down. She shivered, then chastised herself immediately. She wanted to hear it again, so she asked another question.

"What part of the country are you from?"

He seemed surprised she'd changed the topic from books to places. *Oh, well.* She was one of those people who researched exciting subject matter for a living. Everything from "Where is the best place to bury a body?" to "What R&B song is more births attributed to?" had been typed into her web browser. Like dandelions in a garden, topics just randomly popped up in her thoughts. It was her experience that, if she didn't immediately take care of the weed, it was determined to grow stronger until she did. If he was going to write a book, he'd have to research a hundred different topics at a time too.

"The Midwest, originally, but I've lived all over the country. Up and down the East Coast, then some time on the West. I've been back and forth, once or twice."

A stab of guilt hit her for having a combative edge in her tone. She wasn't trying to put him on the defensive, just have a conversation. *Oh, for God's sake!* The only way to fix this was to ease up. "So, where are you on your way to now?"

"Back to Florida. I'm in the middle of a move from Florida to Annapolis, Maryland."

The tactic worked. His expression was a little lazier. Relaxed. But a move to Annapolis from Florida? She didn't understand that logic.

"You're moving *from* Florida? Why would you want to do that? Winter's coming. Maryland is so unpredictable weather wise." Intrigue swept her expression as she silently questioned the sanity of a man who would choose bipolar temperatures over toasty ones. His shrug was indifferent. "Florida's nice, but, honestly, I'm tired of it. A few years ago, I took some time off. I honestly thought I would settle down there. It was only for a short time, I considered it semi-retirement."

"Semi-retirement? You're what? Thirty?"

He laughed at the surprise in her voice. "Yeah. There is that. You can only sit on your ass for so long, you know? It ends up being the same shit, different day—I was bored. And to tell you the truth, I really like Annapolis. I missed the change of seasons, and Maryland in general. It's convenient. Kind of in the middle of everything. Three hours one way, you have the mountains. A few hours in the opposite direction, you have the ocean." His hands went up as he mimicked a balance on a scale. "Beach in the summer. Skiing in the winter. What's not to like? You know, Land of Pleasant Living?"

She was sure she almost gaped. *Retired?* Out of their entire ten-minute conversation, that was the topic that piqued her interest the most. She could paint a house with all the speculations in her head. He was so young!

Wild scenarios danced the cha-cha in her thoughts, each question two steps forward, each answer, a step back. What was he? A lottery winner? Trust fund baby? Maybe she should give him the benefit of the doubt. Perhaps he'd invested better than most people his age. Money from a dead relative? Male gigolo? The possibilities were endless and were more than enough to keep her intrigued.

Now he really had her attention. What she wanted to say was, "Are you crazy? Last winter was brutal. Three major snowfalls. You're nuts!" but decided she might appear to be the crazy one. Instead, she was polite.

"I think I would have stayed where the beach is warm and sunny."

He smiled a naughty grin. "I don't think it would have worked out for me, had I stayed in Florida."

"Really? How so?" Puzzled, she was anxious to hear the answer.

His brown eyes warmed in intensity, competing with the mischief tickling his lips. "Because, if I had, I wouldn't have met a nice girl like you."

Heat rushed up her neck and made a mad dash for her cheeks. Her lips made an O as surprise opened her mouth.

"You're blushing," he said. "And it's quite a pretty, rosy shade."

CHAPTER 3

*D*ash was captivated. He felt the connection between them, and she would be lying if she said she didn't feel it too. Even after years of becoming jaded by sneaky bitches, he couldn't take his eyes off this girl. After experiences with women that would have taken down a lesser man, he could spot an opportunist a mile away. He'd bet the royalties from his next CD that this girl wouldn't hurt a fly if it were within her power. He'd also bet she was single. There was no way she was used to having a man in her life. It was apparent she wasn't used to having help. If she lived with a man, he would have at least taken out the trash. She acted like she was too much of an inconvenience for someone to help her pick up a piece of paper. And the blushing! He didn't think there was a woman left over the age of ten who was modest.

"What can I say? I always blush. I'm Irish."

Her words dismissed the topic, but the color on her cheeks bloomed. "That sounds like an apology for something you can't control. I think it's cute." He gave his approval with a wink.

"Thanks. It's not something I like about myself."

He smiled. Like a fish out of water, she was trying to wiggle her way back to her comfort zone. This chick might be able to write a book, but it was crystal clear she was uncomfortable with flirting. He'd give it to her though, she was giving it her best shot. He wondered if she knew how transparent she really was. Probably not. She sure as hell didn't have an inflated ego. She seemed so self-critical she couldn't even dismiss her clumsiness as an accident. As for being a writer, she was definitely an extroverted introvert. Even he could see that she pushed herself to be "out there" when she was talking to him. He had to admit, she'd honed the skill well. The thing he liked the most was that she didn't seem to recognize him. That was a plus.

"I'll let you get back to what you were doing."

Her sweet smile was a pleasant contrast to the antics of most people he met. Darren "Dash" Barrows couldn't remember the last time someone didn't recognize him. In another circumstance, it would have been a blow to his ego. His band, Boundless Hearts, was all over the airwaves. Everywhere he went people came up to him. It probably helped that he'd cut off his long hair and taken his beard back to scruff. Even the guys in the band hadn't seen the new look. After playing with them for a few years, he'd decided a move was in order. His Florida memories weren't always happy ones.

The band had started playing together roughly six months after his mom's death. It was just a coincidence he'd caught up with several old friends in a bar on Anna Maria Island. He'd known the guys since they were kids. Once they'd graduated high school, they'd parted ways. While he'd made considerable money freelancing up and down the East and West coasts, three of his friends had kept together the garage band they'd started when they were younger.

He asked them if they'd join him, and they took him up on the invitation. Their unique sound quickly caught on. It was a mix of classic rock and roll with a San Francisco sound that was popular back in the '80s. Before they knew it, success hit. They were playing bigger and bigger venues. Their gigs sold out, forcing them to look at larger sites. When festivals overflowed with fans and concerts started selling out in a day, they caught the attention of a record label. Three years later, they were still with the same company. They'd come a long way since their days playing for the neighborhood kids.

Where some people would let the fame go to their head, he didn't buy into the bullshit. He simply considered himself a musician, not some lyrical demi-god. As long as he could support himself on the money he was paid for his music, he felt like he'd made it. That was his definition of success.

Girls, booze, and drugs seemed to be the indulgences of choice when it came to his bandmates, but he was wise with his money, investing it so it could grow. That put him into a different headspace than most of his friends. In the early days, while they pissed away their dollars, he'd planted his in the stock market—and it had grown into a tidy little nest egg. Once the guys got wind of his talent for investing, they asked him for advice. Now they were living off their dividends. Well, all of them except their lead singer, Ian.

A light, feminine laugh trilled through the air, and Dash found himself taking in the catastrophic cutie. She commanded his attention with the way she was so unassuming and had no idea the guy whose interest she'd piqued had been all over the world and found her the most fascinating person he'd met in years. Their conversation about books and literary merits was engaging, but he politely faded into the background when her companion drew her back into a discussion about editing. He wondered what the guys would think of her, especially Ian. His lead singer would have been highly insulted if he weren't recognized.

His thoughts sobered. He didn't even like thinking about Ian being near this chick. It wasn't that he begrudged his friend a good time, he just believed that Ian's drinking and drugging ways would be a real put-off for this girl. Then, again, if his friend didn't change his ways, there wasn't a chance in hell that they'd ever meet—if he could figure out a way to keep in touch with her before their flight ended. If his instincts were right, keeping in touch with her held some future promise. His instincts about Ian said he'd be dead in a few years. It was a shame, too, because he was so talented, but talent didn't save you from a hole in the ground.

A strange rush ran through him. Thinking about continuing his contact with Skylar afforded him a pleasant sensation. After suffering several high-profile breakups, Dash had quickly caught onto the fact there were always more than enough parasites to go around. Most were waiting to make a quick buck with a bogus lawsuit or a false positive pregnancy test. He'd seen it happen to other guys in other bands. Compared to them, he, quite literally, kept himself clean. Nothing snorted up his nose or shot in his veins, not to mention no sex without a raincoat. He didn't have time for any of that shit. These days he was all about the money game. How to plant it and how to grow it. Life on the road was hard. If he kept on the path he'd been following, he'd be able to reap the benefits of investing well while he was still young enough to enjoy it.

While musing through all these thoughts had kept him occupied, it hadn't kept him from stealing a few glances in the cutie's direction. Dash kept an eye on her, his gaze drifting to the side of his laptop screen to snatch a few more details about her. Her eyes were big and blue, of that he was well aware. They'd hit him like a bolt of lightning the first time she'd looked at him. Her hair was long and brown with a bunch of loose waves. When she'd pulled it out of the makeshift bun she had on the top of her head, he'd admired her tousled mane even more. Currently, she was pulling it to the side and twisting the curls into submission by combing them with her fingers. Her lashes were thick and dark and fluttered beautifully against her pale skin. When she laughed, she closed her eyes. It was as if she took a moment to savor whatever it was that had delighted her. She was definitely more "the girl next door" than someone who'd sneak into the bathroom for a quick fuck. *Hell, no.* She had that Bambi-look, all wide-eyed and innocent.

He looked back at his screen. The latest tabloid news had a front-page picture of Ian with seven or eight girls hanging on him. Though he knew it was a different photo, they all looked the same no matter what paper was using Ian for sales. Ian's girls all had bleached blonde hair, heavy, black eye makeup, and a hard edge. Most were so skinny their bones nearly poked through their skin. The guys always joked that Ian's had as many girls as he had coins in his pocket, and they were just as loose. For a cover story, those women didn't give a shit about privacy. In a hotel room or the band bus, they were happy to spread their legs or give a blow job as long as the payout was right. As Dash pinched another look at America's sweetheart sitting across from him, he was glad she didn't know who he was right now. It might better his chances with her.

"Flight 1013 to Tampa will now be boarding at Gate C-26." The announcement over the PA system had her looking over in his direction.

"This is us. Thanks for coming to my rescue." Her blue eyes were gleaming. Sunlight coming through the window caught them as she bent at the waist. She was still smiling at him as she closed her laptop. The effect highlighted the silver within the blue. It shot a bullet of desire through his heart.

"Not a problem. Glad I could help." Suddenly, he remembered that he didn't know her name. He set out to remedy the situation. "By the way, I'm Darren. Most people call me Dash."

"Skylar Harrison." A delicate shrug shook her shoulders. "Also known as Eden Skye. You know, in case you want to read a sexy romance novel." The information was accompanied by a soft laugh. "I know you asked me my name before, but I honestly can't remember if I answered you. I was a little discombobulated at the time."

The tiny confession, so honest and sincere, made him suddenly want to be her priest. At least then he could discover if there were any sins within the heart she, so obviously, wore on her sleeve. He found himself wanting to assure her that her clumsiness had no bearing on his opinion of her.

"You're fine. You aren't the first person to spill coffee in this place, and I'm pretty sure you won't be the last." His words of consolation brought forth another smile, accomplishing the ease he'd intended.

"It was nice talking to you." She turned back toward her editor, whom she referred to as Vince. The two quickly gathered their belongings, and he did the same. He watched them line up according to their boarding position, all the while trying to see where an opportunity might arise to talk to her again. Skylar was lost in conversation with Vince, unaware he was enjoying the feast his observation brought. He intended to look for any chance to get her to remember him.

As he passed her in line, she gifted him a shy smile making his chest ache and his heart squeeze. He didn't know how she did it, but he couldn't remember any woman having the same effect on him. Unconsciously, he rubbed the spot. Yeah, this one was special. Hopefully, by the time they landed, her embarrassment from the earlier clusterfuck would be behind her.

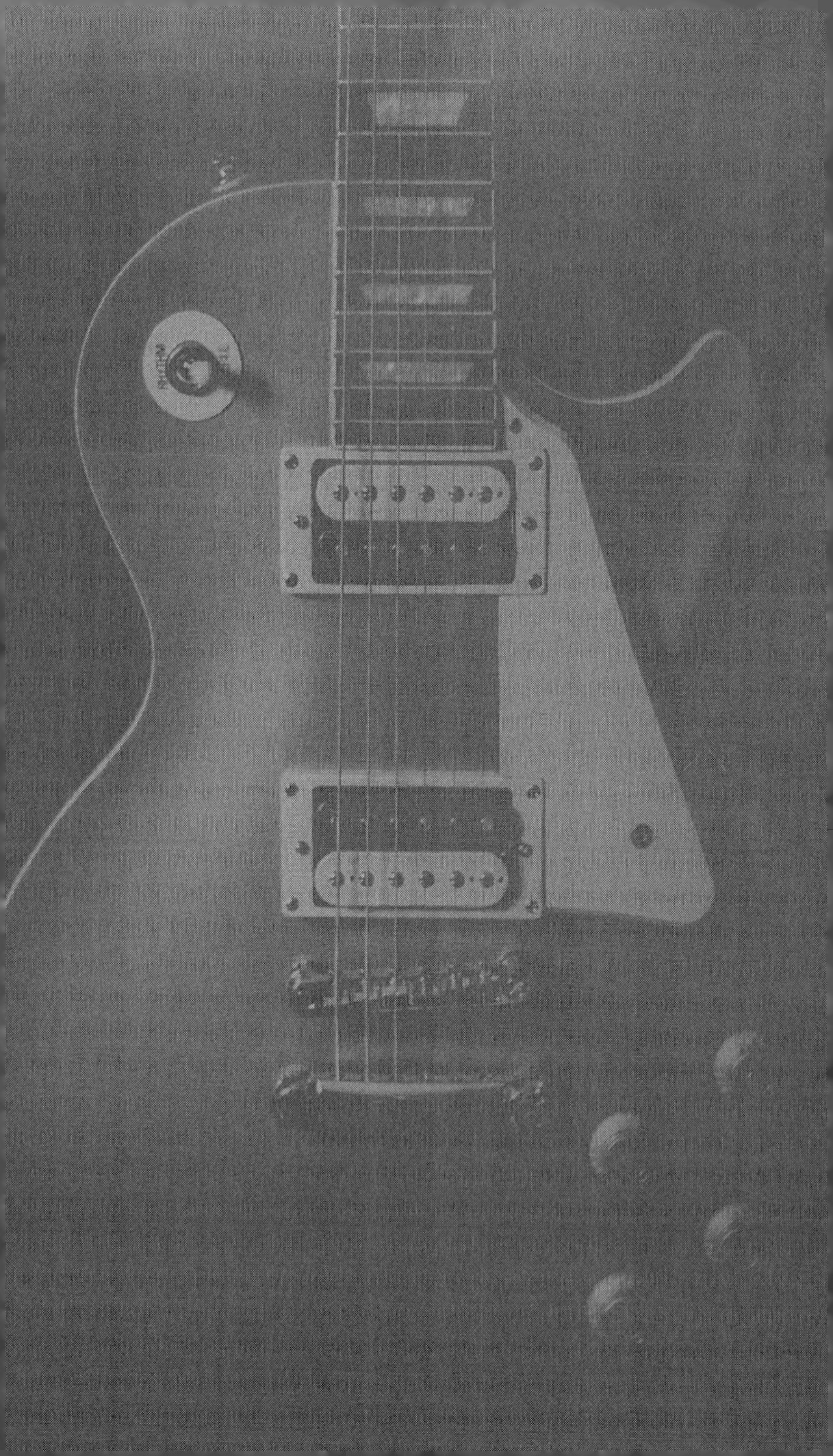

CHAPTER 4

Though he usually thought himself lucky, today, he felt he was even more so. A seat across the aisle from Skylar was the opportunity he needed to have a perfect view of her for the entire flight. Looking up, with his eyes toward the sky, he thanked his good fortune. She looked over at him with a shy flutter of lashes and a graceful smile on her lips. As a passenger held up the line with a luggage struggle, he shifted in his seat, leaning in her direction so he could talk to her across the aisle. "The way you're looking at me says that you're still self-conscious about dropping your stuff in the airport. You need to let it go."

Her tone was hushed. "I didn't realize I was so transparent." Doubt showed in the shrug of her shoulders. "Thanks for saying that. I do still feel weird about it, but it's nice of you to try to make me feel better."

"It could've happened to anyone, sweetheart," he consoled her. "Don't be so hard on yourself."

"Sorry to disappoint you, but that's an understatement. I'm always harder on myself than anyone could ever be."

Pink bloomed in her cheeks making him frown. It wasn't right that someone so perfect was so self-critical. She couldn't see how rare, but how wrong, that trait was. Though he might not know her well, even he could see Skylar's perfectionistic qualities. As if to prove his point, she lowered the tray on the back of the seat in front of her and began to type away on her laptop. It was a sure sign she took her work seriously. That fact alone put her above more than a quarter of the population of the United States.

Dash looked at his phone, though he wasn't really paying attention to it. With his head tipped down, his eyes tipped up and stole occasional glances across the aisle, he made mental notes.

Where he usually took time spent in the air as an opportunity to sleep, he was confident he wouldn't be doing any of that on this flight. Instead, he would look for chances to interact with Skylar. That odd pulling sensation he had toward her grew more potent by the minute. He couldn't explain it. The best he could come up with was the feeling he had when an Eric Clapton guitar went up for auction. The minute he looked at it, he knew it was supposed to be his. Many people had tried to outbid him at that charity auction, but he hadn't stopped until he'd gotten what he wanted. He won that Clapton guitar. He intended to win Skylar too.

* * *

IT WASN'T A LONG FLIGHT, but it was enough time to think of something clever to get her number or ask her out for coffee. He watched her, looking up from his laptop throughout the first hour of the flight. For the past five minutes, she'd been rummaging through the bag that had been tucked under the seat in front of her. He leaned over the arm of his chair. "Missing something?"

"Not really. Just trying to put some order to this mess." She motioned to the bag. "We have about an hour or so before we land. I'll have it sorted by then."

He nodded. "So, what kind of book are you working on? A love story?"

"She doesn't just write love stories," a male voice interjected, making it apparent Vince had been eavesdropping. Since he was a tall man, all he had to do was turn his head to chime in. He could see Dash just fine. "Skylar has two master's degrees: journalism and creative writing. She writes books, articles, and op-ed pieces and she's damn good at it." He smiled proudly. Skylar's cheeks were currently sporting a healthy shade of pink. "She notices everything, and she soaks in that information like a sponge. I wouldn't put it past this girl to win a Pulitzer."

Vince's comments earned him a snarky look from Skylar. A sigh rolled over her lips as her brows pulled together. "Yeah. Right."

"What?" He peered over the top of his reading glasses and looked down his nose at her. "Don't look at me like that. It's possible. You work your ass off, and you're good. People are going to notice."

Her lips tightened, and, again, she rolled her eyes, dismissing him in the process. Dash watched the exchange, amusement curling his lip. They seemed more like father and daughter than business counterparts.

"Right. I'll take that look as a compliment." He turned back to his work, but when Skylar looked back at Dash, Vince quickly turned and pointed his index finger down toward her head. He mouthed the words "she's good" to Dash. Sky must have seen Dash's gaze go above her head because she quickly snapped her head back to Vince. He gave her an innocent look as he pulled his hand back down. Dash was amused by the exchange. He leaned closer.

"So, I'll ask again. What are you working on?"

"I've just finished writing a novel, and you guessed right, it's a contemporary romance. I'm going through Vince's edits on that. As he told you, I also write articles for magazines. I have two galley proofs of those to go through. That's a formality, really. If a magazine accepts an article for publication, I have very little to do with it at that point. When I first started doing it, I didn't think much about it, but magazine and journal topics have been my bread and butter. I like writing novels better, though. I'm hoping that one of them will do so well indie I'll crack open the big five in New York. Of course, if you listen to Vince, I'll have them begging at my feet."

Upon hearing his name, Vince stuck up a hand for a wave, then pulled it back down, making it clear he continued to listen in on their conversation. A protective measure, for sure. *Good for him.*

Her eyes softened, a pleasant expression warming her features. Even when she was kidding, when she talked about writing, her whole face lit up.

Seeing Skylar smile did something to him. His heart lurched. It was as if seeing her happy jump-started his heart. He figured it had something to do with that odd connection he'd first felt at the airport. He was such a cynic when people talked about love at first sight, but there was something about this girl. He sure as hell wasn't in love, but he was definitely "in like" with her.

Skylar turned toward Vince, then stood. She paused a step as she walked past him. "I'll be right back." Dash nodded. In the meantime, Vince moved into her aisle seat and watched until she disappeared into the lavatory. A question raised his brows as he looked over at Dash. It was apparent he was protective of her. If he hoped to get to know her better, Vince wasn't someone he wanted to alienate.

"So, she's that good, huh?"

Vince's head tipped. "She's better than *that good*, and I believe what I said. One day she will have them begging for her work." His confident tone said it was more a question of when, not if, it would happen.

"I would never have guessed. She doesn't seem pretentious at all."

"She isn't, and I'm not sure what a stereotypical writer looks like in your head, but she's the real deal. Her writing is honest. More than that, it's relatable." He paused. Pride softened his brow and lifted his cheeks as he nodded. "And that's what makes her so damn good—even if she can't see it herself. It's a gift, really, how she watches people and sees the stories in their eyes. She writes it how she feels it. She doesn't try to spin the narratives for the masses. She simply observes, plots, and writes the tale as it comes into her head. People resonate with her take on things because they see themselves in her characters. Her biggest problem is that she underestimates herself."

Noting Skylar's return down the aisle, Vince indicated their conversation was over with a nod of his head. He slid back over to his seat and pulled down the armrest before Sky returned.

As she passed by, his eyes lifted to hers. She flicked a glance at him and gave him a responsive smile. Dash watched her with interest. He liked that she was unpretentious. Being humble wasn't as common these days as it was when he was a kid. People bragged on themselves without saying a word. A pair of Frye boots or a Hermes bag silently told people you could afford the finer things. Of course, some people would tell you directly in conversation how wonderful they were. He couldn't count how many people had tried to impress him with "I did this" and "I did that" conversations. It was nice to meet a woman who didn't try to impress, instead she let her actions speak for themselves.

His eyes softened as his mouth took a curve. He watched her scroll the screen of her phone with her thumb. His gaze traced her contours, admiring her assets. Time trudged forward and he realized that, somehow, by the time they landed in Tampa, he needed to come up with a plan to get to know her better. He was determined to see her again. He just hadn't figured out how to do that. One thing was for sure, the idea they would part ways once their flight had ended was no longer an option.

CHAPTER 5

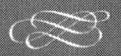

Dash looked at his watch. There wasn't much time left on the flight. Though he'd offered to buy her a drink, she'd politely declined. She never noticed his observations. Instead, she was lost in a universe of words.

He grinned, the lazy curve filling his lips. He liked Skylar, from what little he knew of her. What pleased him most was she had no idea who he was. Not one sign of recognition teased her eyes. To her, he was just another guy. While the band had a two-week hiatus between their concert in Florida and their next gig at National Harbor in Washington, D.C., Dash was using the time to complete his move and take care of some personal business. Running back and forth between Florida and Maryland left little time for pleasure. But meeting Skylar at the airport? That was an added bonus.

For the remainder of the flight, she paid no attention to him. A set of Bose headphones dented her hair as she tuned out everything around her.

"Ladies and gentlemen, we are beginning our final

descent into Tampa. Please make sure your seat backs and tray tables are in the full and upright, locked position."

Dash's heart raced as Vince got her attention. He'd come up with somewhat of a plan during the last half hour. If it worked, he'd see her again.

A smile split his lips as he watched her slide the headphones to the back of her neck. His fingers twitched with jealousy as he wondered what it would feel like to thread his fingers through her long mane. It was crazy, he knew. He should have dismissed their chance meeting, but he couldn't. Somehow, he felt like the fates were smiling on him today. He felt like a schoolboy, the way she made his pulse race. The driving beat against his skin felt like a mini drummer had crawled inside. Thankfully, he was sitting across from her, or he might have scared her away. She missed the way he watched her with anticipation in his eyes.

As if she could hear his thoughts, Skylar stood and turned. A coy smile stretched her glossy lips. Dash read the act as an invitation. It was the extra dose of encouragement he needed to carry through his plan. He returned her smile, watching her as she reached up high to put something into the overhead compartment. Her tight, gently worn jeans hugged her ass in all the right places. The hemline of her top rose above the waistband an inch or so as she stretched, giving him a glimpse of lightly tanned skin. Apparently, she wasn't as much a recluse as he believed most writers to be. He guessed her skin had been kissed by the sun a few times from what he could tell by the slight tan. *Lucky sun.*

Clicking metal filled the cabin space with sound as passengers fastened their seat belts. Dash kicked his bag under the seat in front of him, savoring his view of Sky as she tugged at the bottom of her shirt and took her place.

Reaching into his pocket, he pulled out a piece of gum to aid in equalizing the pressure in his ears. Skylar laid her head back during the descent, and he did the same. Within fifteen minutes, they were on the ground. He'd have to improvise some of what he planned to say and do, but he thought the strategy would work. The last thing he wanted was to use the "I'm in a band" line. Though he knew other guys would take advantage of that status, he avoided that line like the plague. His private life was nearly non-existent, but he would enjoy whatever moments of anonymity he could get. Even if his identity escaped her for a little while, it would be refreshing while it lasted.

* * *

There'd been only six people separating them as they disembarked, but, once up the gangway and into the airport, the crowd grew thick, and he lost sight of her. *Fuck!* This couldn't be happening.

As he scouted the masses, irritation bristled the small hairs on the back of his neck. Taking slow steps, he searched for the girl with a sexy ass and mop of curls. With cautious steps, he quickly scanned through the scores of people. He focused on the restroom area, which was usually the first place people headed once they'd gotten off their plane. Instead of air, stress was now the constant pressure in his head. He was about to give up and move on when he saw Vince come out of the men's room. A sigh of relief escaped his chest when Skylar appeared from the opposite door. He lingered for just a moment, hoping that if he followed a few steps behind them, they wouldn't notice he trailed them.

While on the moving walkway, he saw a week-old poster of the band up ahead. They had finished playing their date in Tampa, but it hadn't yet been removed. A green "sold out" banner was plastered over the date and time. Beneath the bold, black letters was a photo of the band members. Thank God he no longer resembled the man in the advertisement, or his plan could've gone up in smoke. He didn't look anything like he did nearly two weeks before. The bleached blond color that he'd worn well past his shoulders was now lying in a trash heap somewhere between the hair salon and the landfill.

Dash's eyes lingered on the advertisement for a moment. For one millisecond, he nearly fell into the same mindset that made Ian a self-serving asshole. An errant thought raced across his mind, *you don't chase chicks. They chase you,* lit up in red, neon letters. He quickly dismissed it. Though the other guys bought into all that bullshit, he was a bit more down to earth. Besides, Skylar didn't seem like the kind of girl who was easily impressed—and that was okay with him. He liked a challenge.

As Dash entertained the egotistical thoughts, he calmly followed Sky into the baggage claim area. The air hummed with voices. He planned to ease over to where she was standing, keep the conversation light, and hope she didn't notice he had no baggage to claim.

"Hey, man. Aren't you—"

"I am, and if you keep your mouth shut, I'll make it worth your while." The words were hissed, but effective. The kid who'd approached Dash couldn't have been more than seventeen, while the rest of the crowd appeared to be the geriatric set. He'd have to give it to the boy, only a true fan would have spotted him. "See that girl over there?" The young buck went to turn around, but Dash grabbed his arm. "Slow down, man." Eyes now round and wide, the kid slowly crept a half turn. "Stop!" An urgent whisper carved

Dash's tone. "I want to hit on her, and you're gonna blow my cover."

The boy's face turned red. Understanding nodded his head and he curled his upper body, pulling his head into his neck like a turtle. "Sorry, man. I didn't mean to." His expression went from apologetic to disbelieving in a nanosecond. "Doesn't everybody know who you are?"

His response tempted a burst of laughter, but Dash held it in. He reached in his pocket. "You got a pen, kid?" The boy's head bobbed. "Yep!" He slid his backpack off his shoulder and down his arm so fast Dash thought he might have peeled off a layer of skin. His hand went in and out of the bag in a flash, and he nervously thrust the pen in front of him. "What's your name?" Dash took it and began writing on the back of a card.

"Norman."

Dash froze for a minute, then went back to his task. It was almost a given that this boy got a shitload of teasing over something he had nothing to do with. "You live around here, slick?" As he gave the kid a peripheral glance, he decided he wasn't going to ask him any more questions. That head bobbing was sure to draw attention. "Good." He clicked the ballpoint top and clipped it to the card. "I can tell you're a big fan. If you call this number, I'll tell my manager to give you backstage passes to any concert we play."

"Wow! Thanks."

Dash handed the pen back to him with the card attached. "Slip this in your pocket, and don't lose it." He stood near the kid as he quickly scouted the room to see if anyone else might have made the same connection as the boy.

As the young man held the card up to read it, he reached around his back with the other and came back with his wallet. "Oh my God! Two tickets!" He went wide-eyed again as he blurted out the words.

Dash clamped a hand down on his shoulder and walked him a few steps from where they were standing. His heart skipped a rhythm as he looked to see if Skylar was anywhere nearby.

"Shh." He looked down at the boy, whose face was mortified. A chuckle escaped from low in his chest. "Told you I'd make it worth your while, slick. Bring a date. You might get lucky. The concert's sold out."

A knowing look had the boy arching his brow as a naughty smile stretched his lips full across his face.

"Yeah. I know that look." Dash gave him an up-high hand slap and a friendly clap on the back. "Now, do me a favor and get the hell out of here before my girl sees us."

CHAPTER 6

"*H*ey there."

The words at her ear made her jolt as adrenaline shot through her heart. Skylar spun around with her heart in her throat, to see the man who'd snuck up on her. Her expression traveled a smooth path from shock to pleasure as recognition filtered through her. "Hey, yourself."

Though her initial reaction was to turn around and chastise whomever had scared her, there was nothing but delight in her tone. She directed his attention to the blinking red letters above the carousel on an electronic display. "They haven't unloaded the plane yet."

"That's okay. I don't mind waiting with you."

Her cheeks warmed. "Oh?" Her chin dropped as her head fell to the side. She tucked her hair behind her ear as she averted her eyes away from his. She wanted the chance to take another breath before meeting his eyes again. It took a fraction more effort because her heart had leaped into her throat.

BAAAAAWWWWKKKKK

A loud, abrasive buzzing sound pierced the air as the red light at the end of the carousel came to life. As it flashed and spun around, the crowd inched forward. All eyes went to the hole in the wall as each person watched for their luggage to emerge. The black rubber conveyor belt started to move as the annoying buzz ceased. One by one, a rainbow of colored cases emerged. As they both kept watch, Skylar's skin began to hum. It was his nearness that caused the effect. There was something about him that snuck inside of her and made her brain short-circuit. He was so close she could nearly feel his body heat. Her body reacted with a whisper at her core.

"Oh! Mine's one of the first." Though she was happy for the short wait, she was also saddened that their time together was nearly at an end. She curled her fingers into her palms. Resignation melting her spine, her posture slumping at the knowledge that they would never see each other again. The odds of them running into each other again were slim, and, as much as she was distracted by the butterflies in her stomach, she was sorry they would soon stop their flutter.

She stood at the far end of the conveyor belt, suddenly glad her position bought her a few more seconds before she had to say goodbye. As her bright blue, hard shell approached, she reached out. Dash thwarted her efforts, intercepting the case before she had the chance to remove it. He set it on the ground and pulled the handle up. Pushing it toward her, his eyes never leaving her face.

She paused, looking into his gorgeous brown eyes. It was sad to think she'd never see them again. He held a story behind those eyes she was anxious to read. It was too bad she'd never get the chance to turn the pages.

Her heart skipped a beat as she offered a grateful smile.

"Well, thank you." She extended her hand. "It was nice meeting you, Dash. Good luck with your move."

He took her hand, and she gave it a gentle shake. Her grip loosened as she made to turn around and leave behind all but the memory of their encounter. As she took one step forward, her breath caught in her throat. He'd failed to release her. Instead, his grip tightened, and he tugged her back. Her eyes snapped up to his.

"Skylar? There's a concert in D.C. this weekend. Would you like to go?"

She blinked, then hesitated. Her gaze caught his and their eyes locked. Those brown orbs of his could be a woman's undoing with their anxious anticipation. His voice could seduce a girl to throw caution to the wind. Could make her ignore every safety warning she'd placed in her memory's file cabinet. It was crazy for a solitary girl to accept an invitation from a total stranger. And he was a stranger. She'd known him for less than a day. It only made sense to decline his invitation. Perhaps, instead, ask him if he'd like to grab a coffee somewhere near her house and have a trusted friend sitting a few tables over. That would be the safe and smart thing to do. She would give him her prettiest smile and not notice how perfect his lips were and how deliciously the corners of his eyes curled when he smiled. She ran her tongue over her lips, opening her mouth to speak just as she noticed the sparkle in his eye.

"I'd love to."

* * *

I'D LOVE TO?

Skylar cringed inside. It was crazy. She hadn't had much luck in the relationship department, and she sure as hell didn't expect any good fortune by opening herself up to someone she didn't know. She must have some hidden quirk. Some appetite for danger. The last time she'd acted on impulse with a man hadn't worked out so well for her. He'd had a pretty smile too, and her reward for opening herself up to that guy was a broken heart and a loss of appetite. It had taken a while to heal from that fiasco, and, once she had, she was determined to focus on her career and learn to be content with her life.

A ball of regret lodged in her throat as discouraging thoughts crawled through her mind. In spider-like fashion, each spindly step pricked her mind with negative thinking until anxious thoughts spun a thick web.

You should have played a little hard to get.
It could all be a waste of time.
You don't know what kind of music is playing.
What if you don't like it?
Should you bow out gracefully now?
Maybe we'll have nothing in common.

As she continued looking at him, her stare had gone blank. She could tell by his reaction he'd divined her thoughts and was well aware of her hesitation.

"It's just a concert, Sky. You don't have to accept." His hand dropped. He was about to release hers, but she held fast. She could tell he was disappointed, but even then, there was something about him that cut through her reservations. Some silent message was telling her to take a chance on him.

"No. I really want to." She could feel her cheeks hitch, and whatever he saw in her expression made his eyes sparkle.

"Good."

Her reaction to his pleasure was immediate. The brief graze of his fingers against her hand incited a feeling like that of an electric shock. His touch made her skin sizzle, sending tingles of pleasure through her whole body. Her heart lurched a powerful beat. His warm eyes were ablaze. Though she tried to lower her gaze to reduce the effect, she zeroed in on his lips. She blinked, trying to regain control of her thoughts instead of staring at his lush, kissable mouth. Suddenly, and without warning, the lips that had momentarily bewitched her senses and seduced her body, came crashing down on hers.

Her first instinct was to pull away. She should have drawn back to sever their connection. Maybe it would have broken the tie that had the synapses in her brain misfiring. But she couldn't. Pleasurable sensations ricocheted through muscles, nerves, and bones.

Shamelessly, she fell into Dash's kiss. Her typically steely resolve liquified as craving puddled deep in her belly. The lust-filled pool bubbled until an undeniable longing pulled at the apex of her thighs. His lips were hot, his tongue parting hers to claim her. The lusty feelings commanded her attention. Dash kissed her the way every woman dreams of being kissed. His fingers laced through her hair as he cupped the back of her head, and a fresh current of energy raced through her body. Her heart quickened. Her panties dampened. And, just as quickly as their connection occurred, it was severed.

Dash pulled back. He stared at her. She was confident that both of them were wearing the same shocked expression. He cleared his throat, swallowing the awkward moment.

"I'm sorry." His repentant words rushed out. "I shouldn't have done that."

Skylar was speechless. She tried to shake off the mystery of whatever had possessed him to be so impulsive, but the truth was, she felt the same connection. She watched as he looked off into blank space, shaking his head as he toyed with the strap on his shoulder. He sniffed, straightening his backbone as he bought some time. After a moment, he gave her a look. Repentance swam in his eyes.

"I'm really sorry, Skylar. I don't know what came over me. It was just . . . just that I . . . oh, hell!" Dash drew his hand from forehead to chin. He paused, bringing a few breaths into his lungs. Exhaling slowly, his expression slightly composed. "I don't know what to say, except I'm sorry."

Skylar stared back at him, words fleeing her mind. His apology didn't excuse her actions, for she suffered the same guilt. She'd dropped her guard the moment their lips touched. Though she knew she should, she couldn't look away from him. What she'd just experienced was like nothing she'd ever felt before. The power in his kiss had been too mighty to fight. She was conflicted down to her marrow.

If need and hunger were crimes, then they each were willing accomplices. This kind of thing didn't happen in real life! It was something that only occurred in old movies, romance novels, or fairy tales. *A kiss from a stranger?* She conjured an image of the sailor and nurse in Times Square after the war. But people didn't do that anymore, did they? At least not without the threat of being arrested!

She took pity on the man standing across from her. There were hundreds of people around, and yet she felt like they were the only two people there. He felt it too, she could tell, both of them were consumed by a roller coaster of emotions. Her heart still pumped a frantic beat, warning her with every pulsation to beware of a man with such a letha l effect.

"What was that?" She found her voice. Though a hundred reservations told her to grab her bags and run away, her gut told her otherwise. Apology filled his eyes, his expression as sweet as their chocolatey brown color.

"I don't know." He looked as perplexed as she felt. A shrug shook his shoulders while his lips played with a sheepish grin. "I could quote Robert Palmer and say you're simply irresistible."

I'm irresistible? What about him?

Suddenly, they both burst into laughter. Vince had witnessed the encounter from a few feet away. He appeared as shocked as Skylar and Dash had been. For a moment, he froze, watching in disbelief. He approached the two of them, cupping his hand over the handle of Skylar's suitcase to roll it away. "Um, I hate to break up this little tête-à-tête, but I've got an Uber on the way."

The interruption jolted Sky back to reality, yet, still, she couldn't deny that she enjoyed what had occurred a moment ago. The laughter had faded beneath Vince's injection of reality. Dash canted his head, while she traced the contours of his lips. The thrill of highs and lows danced a jig on her insides, while anger sat outside like a wallflower. Instead of the rage she thought she should feel, she felt happy. She was too locked into the residual effect of his kiss to feel otherwise.

Dash's eyes darted between her and Vince. He lunged to put an arm on her hand before she followed him. "About the concert . . ."

Her gaze traveled from his face and down his arm to where his hand rested. As it moved back up, a smile split her face. "When and where?"

He responded with a beaming smile of his own. "Friday. National Harbor. There'll be a ticket for you at the will-call desk. I'll meet you inside."

Still surprised by her uncharacteristic response, she nodded.

"Skylar. Uber's here." Vince tipped his head toward the door.

Skylar searched for something witty to say but could only come up with a quick response. "Gotta go." She turned and followed Vince's path.

"Wait!" Dash cantered over to her. "Lemme see your phone." She handed it to him, and he punched in a few keystrokes. "That's my number. If anything comes up and you can't make it, call me."

She gave him a quick, affirmative nod. With a tip of his chin, he gave her a smile and jogged off into the crowd. Skylar followed suit, heading toward the exit door with a schoolgirl smile on her lips and a spring in her step.

CHAPTER 7

"Hi there. I'm here to pick up a ticket. My name's Skylar Harrison."

Her expression was one of anticipation as she stood at the will-call counter. There was a long line behind her, and the lobby was packed with wall-to-wall people. She'd hoped to find Dash in the crowd, but when she dialed his number, it went to voicemail. She'd left him a simple message but had been confused by what she remembered of their conversation. When he'd said he'd meet her inside, did he mean inside the lobby or inside the seating area?

She hadn't had much time to think about their impending date. With deadlines looming, much of her concentration had been on meeting her writing goals for the day. She hadn't even had time to look up who was playing until that day. When she'd finished working, she sent a document to Vince and spent a few minutes doing a search on the web to learn the identity of the band. When she closed her laptop to get ready, she looked up Boundless Hearts on iTunes. She removed her clothes and entered the bathroom, laid the phone down on the vanity top of the sink, hopped in the shower, and indulged herself in the downloaded tunes while she shaved her legs and underarms.

As she approached the lobby bar, images of Dash came to mind. One of them included a memory of a kiss she couldn't forget. She lingered with her thoughts in one of five lines with at least ten people in each, leaving her to wonder if she'd even get served before the concert started. It made no difference. Either way, she was confident they'd meet up inside. She assumed his seat would be right next to hers.

Finally, it was her turn in line. "White wine, please." Ten minutes spent waiting with Dash on her mind wasn't a bad way to pass the time. She hadn't been able to get his face out of her mind. With eyes the color of candy and lips that tasted as sweet, her dreams were a treat for her senses. In her dreams, she somehow recalled his scent and the way his laugh escaped his throat. She pictured his smile and his snarky side-grin that lifted up one corner of his mouth. She hadn't had much to go on, seeing that they'd spent such a short time together. But the rich timbre of his voice still rang in her ears, leaving her wanting more conversations.

"License." An older man with thick gray hair held onto the stemmed wine glass.

"You're kidding, right?"

"No, ma'am. I'm not."

Her wallet in hand, Sky fished out her license and a twenty-dollar bill. "I'm not sure if I should be offended or flattered."

"Take it as a compliment." He winked at her, glanced down, and handed it right back.

Once the bartender handed the change to her, she

dropped a tip in the glass and turned toward the enormous electronic billboard. Boundless Hearts was on the marquee. She craned her neck to look up to the top. That's why everyone was there. Though, admittedly, she wasn't familiar with their music, her taste was eclectic. She was excited to spend the evening with Dash, and she was also happy to see a band she'd just discovered. She'd played a few more songs on her drive to D.C. Between the bathroom and the event, she decided she liked them. She might not know a lot about Dash, but from what she could gather, he had good taste in music.

Distancing herself from the bar so as not to block other patrons, she slid her finger beneath the rim of the envelope and pulled out the ticket and a note.

Can't wait to see you tonight. Hope you enjoy the show.

What? Sky's brow wrinkled as she stared at the cryptic note. He hoped she enjoyed the show? Wasn't he coming?

Stunned and perplexed, she kept walking as she tucked the note back into the envelope. Like a docile little lamb, she followed along with the herd until she approached the door and showed her ticket. An older woman with dark, curly hair directed her toward section C on the floor. As the concertgoers searched for their seats, Skylar walked along in a daze. Alone.

Her thoughts interrupted the hopeful mood she's started out with. He wouldn't buy her a ticket to a concert he didn't plan to attend. *Would he?* No. That would be crazy —but then, he did kiss a girl he barely knew in the middle of an airport.

She placed a hand up to her mouth to smother her

awkward smile. Shaking her head, she rolled her eyes as a huff escaped. Oh my God! What was she doing? Her mistrustful head kicked into gear. Why hadn't she called him earlier in the week? Maybe then she could have better gauged the guy through the safety of the phone. She wouldn't have been distracted by his sexy smile or been seduced by his eyes. She should have been more cautious. Maybe he was some weirdo kissing millionaire who went around giving women random concert tickets.

And maybe you're overreacting.

Of course, she was. Dash had his own ticket and would show up soon. Maybe he was still at work. A bark of laughter escaped, and she threw up her hand. She had no idea where he worked. She hadn't even asked him what he did for a living. *Why hadn't I asked him?*

Neglect shook her head. She gulped down her wine. Speculation wafted on threads in the air. She needed another glass. At the very least, she should have googled him. *Googled him? What was his last name?*

The more she thought about the details of how she'd arrived at that point, the more she realized she hadn't gotten any details at all. It served her right. She was Miss Detail Oriented. All her metaphorical pretty little ducks had lined up in a sweet little row and just bitten her on the ass. Though she was still holding out hope that Dash would suddenly appear, she also had to face the fact that he might not. The cryptic "hope you enjoy the show" note might hold an explanation she hadn't expected. One thing was for sure, whatever happened, she was getting what she deserved.

A prick of irritation came and went in a flash when she remembered what was in her hand. It was a third-row ticket to one of the hottest bands she'd heard in a long time. Here, there, and everywhere—no matter where Dash was, she was at National Harbor, and she was going to have a damn good time!

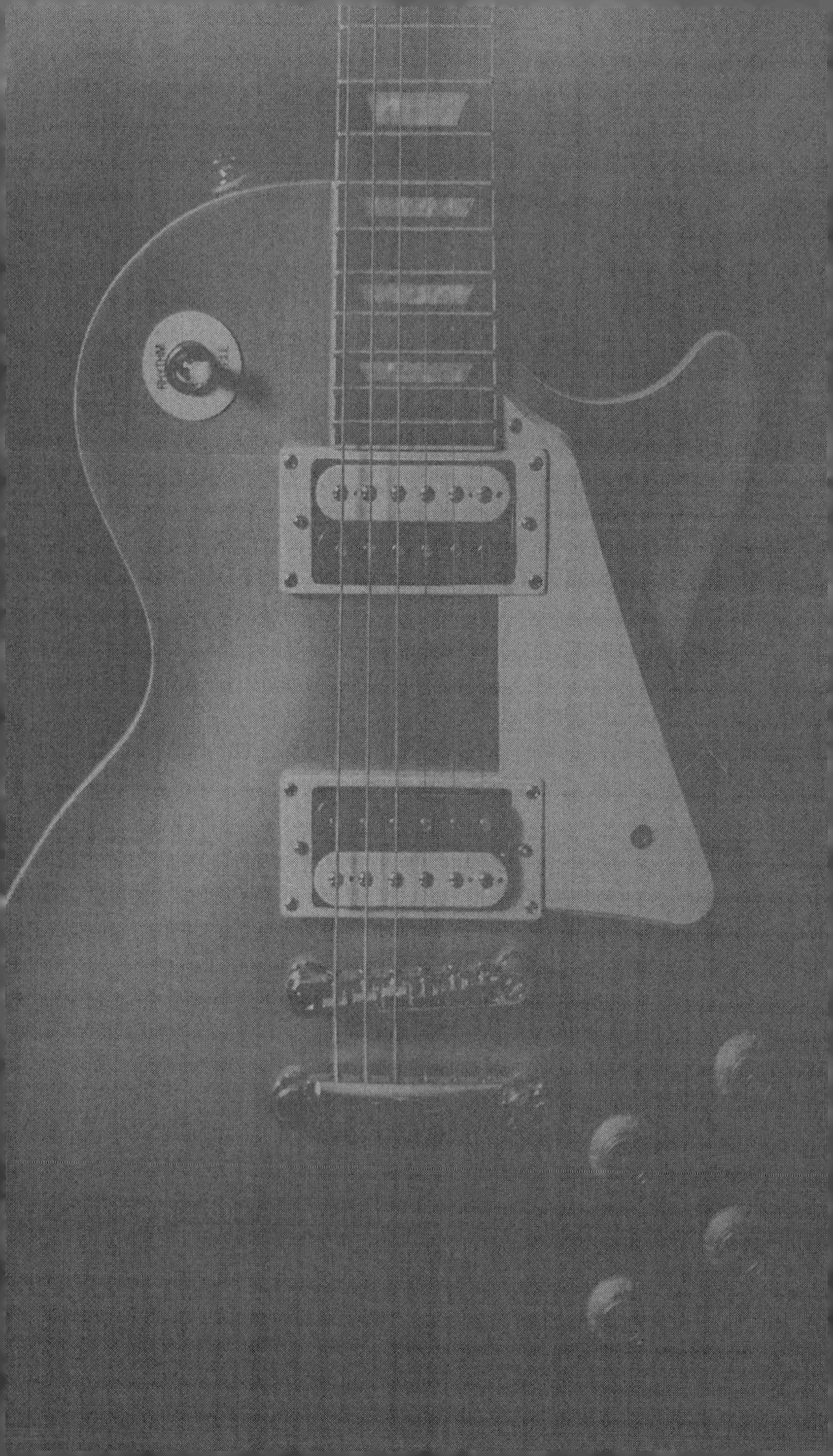

CHAPTER 8

While insecurity roamed through her, Skylar eased the problem with two more glasses of wine. She downed one almost as soon as it was in her hand and carried the other with her. Since she hadn't eaten all day, the alcohol quickly did its magic. What also helped, or hindered depending on your perspective, was that she was a lightweight when it came to alcohol. There was no denying that she was a cheap date. Two glasses down, with a third in her hand, had her very relaxed, and she headed back inside to find her seat.

The venue was easy enough to navigate, and when she returned to the concert hall, an older gentleman with thick, salt-and-pepper-colored hair caught her eye. He wore a blue blazer and gripped a black flashlight in his hand, a dead giveaway that he was an usher. As she approached him, the man broke out a wide, toothy grin.

"Hello, ma'am. How you doin' this evening? May I see your ticket?" His lighthearted tone exposed his jovial personality. She welcomed it, mainly because before the first date had taken place, there was a strong possibility she'd been dumped. Sky handed him her ticket as she scanned the plastic tag citing his name. With squinty eyes, she bent toward his lapel to read the lettering.

"So, Bernie, is it?" She straightened and returned his smile with one equally as bright. "Tell me something good, Bernie. Do I have a decent seat?"

As he perused the ticket, his eyes narrowed, crinkling at the corners. Even in her slightly inebriated state, it was apparent Bernie would have some reading glasses in his future.

"Oh! Yes, ma'am, you do!" He rotated his barrel chest and dipped his chin toward her designated section. "It's right down there, ma'am. Section C. You'll find it real easy. If you have trouble, ask one of those people down there wearing a jacket like mine."

She looked past him and then back. "What do you think, Bernie? Is . . ." she fumbled with the ticket, then held it up close to her eyes. More squinting, and she could make out the numbers. "Is twenty-six a good seat?"

"Yes, ma'am. You're in the third row there. Better seat than the first row, in my opinion. In the first row you go home with a sore neck. Third row is just right. Still close, but far enough away that you can see decently." He used his unlit flashlight as a pointer and Skylar followed it with her eyes. "Just go on down this a'way until you see the letter C. That's your row. Then you can just scoot on over to your seat. The crowd's just coming in, so you won't have many people to climb over."

"Got it. Thanks." She mimicked Bernie's upbeat attitude, gave him an appreciative smile, and continued to her seat. She couldn't help but think Bernie must have a boatload of friends. Each probably had a history with him and could share many tales about their adventures. He was the kind of guy who would make a good character for a story.

She would have liked to have a sit down with him and pick his brain over a cup of coffee. Of course, she'd have her notebook handy. Surely, he had stories that could be fodder for a novel.

As she went along, she scanned the arena for any sign of Dash. Nothing. Surprisingly, the fact he was nowhere to be found didn't bother her as much as it had before she'd gone to the bar the second time. It was amazing how the wine had altered her mood. She was no longer irritated with him. For the moment it had disappeared. As the alcohol filtered through her veins, its inebriating effects melted away any annoyance caused by Dash's absence.

An air of indifference caused her to shrug her shoulders. It was his loss. As a writer, her mind was ripe with possible scenarios. When she added in a little vino, Dash's absence proved to be less of an issue. Not that she didn't care about what happened to him, but she hadn't had a night out in months. Was it selfish that she wanted to have fun and not worry about anything for the next hour or so? She didn't think so. In fact, she entertained the possibility of getting a hotel room if she continued drinking.

A couple of minutes and a few footsteps later, she found her seat. The row was peppered with people but not so many so she tripped over legs and feet to get there. The seats immediately to her right and left were vacant, as were the two directly in front of her. Wherever Dash was, he certainly bought good seats. Though it wasn't likely, Sky couldn't help but think that, if the places stayed empty, it would be perfect. She would have a completely unobstructed view. The stage was so close she felt like she could touch it if she stretched her arm out far enough.

Since there were still a few minutes before the opening act, she took in all the equipment on the ceiling and the stage. Hanging high above were speakers that were as long as she was tall and twice as wide. In her non-expert opinion, it looked like a great sound system. Surely, she would leave with ringing in her ears, but, then, she reasoned, it was all part of the experience.

A few more minutes passed, and in that time, bodies filled the seats. Lights dimmed as the music began to flow. A generous round of applause accompanied the entrance of the opening act. Four musicians and a singer belted out some fresh tunes. They were a local band from the Eastern Shore side of the Chesapeake Bay Bridge. As she looked around, it was apparent many in the audience were there to support the hometown group. For the next forty-five minutes, they played an eclectic mix of music, warming up the crowd for the main event. Some audience members stood, but each song received a round of appreciative claps. Having never heard this band before, Sky made a mental note to look them up and add them to her iTunes.

When the first set was finished and the audience rained applause on the band, intermission followed. She stood and stretched. The lights in the arena were bright as concertgoers enjoyed a break. The marijuana smog gave the room a halo effect. Many in the crowd took the opportunity to refresh their drinks and hit the restrooms. Sky didn't. She scanned the exits nearby, hoping she'd find Dash in the crowd. The search proved futile. All she found was disappointment. It was time to accept the fact she'd been stood up.

Resigned, she took her seat. Most of the crowd was her age or younger. The style of dress was more reinvented '80s than the current day. The only thing she didn't see was the big hair of the earlier period. These guys were somewhat of a throwback, yet current. She only wished she'd had time to do a little more Googling before she'd had to get on the road. Surely, they had an interesting background. As a self-crowned Google Queen, Sky loved research almost as much as she enjoyed writing. It would have been interesting to read some of the pieces that would pop up from the search.

As the lights dimmed, Sky shook her thoughts back to the present. Drifting in the darkness was a track of music, a prelude of sorts. It was the familiar sound she'd been listening to in preparation for tonight. Her body immediately responded. The lower part bounced while the upper half shimmied. Others around her did the same. Feet tapped, shoulders rocked, and legs bounced. She looked around her, feeling the energy in the air. Excitement coursed through her veins, reigniting the effects of the alcohol. The anticipation in the air was almost palpable.

Suddenly, the music faded, then stopped. Simultaneously, the lights dimmed until the room was the color of pitch. A hush fell over the crowd. It barely lasted a moment when the silence was cut by the roar of applause. A spot of bluish-black and white light fell on the stage where a lone guitarist stood in the silence. His head hung low. The combination of spotlight and darkness made him appear ghostly.

With his head down and face hidden, he fired off a ferocious and deafening power chord from his guitar. The crowd went wild. Beneath the expertise of his talented fingers, he continued, enticing the masses with a lengthy, skilled solo. Skylar's heart skipped a beat as the crowd erupted with thunderous applause. The guitarist conjured a frenzy from the multitude. They sprang to their feet, pumped their fists in the sky, and shouted words of praise and affirmation.

Then, silence. As the music ceased, the stage went black. Skylar's heart tripled its beat as light exploded high on the scene in fifty-foot letters.

Boundless Hearts

The band's name hung above the stage, their title ablaze as fiery letters, shaded red, yellow, and orange, burned with electronic flames. Hazer machines dusted the stage, the fog rising to kiss the carbon black outline of the band's trademarked logo. A flash of white light jolted the crowd, lighting the stage. As quickly as it appeared, it graduated to the former blue-black. Looking out from his perch on the elevated platform, the drummer sized up the crowd as he pounded thick wooden sticks to skins. To the left, the bass player slapped his instrument, churning out a monstrous note that equaled the bite coming from the lead guitarist. A growl roared from the amplifier as the keyboard player clawed the ivories. Finally, from high up on a rear truss, a white spotlight focused on the back of the lead singer.

He faced away from the crowd, thrusting his hip from side to side in time with the beat of the drum. An explosion of shouts rose from a sea full of fans. Thinner than a man had a right to be, his jeans hung low on his hips and he used his sexuality to seduce the mob. The glow highlighted his form, casting shadows on a screen hanging from the ceiling to the floor behind the drummer. He raised his arms, the thin, tie-dyed silk kimono unfolded like the wings of a psychedelic angel. Hues of blues and blacks continued to project beneath the shimmering light. Bright light emerged as the singer turned toward the crowd. The combination of man, color, and light ramped up the energy of the group. He expertly fisted the microphone stand, wrapping his fingers around the metal neck, which was adorned with brightly colored scarves. When he pointed a finger out into the crowd, the masses went wild.

More a battle cry than song, he screamed as he belted out the first line of a song. With his chin down and his eyes awash with seduction, he sauntered to the front of the stage as he dragged the microphone and its stand with him. His voice baited the audience, the sound hooking them with his unique tones of mixed gravel and crushed glass. Discordant notes, scratched and ragged, clawed their way from his throat. His appearance cast a spell that was dark, evil, and threatening. As he played the crowd, the deep, coarse tone tempted the sea of bodies to release their inhibitions and become one with the music. Like a needle to a vein, he intoxicated the fans, and Skylar fell victim to the sound like all the rest.

Along with several thousand people, she danced. Sky forgot that her date was absent as she surrendered to the driving beat of the music. Her eyes traveled, first to the singer, then to the bass player. The drummer commanded her attention with a pounding rhythm that her hips obeyed. Finally, the guitarist's solo demanded her notice. His notes were expertly played, the sounds high, shrill, and infectious. She closed her eyes, letting her hips follow the charm he created with his fingers. When she opened them, he captured her gaze with a knowing smile and tempting brown eyes.

Dash!

Skylar shrieked. Her heart seized. Oxygen rushed from her lungs while her legs wobbled.

How could she have missed the connection? *Ignorance. That's how.* It was her only excuse. In between the time she last saw him and tonight, her time had been consumed with work. Even while looking at his larger-than-life image in the lobby, she hadn't made the connection. The man she'd met at the airport looked nothing like the man in the publicity shot. In the photo, he wore a beard. His hair was well past his shoulders and wavy. Now he was clean-shaven. His style was trendier, short on the sides and long on the top. There was only one thing that hadn't changed. The one feature that, even now, pinned her as it caused the familiar energy to seep quickly into her veins. His gorgeous brown eyes—and they were looking right at her.

Skylar's grin widened, so much so that it threatened to split her face. At the exact moment their eyes met, his smile extended across his handsome features in equal measure. His gaze intensified, his smile growing as he looked at her while shredding his guitar strings. As he played the notes of the song his eyes locked with hers. Once he was sure they'd made a connection, Dash lost himself in the music.

Skylar watched as he played. His hands were magic. The fingers of one danced on the guitar's sleek neck, while, with the other, he effortlessly charmed the strings with a pick. The weighty, ominous rhythm lured her as it filled the air with heart-pounding moxie. The notes penetrated her skin, making reason melt away. Any concerns she had earlier in the night withered, disappearing within the mass of moving bodies. Some jumped, others slithered, and still, others swayed. Like a sensual snake, Skylar's body gyrated in time with the music. Unlike those who were simply trapped by the rhythm, she was snared by the man himself. He hadn't stood her up. He'd wanted her in attendance. The knowledge liberated her anger. She let go, dancing before him, becoming one with his music.

It was mind-blowing.

And it was all Dash's fault.

CHAPTER 9

No longer able to think clearly, Sky gave into her relaxed state. As the band traveled from song to song, she responded by swaying her body and grinding her hips like all the rest. When was the last time she'd let go? Most of her experiences were played out in her own imagination. She couldn't be sure if her euphoria was the electricity emitted by so many bodies or if the source was the bewitching power of the men on stage. Dash, still sporting the sullen posture of a brooding rock star, broke out the notes of the band's first number-one hit with skillful precision.

The frenzy of the crowd went chaotic, half of them jumping on their feet, their voices at near screaming volume. They sang the words to the song with abandon. A person's self-consciousness could die in this atmosphere. Inhibitions fell, the point emphasized as she and others pumped their fists in solidarity, paying homage to their gods of rock.

The band flowed seamlessly from a pounding song to a quiet one, the tempo slowing down just a bit to let the audience catch their breath after so powerful a performance. The crowd clapped together in time with the musicians, creating a solid beat that complimented the band's music.

Harder.

Louder.

Stronger.

As everyone fell into the tunes, the skunky smell of pot further thickened the air. Skylar wasn't immune. The mushrooming cloud had begun to develop during the opening act and quickly circulated. Now, even more dense, those who hadn't indulged were feeling the effects of the smoke. Vapors lingered, joined with a fresh supply now that Boundless Hearts had come to the stage. She inhaled the same as the rest of the crowd, finding relaxation in the contact high.

The energy in the room was as potent and infectious as the driving music. Heart-pounding notes vibrated against the walls. Sky was of the opinion that all rock was musically scored sex. Excitement hovered in the air as rabid fans danced along with the songs of their favorite group.

Skylar danced her ass off. Gone was the cautious bookworm, at least for the night. For whatever time remained this evening, she was going to ride the high. She was a girl intent on having fun. Tomorrow would come soon enough, and all of this would be just a memory. *Like the memory of the airport kiss.*

Shit! The thought sobered her. While Dash was hot as fuck, and she would forever remember this night, they came from two different worlds. It only made sense that she'd replay her fond memories of him over and over again but, to him, she would be just another girl he met on his travels. Tomorrow, memories of her would fade from his mind.

* * *

WHITE LIGHT ILLUMINATED the arena bringing everything into focus. The brilliance served to cut through the residual fog of smoke and clarify the aftermath. Skylar's thoughts were equally as clear.

Now that the concert had ended and the crowd had thinned out, she sat in the near-empty theater, hoping for an opportunity to see Dash. In the past two hours, she'd experienced more excitement than she had in months. Maybe years. Now that the plug had been pulled and the energy had died down to nothing, her clearer head put things into perspective—and she was still trying to make sense of it all.

The entire night had been electrifying, a balance between excitement and exhaustion. Though she was tired and sweaty, she didn't want to leave. If there was a chance she might connect with him, she would . . . *You would what, Sky?*

If the truth be told, she had no idea what she was going to do if she saw Dash. All she knew was she'd felt the link between them again tonight. She couldn't explain it and entertaining the idea that there might be more than something casual between them might make her a fool but, then, so did making out in an airport with a total stranger. There was no way to categorize what she felt whenever he was near; it defied logic.

When she looked into Dash's eyes, she found something more than she should. A need in her blossomed when they touched. Though it made no sense at all, every emotion she'd attempted to put into words in a love story was happening in real life to her. She was the girl falling for the guy. The unlikely pair whose worlds and circumstances would eventually resolve into a happily ever after. She was the fictional character defying all odds. The girl from the small pond whose desire was to swim with a big fish. But it shouldn't be. There were a million reasons why she and Dash shouldn't start a relationship, and only one reason why they should—kismet.

Was she kidding herself? Was it all fabled bullshit? Truth was what she could see in front of her own eyes. Surely some scientist somewhere had figured out a logical, mathematical formula that would prove that there was no such thing as predestination, and that all things were random. But she wanted to believe. Her head hurt as she warred with herself.

Why was she trying so hard to figure this out? Dash was probably long gone from the venue. What she needed to do was go home, take a hot shower, and climb into bed. After a good night's sleep, her scattered thoughts would clear. She'd return to her fictional worlds and write out this story with an ending of her own choosing.

Sky grabbed her purse. She didn't need a hotel room; she'd sobered enough to drive. At least now the concert area was nearly empty. She'd lagged behind long enough for the crowd to have thinned out. Once she got home, she could write about her experience tonight in detail. It would make an excellent premise for a story. She could use her imagination to create the relationship and the ending she wanted. That was a much better idea than the alternative, hanging out like a little groupie to get a glimpse of the rock star.

Her spiked heel boots made a clacking sound as she made her way out of the row. Roadies were on the stage, busy breaking down. As they dismantled lights and sound equipment, the cleaning crew busied themselves in the seating area. The members of the band had probably been shuttled away to wherever it was that would afford them the most privacy. There was no need for her to stick around. She had Dash's number. She'd give him a courtesy call tomorrow and tell him she appreciated the night out. Her original idea of reconnecting with a guy that had turned her on was foolish anyway, especially now that she knew who he was and what he did for a living. There was no way the two of them would work out, coming from such different worlds.

"Excuse me, miss?"

Skylar paused. A huge man with a booming voice approached her from behind. As she turned, she recognized him as one of the men who'd been rolling equipment cases up onto the stage after the concert. He wore a black tee shirt and had a lanyard around his neck.

"This is for you." He reached toward her, his thumb pinching a piece of paper between it and his other fingers.

As Skylar took it from him, she couldn't help but notice his hands were two times the size of hers. "Thank you."

He smiled a pleasant smile and inclined his head as he left. When he turned, she noted the word "STAFF" in white letters stretched across his broad back. She waited until he was a few steps away before opening it. There, written in beautiful penmanship, was a note from Dash.

Butterflies, once again, fluttered.

If you can stick around for a few minutes, I'd like to see you.
Dash

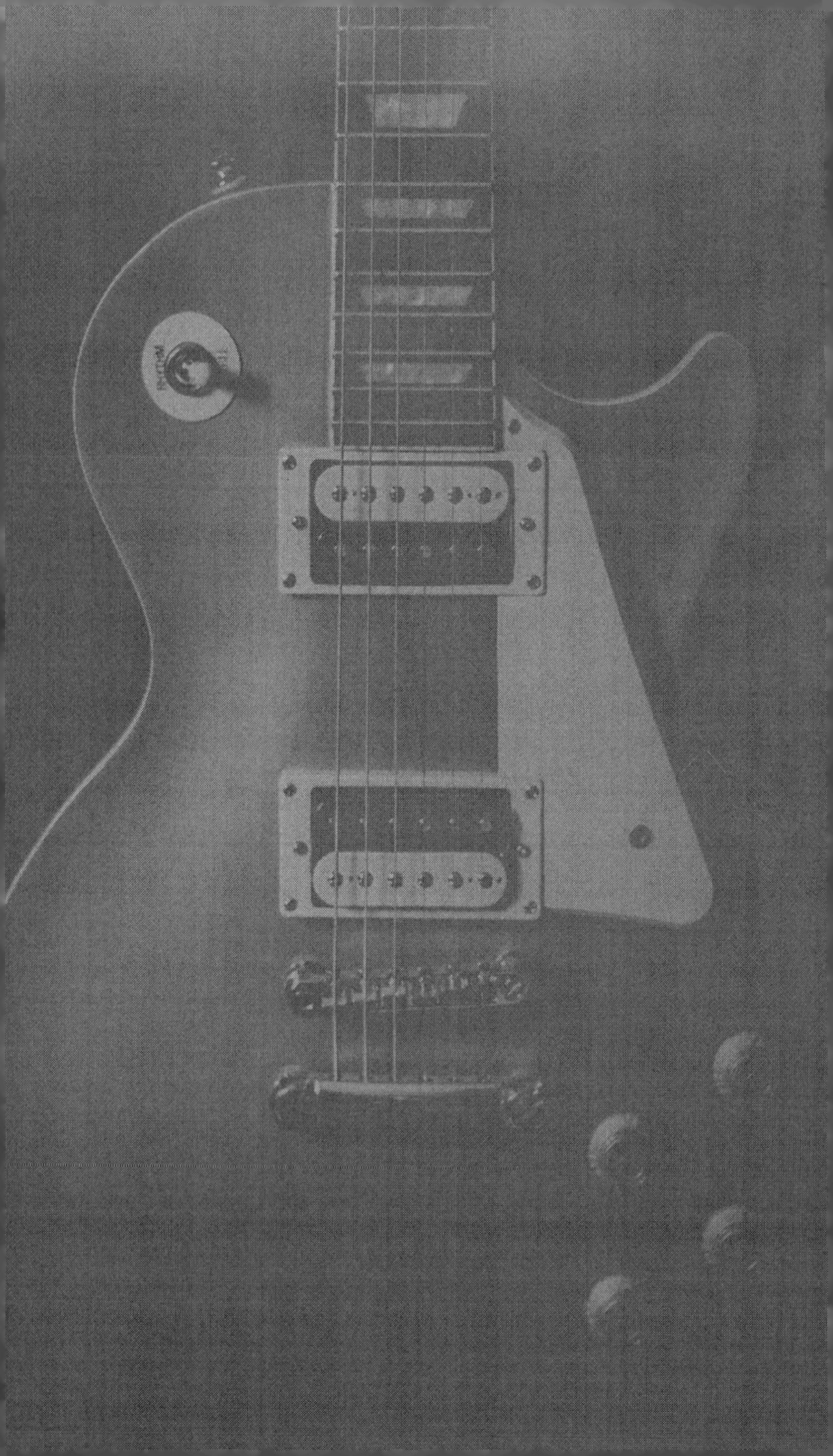

CHAPTER 10

What exactly was it about Dash that made her tummy flip and her thoughts scramble?
Anxiety? Maybe.
Excitement? Probably.
School-girl crush? Definitely.
A waterfall of emotion showered over her, leaving a thin film of doubt in its wake. What did a man like Dash want with a girl like her? His life was most certainly more exciting than hers which was quiet and spent behind a computer screen. Every cliché occupied rent-free space in her thoughts. She'd heard the stories and read the tabloids. The rumor was that musicians had a girl in every city and were only out for an easy piece of ass. Ugh! The plague of an overactive imagination. She could go around and around for days with different case scenarios and still come up with no answer.

Sky walked to the edge of the stage. Like a kid on a carnival ride, her thoughts went askew, and she wondered which persona would appear when she saw Dash. The sweet guy from the airport, or an arrogant rock star?

Behind her, the sound of boots scraping against a cement floor interrupted her fast and furious thoughts. When she turned, the objections and concerns at the forefront of her mind withered at the sight of a pair of warm, brown eyes. Heat blushed her cheeks as a lazy smile stretched her lips. "Thank you for the ticket."

"Thank you for waiting."

And there it was. A combination that could only be described as "Mr. Sex on a Stick" with a voice that was as smooth as Kentucky bourbon. He stood tall above her and, as she looked up, her neck craned to take in the whole effect. His eyes and hair were darker up close than they were from a distance with lights beaming down on his head. She surveyed his body, remembering what it felt like against her. With narrowed eyes and disapproval on her lips, she smirked. "You could have warned me, you know."

Dash canted his head to the side as his brows pulled together. Questioning lines furrowed the space in between. "You didn't know? I thought you might have put it all together."

Skylar shook her head. "Nope. I was busy with deadlines. I Googled the band so I could listen to some of their, correction, *your* music, but that was all I searched for. Just the music. I guess if I'd spent more time researching, I would have put two and two together."

"Sorry 'bout that." He shrugged it off, sheepishly. His eyes sparked as if a thought occurred to him. He tipped his head. "If you want to know the truth, I'm glad you didn't know. You'd be surprised at the shit people will do to meet the members of the band." Retreating a few steps, he leaned back and rested his weight against the edge of the stage.

Taking a cue from him, she took a seat across from him in the now empty row. "I'll bet." She nodded. Pausing as an image came to mind, she then scrunched up her face. "I'll go out on a limb and say I'll bet none of them have dropped all their stuff in an airport to get your attention."

As he laughed at her answer, she fell into the sound. It wrapped around her like a cozy blanket. How was it possible she could feel homesick for a sound that wasn't yet familiar?

"No. I can, quite honestly, report that no one has ever used that one."

At the awkward memory, Sky was desperate to explain yet again. Her hands raised in a surrendered gesture. "I assure you, that was not my plan."

Another pause passed between them yet Dash never released his gaze. She, however, grew more self-conscious beneath his scrutiny.

An awkward moment ticked by. Then two. Then three.

She stood as discomfort pricked her skin. She reached out, extended her hand, and gave him a grateful smile. "It was really nice seeing you again. Thank you, again, for tonight."

Dash blinked, momentarily stunned by the change in her demeanor. A question quirked his brow. He took her hand. "Sky, don't go." His eyes begged her to stay. He spoke easier. "You're really beautiful, you know?"

Her expression shifted as his tongue loosened. She felt a wry grin creep into her lips.

"Shit! I didn't mean that."

Morphing once again, lines etched her forehead as she watched him in silence. Her shoulders stiffened as she tipped her chin. Certainly, he didn't mean to renege on his compliment.

Mortified, he clicked his tongue. "I mean, I'm not a psycho or anything. It's just that your face . . ." He fumbled the words as he ran a hand over his face.

An awkward smile scraped her lips. "My face, what?"

With a quarter turn of her head, she presented an ear to indicate she was waiting for an explanation. From this vantage, she could still see him, and most certainly could hear him. Though she toyed, it would be fun to watch him walk over the eggshells without cracking them further.

He dropped his chin to his chest, then looked up at her through sheepish eyes. "I'm really fucking this up, aren't I?"

Amused, she acknowledged the point with a tip of her chin and a bob of her head. "You're doing a fine job of it." The phrase misery loves company ran through her mind and, though she hated to admit it, his discomfort made her feel less self-conscious. Gone was her preconceived notion that he would be all cool and arrogant. Now that he was the awkward one, she felt refreshed. Instead of meeting up with a stuck-up, egotistical public figure, he was just a regular guy.

"I didn't mean to say you were ugly or anything like that."

Her eyes rounded further as he, once again, put his foot in his mouth.

"Shit! I did it again!"

Clearly irritated with himself, she saved him by closing the distance between them and placing her finger on his lips. "Stop talking. It's fine."

His expression relaxed as he realized she'd kept him from digging the deeper hole. He wrapped his hand around hers and removed it from his mouth. "So much for making a good impression."

She remained quiet, yet her thoughts scattered again. All that mattered was Dash and this moment. The rest of her thoughts could wait.

"I don't know what it is about you, Skylar, but you rattle me—and then you see right through me." He spoke easier, squeezing her fingers as he made his confession.

She swallowed. She walked the same clumsy road he did. Maybe that's why his honesty was refreshing. The color of his eyes intensified as his expression turned serious. Now nearly black, they spilled their secrets.

"Everybody thinks I'm cool, and maybe I am in some things. But when it comes to you . . . I don't know. There's something there. Something more." His baritone fell an octave. "I guess it's better that you know the truth. I'm really a fuckup—at least when it comes to impressing you."

"You're trying to impress me?" She lost her poise as she blurted out the words but couldn't silence the surprise in her voice. "Why would you want to impress me?" Her thoughts scrabbled for an answer to her own question. Dash could have any woman he wanted, yet he was trying to impress her? She waited to hear the explanation as she watched him swallow what she could only imagine was a bundle of nerves.

"Because from what I know of you—and I know it's not much—I like you. You're genuine and kind and funny. It's crazy, but you're one of the most fascinating people I've ever met. I thought that before I kissed you. After the kiss, I wanted to do it again and again."

Skylar shivered, fearing the intensity in his gaze because she was sure she would drown in its naked truth. Dash reached around her waist, pulling her in to remove any space between them. Like a war drum, her heart pounded out an emotional beat. Dash fought to find the right words to express himself. He reached up and tucked a loose curl behind her ear. Tender feelings blossomed inside of her. The solace that most people search a lifetime for was right in front of her, reflected in his eyes. His easy smile tormented what was left of her reservations and she released them.

"Before you write me off, just know that shit like this

doesn't happen to me. I like you, Sky. I want to get to know you better. All you have to do is let me."

CHAPTER 11

Skylar's heart tore open. It wasn't just Dash's words that won her over, it was the sincerity with which he'd said them. Their conversation could have lasted a minute or an hour, but time seemed to stand still when she was with him. The buttery smooth tone of his voice made her feel all warm and fuzzy inside.

"So, you'll go out with me?"

"Was that a question or a statement?"

"Both."

She looked around the auditorium as she lured him from his serious tone to her more playful one. "In case you didn't notice, you did ask me out, and I'm here."

A line of disapproval filled his lips. "Not a date like this—although I'm glad you came tonight. I'm talking about a real date. We could do something easy like coffee, or we could go to a fancy restaurant. Your choice."

The smile on her face was the outward expression of her inner happiness, yet so much more bubbled beneath the surface. If Dash could really see how genuinely excited she was, he might have run the other way. Her gut told her to go for it. He seemed like such a nice guy. Not like some of the men she'd dated in the past. They'd droned on and on, mostly about themselves. She'd only been able to take so much of their egos before she'd had to end things. Although this was only their second meeting, she felt the contrast. Those guys bored her with their constant bragging, while Dash had every right to boast, yet didn't.

Then, a sudden case of nerves hit. Was she setting herself up for disaster? Dash *did* have every right to brag, so what did he want with her? He could have any girl he wanted.

Sky needed air. Distance. The hair on the back of her neck was standing at attention and her palms were clammy. As she took a few steps back, she wiped her hands on her jeans. Her insides rattled, she had absolutely no idea what to do next. Precisely what was the proper protocol when the guy who kissed you and asked you out was one of the most eligible bachelors in the United States?

"Um, okay?"

Dash stretched to his full height, his tone tentative. "Now I have to ask if that's a question or a statement. Really?"

She shrugged. "I guess so. I mean, why not? What do I have to lose?" She managed a twisted smile. "Let's tell the truth here. You already stood me up so you could go play music with your friends in front of a couple of thousand people. Coffee seems pretty tame compared to sitting next to an empty seat." She tossed him a smirk. "You are going to sit down at a table with me, right? I mean, you're not going to turn out to own the restaurant or be a barista, are you? Just asking."

Dash let out a laugh. "How did you like those empty seats? I wanted to make sure you had a good view."

"You did that?" Surprise rounded her eyes. "I thought the ticket holders just didn't show up."

"Nope. That was me. When I remembered your height, I had them reseated."

His expression was sweet. If nothing else, he was certainly thoughtful. Again, something uniquely different from other men she'd dated. But the sudden fear crept back in and seized her heart. This roller coaster of emotions was not a ride she wanted to be on. A not-so-pretty scene that included press and paparazzi played out in her anxious thoughts. One that might alter their course. Now that she was aware of Dash's notoriety, she had to think more clearly. This wasn't just a date anymore. It wasn't only Dash and her. Now it was Dash, her, and the public. The mental image was overwhelming.

Taking a few steps back, she distanced herself from him. "On second thought, let me think about it, okay?"

"Whoa! What just happened, Sky? I saw it in your eyes. You drifted away." Disappointment shadowed his eyes as his expression turned serious and guarded. He studied her for a moment, wariness written across his face. "If I say yes, you have to tell me what changed your mind all of a sudden."

She made a quick attempt to gather her thoughts but uttered not a word. If she did, she would prove herself to be a coward. A million case scenarios were screaming in her head, but one took center stage. It was the only explanation she could give him at the moment. "Because you're larger than life, Dash—"

" Barrows. Dash Barrows," he interjected.

"Ok. YOU are larger than life, Dash Barrows, and I'm a bookworm. An introvert. Chances are someone, somewhere, will snap a picture of something as innocent as coffee and make it into something else. You're used to that kind of attention. You live a billboard-sized life, where mine is the size of a postage stamp. It isn't just me I'm thinking about. I'm thinking of you, too. I don't want you to put either of us in an awkward position." Though her expression softened, her mind battled with conflicting thoughts. Dash's personal life wasn't personal. She couldn't imagine what that kind of scrutiny might be like, and she wasn't exactly sure she wanted to know.

Instead of backing off as she'd expected, Dash doubled down. His jaw stiffened, and his lips tightened into a tense line. Determination corrupted his usually kind eyes. "My life might be billboard-sized, as you said, but underneath all the hype, I'm just a regular guy. I can't help that my life is more public than private, but I want to get to know you better. Me, Dash Barrows the man, not Boundless Hearts's guitarist. What you see on the stage is two hours out of a twenty-four-hour life. That guy you see up there is a much more cautious fuck than you think. That is work. This is me." He took a step closer. "What I do on stage is just like any other guy going to work for a paycheck, just more visible. Those stories you might have read about me? They're all hype. Believe it or not, Sky, I don't drink, smoke, or do drugs. I am very responsible in my private life." He tossed back her earlier smirk. "Except for laundry. I hate doing laundry."

While she appreciated the explanation, she was lost in her own thoughts. They were conflicted at best. While he'd presented more reasons why they should have, at least one, real date, she tried to define the hollow feeling she got when she thought about never seeing him again.

With a slow shake of his head, he caught her wrist. Her gaze fell to the point of their connection. Though the tiny, comforting circles he traced on the top side sent soothing messages, her stomach was still doing flip-flops. He took her chin between his fingers and lifted. His jaw was set while resolve filled his gaze. "You really should give me a chance, you know?"

His voice dropped low, the tone sounding dark and severe. His purposeful expression wrapped around her, convincing her he wasn't going to give up. How could she resist those gorgeous eyes and oh-so-kissable lips? The uneasy feeling in her belly grew to epic proportions. There would be no second chance for this. If she walked away now, regret would be her constant companion. Those familiar goosebumps that had begun at the airport were presently skating over her skin. If she gave into doubt, they might never come again. His eyes begged while his tongue traced his bottom lip. Suddenly she wanted to kiss away his unsettled expression.

"I promise, you have nothing to lose by going out with me and maybe everything to gain. Take a chance, Sky. You might just find that we have more in common than you think."

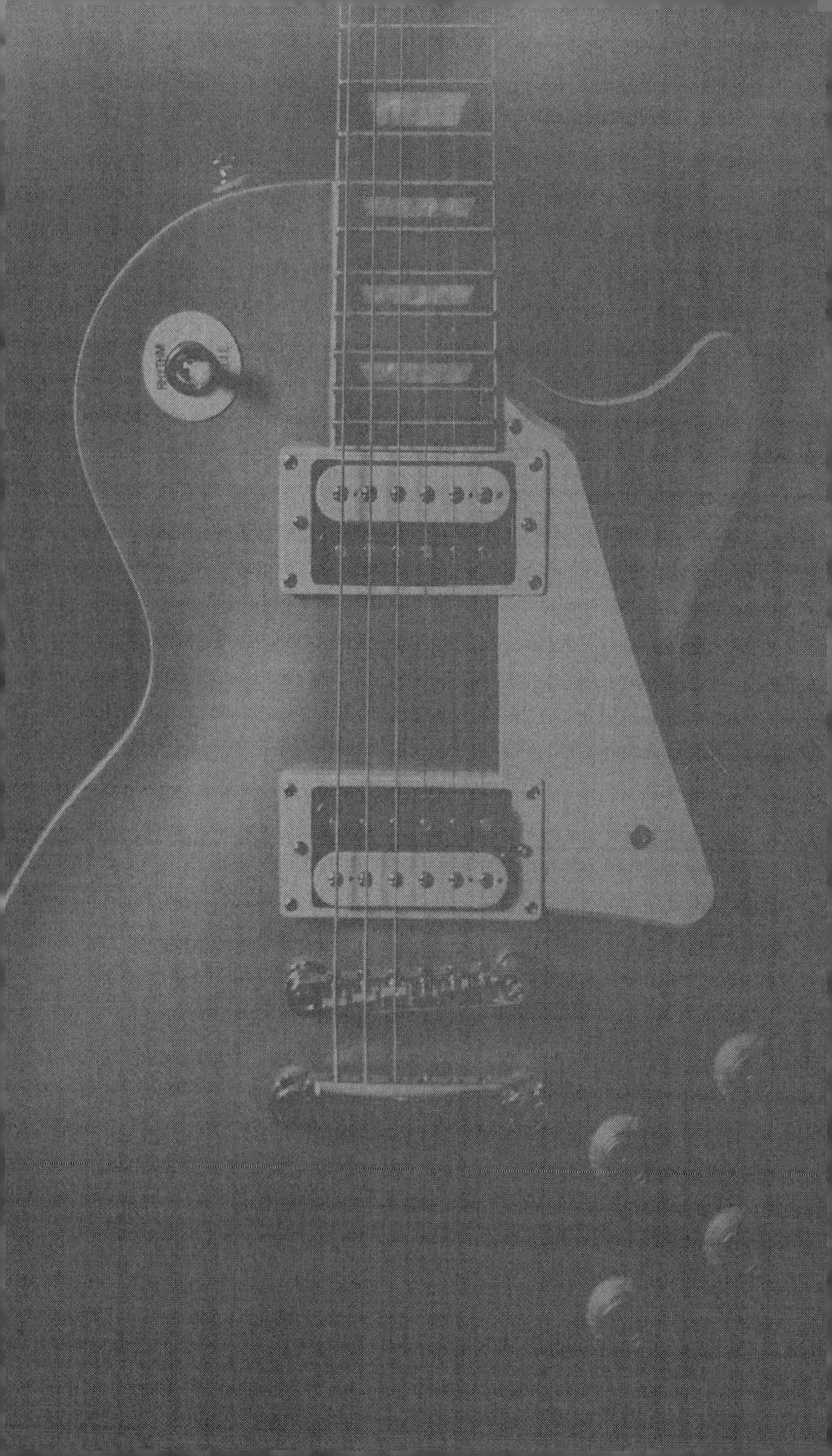

CHAPTER 12

The drive home did little to clear her head. Though completely sobered after her conversation with Dash, there was still much to think about. As she inserted the key into the lock of her red-painted front door, Skylar promised herself she would do as Dash had asked and give his offer serious consideration. There was much to contemplate.

As she crossed the threshold of her house, the top hinge made a tiny creaking sound. Strange how the minute she closed the door behind her, she immediately felt better. The little town house in Fells Point was her safe space. At least there she could unravel her thoughts. The prickly needle ones she'd experienced on the way home had been less than helpful.

She wondered if things were as complicated as her fear made them out to be. Sky kicked off her shoes, set her keys on the small table nearby, and shucked her jacket. As she hung it on the coat rack, her posture deflated.

Pulling a folded blanket from the back of the sofa, she

draped it over her body, sinking into its soft comfort. She told Alexa to dim the lights. It was so much easier to think at home than when she'd been staring into eyes that seemed to see into her soul.

A crack of thunder split the silence as lightning cut a flash across the sky. A pang of guilt shot through her heart. She regretted making Dash feel bad. That had never been her intent. Caution seemed to rule during their conversation. She wished she could have just said yes to his offer. After all, it was only one date. Though she could tell he was disappointed, she was equally disappointed with herself, if not more so. A life like the one Dash led could be exciting but could also swallow her whole. When had she lost her adventurous spirit? More importantly, had she ever possessed such a trait?

The wind blew the rain sideways, pelting it against the windows and door. Skylar closed her eyes, and a deep breath steadied the beat of her skipping heart. There was something soothing about the sound of rain. Though some detested a downpour, she felt the opposite. Stormy weather was when she was the most creative. She'd plotted many stories beneath a turbulent sky. Her house was across the street from the water. Most days, the view from her Thames Street home featured boaters and water taxis transporting tourists from Fells Point to the Baltimore Harbor. Tonight, all she could hear were massive drops beating down on the street. As the water poured from the sky and hit the old cobblestone, the sounds lulled her into a deep state of relaxation. Still, Dash was the one who consumed her thoughts. Did she dare imagine what life would be like to date someone so visible?

The thought rattled her, and she flipped over to her side. A familiar weight settled on her thigh. She opened her eyes as her cat gracefully tiptoed to her hip, then jumped to the hollow curve between her stomach and breasts. The familiar, soothing purr started the moment the cat curled up beside her. "Hi, Hemi." Skylar ran her fingers up and down the cat's back, and the sound stayed constant. "How's my sweet boy?"

The animal, aptly named Hemmingway for her favorite author, had incredible mousing skills. That trait came in handy when one lived in a house that was more than a hundred years old. An occasional field mouse could find the tiniest crack and make its way inside, looking for a warm, dry place. Hemi made sure they knew they weren't welcome.

As he positioned himself for a belly rub, she splayed her fingers and ran her hand through his soft, downy fur. The display of mutual affection was their routine. Every night she petted Hemi, and every night she fell asleep to his purr.

Sky readjusted, settling in to get more comfortable. She pulled the blanket up over her shoulder until the edge kissed her throat. As she closed her eyes and drifted to sleep, her last thought had nothing to do with stories or edits or a deadline. Tonight, only one consumed her dreams, and his eyes were hypnotizing.

* * *

HER BARE FEET padded against the hardwood floors. Sunlight crept through the curtains. Skylar picked up her phone to look at the time. Early morning. She needed coffee.

The hardwood floors stopped at the kitchen where the tile began. At least they weren't cold. When she'd had the stone installed, she made the wise decision to have them heated. Though it would always be an ongoing project, her little home now bore her personal stamp. One by one, the renovations had turned the small, cut-up row house into an open and inviting area. Though her friends had thought her crazy, she'd known when she'd looked at the house that the countless projects necessary to make it a home would be well worth it. The property had sat empty for nearly five years. It had needed many repairs—almost a complete overhaul—but Sky had been up to the challenge. Instead of feeling cramped and overcrowded, the new concept welcomed visitors. She'd upgraded all the appliances to the consumer's equivalent of a chef's kitchen. The house was listed on the historical registry and would bring her a tidy profit should she ever sell—but she wouldn't. Her home was her safe space, the place where she could think without distraction.

Though it was morning, she reached into the cabinet to get a mug and poured herself a smooth bourbon for a Kentucky Coffee. After last night, she needed a drink, and there was certainly more than a shot in there. Had Dash Barrows really asked her out, and she'd hesitated? She mixed together the rest of the ingredients, shaking her head in disbelief as she brought the cup to her mouth. The mild burn of the alcohol against her lips coated her tongue and throat as it went down. She released a breath, exhaling the slight burn. What had she done last night? She wouldn't be surprised if Dash called her today and reneged on his invitation. If he did, she couldn't blame him.

A long sigh escaped her as she closed her eyes and stretched her neck from side to side. She should have been like every other female and jumped at the chance, but she couldn't. It wasn't in her nature. How she envied those women. She'd never been a girl to throw caution to the wind. Consequences, good or bad, were always weighed carefully before she made a decision. Her grandmother had called her an "old soul," and that's exactly how she felt: ancient.

She tossed back the drink. Her eyes pinched and nose scrunched at such an early-hour assault. Hopefully, she could loosen some of her stuffy thinking with the help of the drink. Her quirky DNA required that she have checks and balances in all things, and she wanted to do the right thing. Last night was a beautiful memory, and though her tired mind had been assaulted by the adrenaline rushes, she'd promised herself the decision would be made today. No more skirting the issue. After all, it was just one date.

As Sky finished off the drink, she thought of the last thing Dash had said to her before they parted ways, that he was a regular guy who hoped she would give him a chance.

Dash knew about as much of her background as she knew of his, which was nothing. He didn't know the circumstances that had made her so cautious. Countless doctors, wearing their best poker faces, had let promising words fall from their lips when her father had been diagnosed with cancer. "We're hoping for the best outcome" was the most used phrase. Her dad had hung onto the word "hope," and all it implied. One more day, then one more hour, until the final, last minute. When his human body could take no more, she told him how much he was loved. In the aftermath, she'd clung to what was left of her faith. It hadn't eased the sting. Not one thing the doctors had promised came to pass. The experience had jaded everything in her world, and she had become very cautious in every aspect of her life. People were careless with promises. Was Dash one of them?

She stared up at the ceiling. "C'mon, Dad. I need a little help here. I don't know what to do." Neither lengthy nor wordy, she sent up the plea. If there was any way her father could help clear her mind from wherever he was, he would. When he'd been alive, their meaningful conversations always ended with an "aha" moment. The minute when confusion became clarity. She needed one of those now.

CHAPTER 13

Three weeks. It took her that long to muster up some bravery and agree to go out with him. For twenty-one whole days and nights, their relationship grew over the phone. Sky had to give it to Dash; he was persistent and patient. After each conversation, she ran countless scenarios before she finally asked herself if dating Dash was worth the risk of having her privacy invaded, being judged by his adoring public, and, most importantly, the chance of heartbreak. Her conclusion? It wasn't about him at all—but her. It was time that she stepped out of her comfort zone.

Throwing caution to the wind wasn't Skylar's forte, but today she was doing it bravely. Now she stood on the curb of her street staring at the object of her first test at trusting Dash. A monstrously large, black Harley Davidson. Surely, she was out of her mind.

"Ready?" A determined tone nearly masked the question that rumbled from Dash's chest.

She wasn't quite sure how in the hell he'd convinced her to get on a Harley. There'd been something about his confidence that made her feel at ease about the journey. Of course, that had been over the phone. She could be brave from a distance. But there she was, standing next to the big metal beast, ready to ride through the countryside. A growing sense of adventure warred with her common sense. She was both excited and terrified. Somewhere between the two feelings was her fragile line of acceptance. Trust was the most important thing she was giving to him, and today it would be sitting with her on the seat behind him.

Her fingers tightened on his shoulder. "What do I do?"

"Right foot on the peg. Right hand on my shoulder. Push yourself straight up, then slowly swing your left leg over the seat. Try to stay balanced. Once your leg is over, sit your ass down."

Her slight nod seemed to take forever as she tried to visualize his instructions. She could do it. His confident smile told her so.

Noting his firmly planted feet and steady grip on the handlebars, Sky stiffened her spine, inhaled a deep breath, and readied to mount. He tipped his chin to indicate he was ready—but she wasn't.

Dash seemed to sense her fear and turned his head toward her. When he let go of the throttle, the scream of the engine quieted down to a more mellow rumble. "What's the matter?"

Her gaze dropped to the black boots she'd purchased just for this trip. Though she struggled to put her feelings into words, hesitation sealed her lips. She found it hard to look at him.

He reached for her chin, lifted it, and checked the latch on her helmet. "Are you scared?"

His leather-clad fingers felt rough against her skin. Sheepishly, she nodded.

"You don't have to be embarrassed about it."

She looked at him with an unsure gaze. "It's not that I don't trust you, it's just that there are so many things that could go wrong, you know?" Her voice trailed off beneath the weight of her trepidation.

"I'm glad that you're cautious, but fear is never good for you or the driver. I'm as safe as I can be, Sky, and with you on the back, I'll be even more so. I can't control the other guy, but I never let my guard down when I'm on the bike."

She rolled her shoulders and shook the tension out of her arms and legs. "This is all strange to me. Trusting someone like this."

"I get it, but you have to relax and stop thinking like that. Instead, think like this: it's a beautiful day, the sun is shining, the birds are singing, and we're going to enjoy the road less traveled. Concentrate on the here and now. I take the back roads, mostly, and there's not much traffic." He revved the throttle. "Let's go through this one more time. Foot here. Hand here. Swing your leg behind me. Sit your ass down. Got it?"

"I think so. It sounds like mounting a horse." She scrunched up her nose and pinched her eyes. "I'm not really good at that, just so you know."

"That's fine. Thanks for the warning," he laughed. "Just make sure you don't swing that leg like a gymnast. Just straight up and over slowly. If you tilt our center of gravity, you can make the bike go down."

Holy shit! No. That wasn't something she wanted to do. A wave of adrenaline hit, but she wasn't wimping out. She was determined to do this, even if all she did was prove to herself she could.

Her stomach did a little flip as she grabbed hold of his shoulder. She did exactly as he'd instructed, finishing the task with a perfectly balanced half-pirouette. He did as he'd promised, holding everything steady until she was seated.

He twisted the throttle again, breathing life into the nine-hundred-pound beast. "Ready?" He watched for her nod over his shoulder, his voice loud so she could hear him over the roar of the engine. "You can either hold on to my waist or my belt loops—but I'll let you guess which one I prefer." His brown eyes studied her as she wrapped her arms around his waist.

An unexpected ripple of excitement skated over her skin as she blew out a breath. "So, we're good to go?"

Again, she nodded.

"Great. Let's do it!"

Dash took off, the sudden motion eliciting a yelp from her. The action shot her with a mix of fear and excitement that penetrated all the way to her insides. Instantly, she felt guilty. She wasn't as fine as she pretended. Though she'd said she was okay, she really wasn't *good* at all. Terrified would more accurately describe what she felt, but she covered it with a smile. Her mind was spinning like a wheel, with many emotions vying for the coveted top spot. She forced herself to stay in the moment, refusing to let her feelings rule her. *Concentrate on the here and now.* Wasn't that what he said?"

With her hands around his waist, she felt his muscles ripple and vibrate. She looked and saw the landscape whizzing by. Her eyes slammed shut. *I'm okay. I'm fine. This is fine.*

Relax.

Relax.

Relax.

As she repeated the mantra, her hands loosened their grip and she sucked in deep rushes of air. Dash had slowed the bike to a more leisurely, steady pace, and she inched her eyes open. Breathing became a little easier.

When he'd told her he loved to travel the back roads on his motorcycle, she never gave any thought to what that meant. She guessed it would feel like it did when taking a drive in the country. In a car. This was nothing like that. It was different. Distinct. Even behind the tinted lenses of sunglasses, colors were more vibrant. Where a few minutes ago, she'd locked her body tight, her shoulders were now relaxed. The tension that had held her back ramrod straight was now melting away as it trickled down her spine. Her hips loosened. Her legs fell open. She let go of his waist and sat a little further back, hooking her thumb, index, and middle fingers through the belt loops on his jeans.

How to phrase the rush of exhilaration she was riding? Words seemed to fail her writer's imagination. To say it was a beautiful day seemed unjust. Everything about their surroundings overloaded her senses. Unchained and free from the usual modes of transportation, everything that caught her eye was fresh. Her terror calmed to wonder. Not surprisingly, words for a story swirled around in her mind as she cataloged the ever-changing scenery.

An early morning chill hung in the air as the sun broke its way through the night sky. The autumn landscape was covered by a blanket of morning dew. I inhaled the fresh smell, thankful I was witness to this perfect time of day, when the world awakened.

It was crazy how, when emancipated from her computer screen, her synapses fired in a different direction. It was as if she were looking at nature for the first time. All the pigments of creation had stippled the landscape. Pinks were pinker. Blues were bluer. The view pulled at her heartstrings as the slightly chilled breeze chapped her face. While Dash focused on the road, she casually held on to his belt loops. He reached back and patted her leg.

"You like?"

"Yes." How could she not? The residual beauty from the morning soaked into her bones and saturated her soul. As the sweetened smell of oxygen bathed her lungs, her worry evaporated. Like sprites hitching a ride on a dandelion wish, her concerns floated away. In their place was tranquility. Fear no longer shackled her heart and mind.

Was this what it would be like to be with Dash? Every day would be an adventure? He was a mystery she wanted to unravel. She wouldn't deny that she was attracted to him—an air of raw sexuality emanated from him—but there was so much of his personality buried beneath the surface. Seeing him play in concert was exciting, but this kind of day was more her style.

She toyed his leather belt with her thumb. Suddenly she felt like they were more kindred spirits than she'd originally thought. She lifted her eyes to take in the lush rolling hills and something inside of her clicked. Maybe today was the evidence she'd been waiting for all along. A sign that he was just a normal guy who enjoyed the quiet. Not that a Harley was quiet, but spending a day enjoying simple things like fields of budding flowers and a back road beside a creek spoke of his love for simplicity. Life was complicated enough without spending days constantly living up to the expectations of others. Even though their circumstances were different, the pressures to perform were the same. She felt none of that today and, from what she could see of Dash's face in the side view mirror, neither did he. He was a study of serenity.

Dash inclined his head, directing her gaze to a large field. "Look."

Ripples of excitement filled her belly as they spied a family of deer near the tree line. With childlike wonder, she pinched the loops at his waist. The scene was too perfect, the deer too beautiful. She leaned into him, placing her chin on his shoulder. "Is it always like this? So peaceful and beautiful? So free?"

A soft bark of laughter shook him as she spoke into his ear. He turned his head just slightly. When she caught a glimpse of the side of his face, she noted a hint of humor. The corner of his mouth hooked into a smile as he stole a quick glance over his shoulder. Even behind his sunglasses, she caught the crinkle of delight at the corner of his eye.

He leaned back, taking one hand off the handlebar as he again reached back to give her a reassuring pat. "It's never the same, babe—and it never grows old."

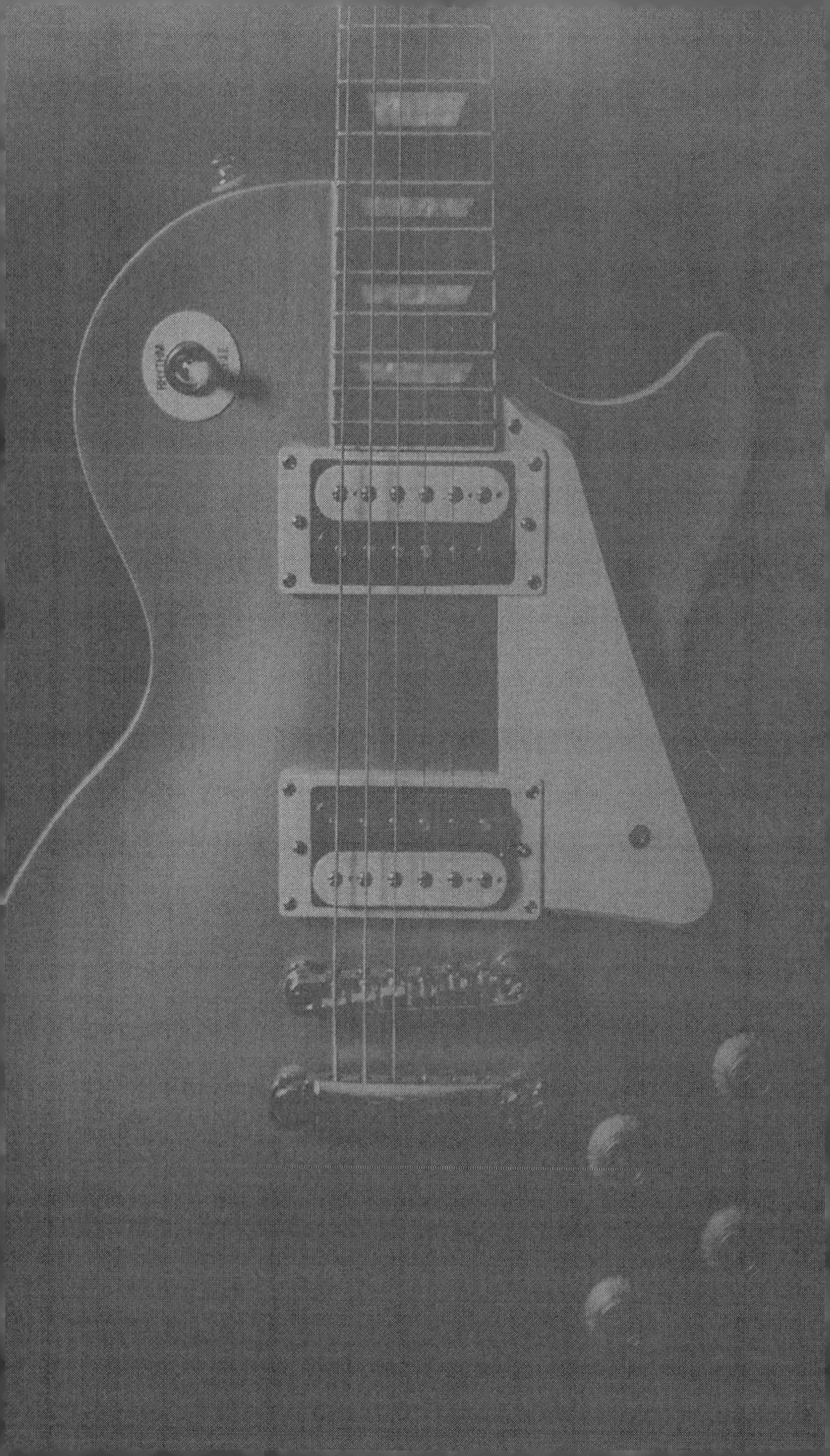

CHAPTER 14

Skylar set her laptop to the side and took a long stretch. She'd been awake since the crack of dawn. Three cups of coffee later, and she was finished. It had taken her nearly a month to put down the first draft of her new novel. This one was much lighter than her previous stories, and she couldn't help but wonder if the change was due, in part, to her ongoing relationship with Dash.

She rolled her desk chair over to the window. The morning sun glistened on the water across the street. It was ten o'clock, and the stores in Fells Point were opening for business. The tourists would be taxiing over from the harbor. With too lovely a day to stay inside, she expected there would be scores of them. Broadway had an eclectic mix of restaurants and bars, as well as antique and vintage clothing stores. Dash appreciated the area as much as she did. Their walks around the neighborhood always had them discovering something new. Since finding classic treasures was something they both enjoyed, they did it often.

Skylar placed both hands against the wooden window frame and with a hard shove, pushed it open. Fresh air mixed with the dank smell of harbor water filtered into the house and billowed the curtains as she scooted back to her desk. It would be nice to escape the confines of her house with Dash today. Why she was so vigilant about her writing routine, she didn't know. She kept herself chained to the desk. Habit? Maybe. Dash reminded her that she could write from anywhere, and often encouraged her to get out of the house. Though it was an interesting thought, she'd never done it. She was a pain in her own rear end and was so particular about so many things it seemed like she'd created a bit of an OCD ritual for herself. It also wasn't as easy as he would think. Inspiration hit her at the most inopportune times. Often, when most people were going to sleep, her mind spun storylines. Thoughts and ideas were most malleable for her in the dark of night. Having Dash in her life also added another element. Nighttime was also when longing seeped in. Images of Dash would corrupt her thoughts and filter into scenes. The way he kissed her. The way he held her. The way her hand felt when he captured it in his and refused to let go. All those things found their way into her romances. And why wouldn't they? The way that she felt about him had changed her perspective about many things, and she described them now in greater detail. This latest story had a couple meeting at a bus stop. The girl fell hopelessly in love with the boy. Through tragedy, they triumphed and found their happily ever after. Though Dash spent as much time with her as his schedule allowed, he was away more often than not. The thought that she and Dash might have a happy ending of their own whispered through her thoughts. Anything was possible.

The rocker and the writer, such an unlikely pair. Dash regularly made jokes about how they were perfect for each other. Opposites attract, he would say. Neither was able to offer an explanation for their attraction, so they compared themselves to Forrest Gump and Jenny. Peas and carrots. Carrots and peas.

Sky rolled her head from side to side, giving her neck a good stretch. As she pushed the chair away from her desk, she arched her back, raised her hands up toward the ceiling, and reached as far as she could. Stiff muscles, cramped from confinement, burned deliciously as she positioned her body to help unkink and unravel. Though the chair was comfortable enough, spending all that time in the same position took a toll. Creaks and pops came from stiff, underworked joints. Hemmingway jumped up on the desk, his meow a cry for attention. "Ah. No more today, buddy. We're done." She reached underneath him and cradled him just above his belly. Hemi was content to ride her hip from the office to the kitchen. Setting the furball on a cushioned chair, she rubbed behind his ears. Gratitude fed his purrs. Sky was in such a good mood. Not only was the first draft complete but, today, Dash was coming home.

"That's all you get, pretty boy. I've got to eat and shower." The words fell softly from her lips, piercing the quiet room. She popped a bagel into the toaster and grabbed the apricot spread from the fridge. She had plenty of time for a bite. The last thing Dash said on the phone was "Have your britches ready for a ride." She glanced at the clock, rubbing her eyes to help her focus. She'd been staring at a screen for so long her eyes felt like they had sand in them. Working from the middle of the night into the early morning had its advantages. She'd have a few hours before he arrived. It might be enough time to do everything she wanted to, eat, shower, and nap. In her current state, rest was an excellent idea. The last thing she needed to worry about was falling asleep on the back of a motorcycle.

One of the things Dash wanted to talk to her about was about traveling to meet him while he worked. While Dash's life on the road didn't appeal to her, she'd promised she'd give the idea some thought. Though familiar with travel due to book signings, it wasn't her favorite thing to do—but it could work.

As she removed her jeans and shirt, she tossed them into the hamper. A shower sounded good after the push to make her self-imposed deadline. Indie authors were entrepreneurs. Everything fell on their shoulders. Writing, covers, editing, formatting, and publishing. Then came marketing. If you were lucky, you formed a great team. If not, your book could end up at the bottom of the retailer's list. There were pros and cons, but she'd been lucky enough to be on the pro side of the list more often than not. It worked if you were a self-starter and a go-getter. Thankfully, she was, and Amazon had created the ability for authors to independently upload and sell their books. Still, she hoped that one of her books would catch the eye of one of the big five.

The shower head sent out a gentle mist, but she changed that to the massage setting. As the steam fogged the bathroom, Skylar slipped beneath the spray. The pounding water relaxed her neck, loosening the damage she'd done from countless hours spent over a keyboard. It didn't take long for her skin to turn lobster red, a sharp contrast to the comfy white bath sheet she draped around her body before wrapping her mass of wet hair in a smaller one.

Sky took a close look at herself in the mirror. Beneath the bright vanity bulbs, she noted the dark, bluish circles under her eyes. Hopefully, a little concealer would fix that problem. She rubbed lotion on her damp skin, indulging in kneading arms and legs that had been kept in one position for too long. She patted moisturizer to the darkness beneath her eyes with the gentle touch of her ring finger, then took herself to bed. She could only hope the puffiness would be gone by the time Dash arrived.

Exhausted from ten hours of writing, Sky slipped between the sheets. The stiff cotton was cold on her bare legs and feet. She thrashed her legs back and forth beneath the covers, trying to conduct a little warmth. As she tucked the blanket beneath them, she raised her legs so the material surrounded them. She yawned. Fuzzy socks would have provided needed relief, but she was too lazy to get out of bed.

As she closed her eyes, anticipation and memories formed a blissful cocktail. While on the phone, Dash had confessed to missing her. He admitted that even when playing to sold-out crowds, she was in his thoughts. She hugged herself, a smile tugging at her lips. Though she and Dash laughed about their strange connection, she agreed with a statement he'd made to her:

"What we have is rare, Sky. We can't let anything ruin that."

Though many would think otherwise, Dash Barrows was nothing like his stage persona. He was so damn serious while performing, choosing instead to leave the theatrics to Ian. Dash was, indeed, a gentleman full of old-time charms. An old soul. He still liked opening doors for her and bringing her flowers. It was refreshing from the assholes she'd dated before, and precisely what she found most endearing about him.

She turned over, adjusting on her side. She tucked the pillow beneath her towel-wrapped head and immersed herself in thoughts of him. What would he bring back from his trip this time? Though she didn't expect anything, he always brought her a little something from his travels. He seemed to find joy in the little things. The world would be shocked to discover what a romantic Dash was, and, because of that, he'd completely stolen her heart.

CHAPTER 15

Skylar reached over to the empty pillow. Though half-asleep, she splayed her fingers as she slowly trailed over the light blue, cotton pillowcase. An image of the two of them making love had her pressing her thighs together. A shiver trailed down her spine as she imagined lying next to Dash, skin-on-skin. Goosebumps pebbled her skin. Though it was something they both wanted, their schedules always got in the way. She didn't know how long she could stand postponing the inevitable. Just the touch of his fingers skimming the back of her neck hardened her nipples. The timbre of his voice on the phone sent rushes of pleasure coursing through her bloodstream.

Through half-closed, sleepy eyes, she stared at the place where she pictured Dash resting his head. Gingerly, she traced the pillow. This separation had been too long. She was eager to touch his face. Look into his eyes. *Soon.*

She took a deep breath and flipped onto her back. As she stared at the ceiling, exasperation rushed a sigh past her lips. Sleep was fleeting, giving her short periods of uninterrupted rest only to find her fully awake with each movement. She threw aside the comforter, sat up on the side of the bed, and shuffled her feet on the floor. She looked over at her cell. Three missed calls. As she picked the phone up, it lit up and buzzed in her hand.

"Hello?"

"Hey, babe."

Upon hearing his voice, desire thickened her tone. "Hi."

"I'm on my way over. I'll be there soon. Less than an hour."

She stood, walking circles around the room. "Okay. What's the plan for today?"

"It's a surprise." Amusement lifted Dash's voice. Spontaneity was his strong suit, not hers, and he knew it. She was a list girl. A planner. And Dash? He loved catching her off guard to make her expect the unexpected.

"I hate you," she countered.

"I know." With a laugh he blew out a breath. "Be ready when I get there."

An eye roll was in order. It seemed she did a lot of that when it came to Dash and his antics. "See you when you get here."

It was apparent the resignation in her tone made him chuckle. "See you soon."

Skylar threw the phone on the bed and started rummaging through her bureau drawers. She slipped into her underwear, shimmied into a pair of jeans, and pulled a V-neck tee shirt over her head. She smoothed the shirt over her breasts and noted the pale triangle of skin at her throat. She'd been spending a lot of time inside. Hopefully, being outside today would gain her a little glow.

She lifted the brush from the dresser to put some order to her messy curls. With each long pull of the brush, smoothing her hair, excitement fluttered in her beating heart. The culprit was her imagination and the heated gaze of deep, brown eyes.

* * *

THE TELLTALE SOUND of Dash's Harley could be heard from three blocks away. She'd finished pulling her hair into a ponytail just as she heard the machine pull up in front of her house. Though their time spent apart might not seem long to some, the anticipation of seeing him again had reached an almost unbearable level. Her lovesick heart picked up its pace, making her desperate to see him.

Though she was anxious to see him, she hoped they would have some time to talk about his latest venture on behalf of the band. Marketing was so important, as she well knew, and Dash wanted to monetize the band's brand. Ian and the other guys were supposed to have been in the meeting. Hopefully, Ian had attended sober.

She was looking forward to being with the man whose playful sarcasm always outweighed her concerns, even those about Ian. Dash read her moods well when they were together. She didn't know quite how he did it, but somehow he even seemed to read her feelings through inflections in her voice, knowing exactly what she was thinking before she opened her mouth to tell him.

When she opened the door and saw the broad smile on his handsome face, it only further drove home the fact she would never want to be a part of something that would cause him pain.

"Hey, sweetness." Skylar's front door was only six feet from the street, as were most of the rowhomes in Baltimore. Dash pushed the kickstand down with a leather-clad foot. In a heartbeat, his arm was around her waist, locking her in his embrace as his lips met hers.

What was it about his kisses that made her feel like a schoolgirl? His embrace was always a moment longer than she expected; each new kiss was sweeter than the last. When he pulled back, his eyes took her in. "Ready?"

Pleasure edged his voice, making her anxious for the day to get started. She made quick work of mounting the bike, always being mindful of his first instructions. She fastened her helmet and put on her sunglasses. Once he checked to be sure she was ready, the familiar jolt of excitement mixed with terror hit.

She let out the breath her lungs always seemed to hold captive at the exact moment he took off. There were times she was sure her fingernails punctured holes through his leather jacket and was equally certain he heard her little yelps through barely parted lips. Still, as their rides increased in number, she was just as amazed and distracted by the beauty of nature as she had been that very first time.

"Why won't you tell me where we're going?" She leaned in close, her voice raised so that he could hear her over the engine.

"Because you're a hard girl to surprise. You'll see it when we get there." He loved to surprise her.

No matter how much time they spent together, every dinner, phone conversation, and stolen moment was imprinted on her mind. Something she'd promised herself she'd have to get used to was that she shared Dash with the world. Everywhere he went, and everything he did was open to anyone with a cell phone to document. But times like these were theirs alone. She appreciated these little moments. The simple act of holding him in her arms made her happy. She inched her butt forward, pressing her breasts into his back. After weeks apart, his nearness seduced her. She rested her cheek near his shoulder. She wanted him lying beside her. Holding her. Loving her.

Dash rounded a corner and pulled over to the side of the road. Immediately, Sky's senses engaged. Beauty was everywhere. Beneath a shimmering blue sky dotted with fluffy white clouds sat an immense field of lavender. Rows and rows of various colored flowers seemed so perfectly spaced that they created an illusion that they stretched out forever. The sensory assault continued as she inhaled. Deeply filling her lungs with the sweet, relaxing scent, she could feel their relaxing effects soak through her skin. She'd been under the impression that all lavender flowers were purple but now knew she'd been wrong. Blues and purples in various hues spread out as far as the eye could see. It was a most beautiful sight, almost too wondrous for words.

"What do you think?" He removed his helmet and dismounted the bike, then offered her his hand for assistance.

As she took it, she slid her leg over the seat. The soles of her boots crunched on some loose blacktop. How to answer his question? Words seemed inadequate to describe such perfection. "It's stunning." She leaned into him and found his focus wasn't on the field but on her.

"I missed you." His rich baritone made her insides quake.

Without hesitation, he claimed her lips. Sky's head fell back, a victim of desire. This was no sweet kiss. This was the kind of connection that turned blood into lava. As it coursed through her veins, it left an imprint. The heat burned away her reserve and opened her mind to all sorts of lustful thoughts.

He pulled back, their connection remaining as they gazed into each other's eyes.

"You're cute and hot."

Skylar's lips pursed in a crooked pucker as she

dismissed his compliment. "You always say that. A hot mess is more like it."

"*My* hot mess," he corrected. "I thought you'd like this. Something wide open, with no paparazzi, and beautiful—just like you."

He released her, turning to the saddlebag on the side of the bike. He pulled out a thick, black canvas bag with a Harley Davidson logo on the side.

Puzzled, she canted her head. "What's that?"

"Our food." He gave her a playful wink. With one hand on the bag, and the other taking hers, he led them over to a grassy plot.

Skylar looked around. "Are we allowed to be here?"

Dash managed a soft laugh as he looked at her. "Always the rules girl, aren't you?" He paused, dropping the bag to the ground. "This looks like a good spot—and, yes, we're allowed to be here. It's the picnic area."

A relieved sigh relaxed her shoulders. "I'm surprised we're the only people here. It's so pretty."

Dash unzipped the bag, removing a thin blanket and spreading it on the ground. He then placed utensils, glasses, and plates in the middle, finishing the set up with sealed containers of food and bottles of water.

Dash held Skylar's hand as she took a seat on the corner of the blanket. Dash did the same on the other side. "I can't believe all of that fits in there."

"Yeah. I got lots of gear for the bike. I just thought it would be a good day to get away."

Appreciation filled her expression. Dash was great about doing little things that others underestimated.

He opened the containers, filling their plates with fruit, cheese, and crackers. Handing one of the plates to her, he then took his own.

"How did everything go on your trip?" She took a bite of cheese, then washed it down.

Dash did the same, waiting until he swallowed before answering. "It went okay. We settled on a few branding ideas. Ian didn't like a few of their ideas, but he was outvoted by me and the guys. He thinks that stuff like the band's logo on coffee cups and beer cozies is selling out. Me and the other boys think it's smart merchandising."

Sky noted the drop in his tone. "Why do you all put up with him?"

He shrugged. "He's like the bratty little brother in a family full of boys. He's a pain in our asses most of the time but, honestly, deep down inside, Ian's got a good heart."

Skylar let the topic of Ian die with Dash's last comment. It was apparent the subject weighed down his good mood, and on a beautiful day like today, the last thing she wanted to do was waste their time thinking about Ian.

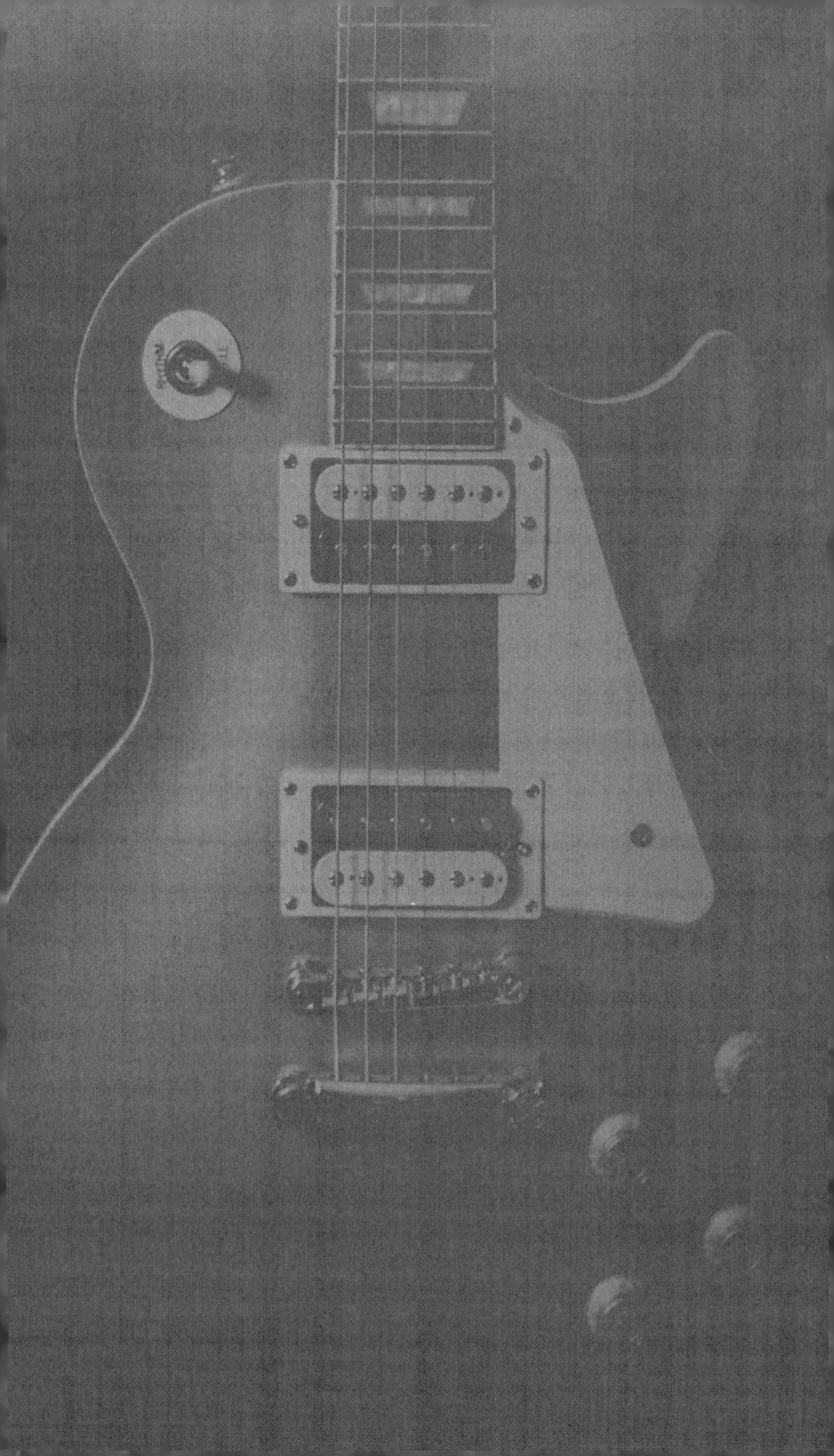

CHAPTER 16

*D*ash pulled up outside his house. He turned off the engine and pressed the heel of his boot onto the kickstand. The metal tip scraped the asphalt driveway. It always amazed him how such a small piece of metal could support a nine-hundred-pound machine. Dismounting, he turned and extended an assisting hand to Sky.

He could tell her hips ached from the ride. It was her longest yet. Although getting her ass in the saddle in the first place had been a challenge, he was satisfied he could now put her in the seat and go. He was proud of her. She's pushed past all her reservations to embark on a new experience. In return, he noted her every need. When a break was required, he'd stop. When she got a little anxious, he'd reach back to her with a reassuring pat. Hopefully, the time would come when they'd take a real road trip and explore the country.

They'd started out at her house and ended the journey at his. His cock twitched at the idea of taking her to his house. He wanted time to reconnect and, hopefully, move to a new level in their relationship. The thought of Skylar bare and beneath him sent a rush of blood to fuel the fire within.

Sky walked the path to the house in front of him. He studied her, noting every flex of muscle and every sway of her hips. If she could read his sinful thoughts, she'd run away screaming.

He put the key in the door and pushed it open. The hallway led into the living room, although he would rather have headed to the bedroom. This was the longest he'd ever waited to get a girl into bed, but then Skylar wasn't any other girl. He felt something more with her, and, because of that, he wanted more from her.

Dash plopped down onto the sofa and pulled Sky down with him. The edges of the cushion bowed beneath their combined weight. As his legs spread and knees fell apart, her ass settled in the space in between. This was what he missed when he was away. The feeling of connection he felt whenever he was with her.

Skylar draped her arms around his shoulders, studying his expression. For a moment, he was speechless. There was something about looking into her eyes. Some feeling at each reunion he couldn't describe. His body reacted, but not just his cock. His heart swelled inside his chest when he held her. She made him feel like a kid on Christmas morning.

He took her chin in his hand and skillfully guided her lips to his. Primal craving swirled deep within him, driving the kiss with lust. His body demanded more. He wanted all of her, but he respected her caution and tried to move a little slower, leaving her with a taste of what was to come.

"I made dinner," he announced. "It's in the crackpot."

Surprised and amused, Sky's eyes widened, her blues still swimming in a lust-filled pool of his making. "You made dinner? And do you mean crockpot?"

"Yeah. That. It's my first attempt." He shrugged. "I could have just made sandwiches, but I thought that you might want a real meal. I looked up a recipe online and dumped everything in there this morning. I figured it would cook while we were out. Hopefully, the food is edible."

If he read her as well as he thought he did, she definitely just melted a little. That look on her face warmed his insides as much as a smooth whiskey. Christ, the girl affected him! He'd never get tired of studying her many expressions.

"So, what do you want to do? You want to eat now or, maybe, watch a movie?"

His eyes swept over her, lingering on her breasts. "I think I'd like to stay here and enjoy the view if you don't mind." His brow quirked as he watched her cheeks flame. He traced the vee of material at her neckline and noted the heat flashing in her icy blues. His hand slipped from her waist to her ass. "Besides, I'm gritty from the road. I'm going to shower before we eat."

She looked down at herself, suddenly aware that a thin, tacky mix of pollen and sweat clung to her exposed skin as well. She swiped her forearm with her hand. "I feel a little icky myself."

Both brows inched up now, a playful arch forming between them. His whiskered jawline ticked as a hint of mischief stretched his mouth with a sly grin. "Want to join me?"

Her expression blanked. His fantasies did not. The sudden reality of being wet and naked with Skylar caused a pinch as his member stiffened. He ached to be between her legs. His lip pulled up, the look on her face feeding his telltale erection with a new pulse of blood. "You say you care about the planet. Showering with me would save water, you know. Reduce your carbon footprint and all that shit."

He teased her with the tone of his voice. The backhanded invitation was thick with lust. A tiny moan escaped her. It was so subtle he doubted she knew it had slipped between her lips. The sound caressed his ears. Excitement rushed through his veins, heating his blood. The warmth had his dick straining against the metal zipper. His eyes locked with hers. "You're thinking too hard about this, sweetness." His hand slipped off her ass. Gripping the bottom of his tee shirt, he pulled it up and over his head.

A sexy grin played with her mouth. "Something tells me I might be in there long enough to get waterlogged."

He responded with a quiet, affirming, growl, and a nervous laugh escaped her. She averted her eyes, and his brain played tug-of-war with reality and fantasy. "You're so damn cute when you blush."

A nervous laugh escaped her as heat continued to curl through his body. Like smoke, it wafted, invading sinew and bone. Its effect turning him from Dr. Jekyll to Mr. Hyde.

While away from her he'd played this scene over and over in his imagination. Still, now that the reality was staring him in the face, he hoped to push her boundaries. His fantasies sat at the cusp of reality, and he eagerly awaited their realization with bated breath. He slid her legs off his until her feet hit the floor. Rising from the sofa, he took her hand. "Let's go."

He steadied the beat of his heart as she trailed obediently behind him. He wanted to take his time and enjoy every inch of her. Intertwining their fingers, he took control. Unless she showed a serious inclination to disagree, he was playing this dream out. By night's end, he would be inside of her.

When they reached the bathroom, Dash wasted no time shedding the rest of his clothes. He kicked them off to the side where they landed in the corner in a messy pile. Now, naked before her, the evidence of his desire high and proud, his heart pounded. It wasn't fear that stroked the beat. Sex had always been a means to an end for him, but this was a deeper kind of need, and so much more poignant than just a physical act.

A switch flipped in his mind as he engaged with his inner beast. A primal feeling came over him. He craved the taste of Skylar. The feel of her. Excitement gnawed at him from deep down inside, gripping him with an appetite that could only be satisfied once he'd claimed her.

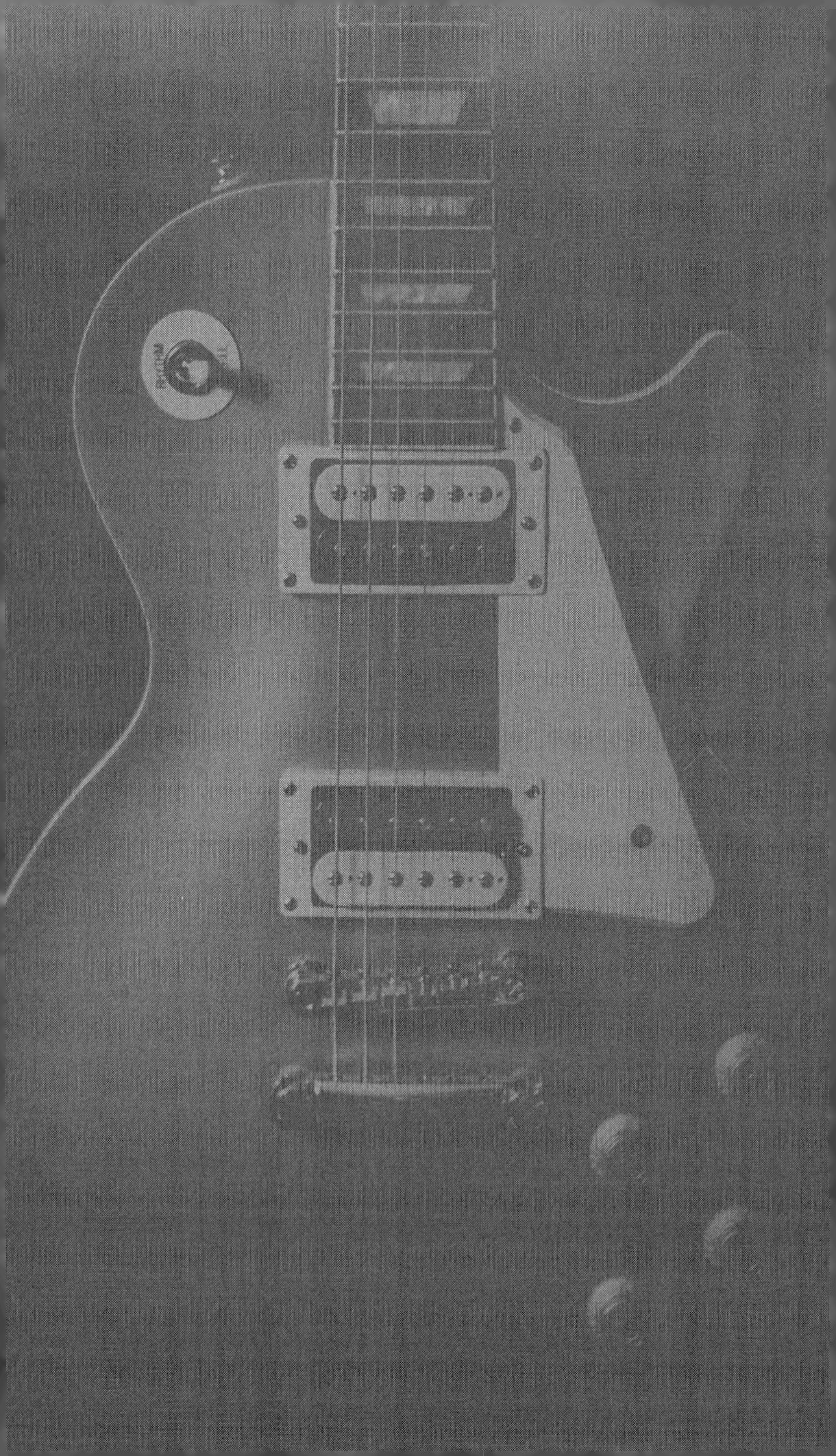

CHAPTER 17

Seeing Dash bare before her, a pool of heat collected in her core. A slight tremble shook her knees. Though she tried to avert her eyes, she couldn't tear them away from his stiff, swollen erection. It stood proudly at attention, jerking beneath her gaze. His arousal fed her own, the shuddering inside her gripping her core with lust. She reveled in the passion it produced.

Still clothed, she dragged her eyes from his cock to his face. His stunning brown eyes had darkened to near black. His nostrils flared as he struggled to hold back his urges. He looked like an animal untamed, ready to devour her. A thrill rushed through her veins. Carnal energy bounced between them as he filled her space and closed the distance between them. Her scalp tingled; a million bees buzzed beneath her skin with a vibrating pulse. Nothing could have prepared her for the effect of the raw desire Dash incited.

The chaos inside of her head refused to quiet. The heady cocktail of longing and lust flushed her body with heat. Her gaze fell beneath the intensity of his, her view fixing on his bare feet. He caged her in as he moved each naked one outside of her booted ones.

"We could stand here all day like this, sweetness, but then we'd never get what we both want." He'd dipped his head, his words vibrating on the spot just beneath her ear. She sucked in a breath, her head falling to the side. A shiver possessed her as he inhaled a trail along her neck. From her earlobe to the hollow of her throat, he took in her scent. He was so potently male that it unnerved her, the imbalance he set into motion tossing her senses into a tailspin. She lost herself in the intensity of the moment but needed to breathe.

She pulled back to look into his eyes, the corners creasing beneath the tension of desire. He stalked her with his burning stare, his nostrils flaring as he inhaled a snorted supply of oxygen. The primal effect shook her to her core, and her body responded, sending a rush of wetness to the apex of her thighs.

These sensations were more than she could have anticipated, her experience had been limited at best. His intensity cut her like the blade of a knife. Craving erupted through the surface. She felt like she was drowning. The intense feelings were equally frightening and thrilling. Not even her wildest fantasies corrupted her like the current onslaught of sensations taking over her body.

Suddenly, fear rippled her spine. Intense chills raced up the back of her neck. Skylar froze, barely breathing as her lungs struggled for oxygen. Dash was instantly aware, stepping back to give her an inch of space.

"Skylar, stop. I'm not going to hurt you or do anything you don't want. Don't steal this moment away from us because you're afraid."

His tone was commanding and had a drugging effect. Her neck and shoulders relaxed as he guided her backwards. He pushed her back until her butt rested against the edge of the vanity. With confident fingers, he undid the button on her jeans and lowered the zipper. His hands dipped inside the waistband, separating the hugging denim as his eyes bored into her.

The space between her thighs was wet, but her mouth was dry. Excitement pitched a high ring in her ears. Her pulse beat a clamoring drum that kept pace with her racing heart. Tsunami-strength emotions closed her eyes as she took a breathless moment to sink into the heady feelings. Dash's touch electrified her as he pushed her jeans and panties down over her hips. As he guided them over her ass and down her legs, his fingertips left a scorching trail. Down on one knee like a dark but charming prince, he unzipped her boots, removing them one by one. His thumbs hooked the rim of her socks, his calloused digits grazing her skin. Nerve endings stood at attention as they traveled the delicate arch in her foot, causing her toes to curl. As he looked up at her, the plea in his eyes begged her to surrender completely. Suddenly, she understood that a woman submitting to her own desires was the most significant power she possessed.

The minute she let go, surrender unleashed a violent rush of carnality. Passion scratched its way through her core with blazing claws. She helped Dash remove her jeans and then moved so he could easily lift her other garments. After he tugged her shirt over her head and slid her bra from her shoulders, she gathered her hair and moved it to one side. His lips seared kisses on her neck, making her moan. His hands cupped her ass cheeks, and her hips writhed a response.

"Maybe you should be afraid." Dash's low laugh tormented her sex. Moisture rushed to prepare her for his entrance. He claimed her lips, crushing them with his own.

She welcomed the sweet bruising she was sure would follow.

Reluctantly he released her. In his eyes was a wicked plan. He reached inside the shower and turned the knob, then covered his dick with a condom. Within minutes heat-swirled steam filled the air. The foggy mist enveloped Skylar's skin with a slippery veil. Her muscles ached, especially her thighs. Straddling a leather seat for hours had caused the soreness. She was hopeful for pain of a different kind before the night was through.

Dash stepped beneath the hot spray and extended his hand to her. She took it, catching her breath as the hot and heavy droplets softly pelted her sensitive skin. She tipped her face up for its full effect. Water streaming through her hair, saturating the strands as it washed over her head, face, and neck. The heat stole away the tension that remained between her body and mind. She closed her eyes and braced her hands up against the wall. She could feel Dash's naked body behind her as he closed the gap between them. Her desires sweltered, raising the heat within her core as her sex clenched.

"Relax, baby. Let me take care of you."

Her fingers curled into her palms as he kneaded her shoulders with steady hands. She groaned, her head falling forward as muscles unkinked and unraveled beneath his ministering touch. He trailed down her spine to her lower back. With her eyes closed and Dash's erection throbbing against her backside, her thoughts tumbled into an erotic dream—except she wasn't dreaming. She was living out a fantasy.

He gave her hair a tug, and her head fell back in response. An unsolicited moan escaped her, and his cock jerked out a reply. He thrust against the crack of her ass. As he continued his seduction, he reached around to her front. With both hands, he cupped her breasts and pulled her against him beneath the full force of the water.

She gasped. Her nipples pebbled, the tips now hard and wanting. Dash massaged them as well. He teased and stroked as his hands traveled her wet skin, tracing beneath the heavy globes. With eager fingers, Dash moved lower, skating the tips over her hips and belly with just enough pressure to loosen the knots. When they reached the top of her thighs, he pulled her hard against him. The feeling was sublime, sending a fresh coating to the inside of her thighs. He pressed his powerful, ripped chest to her back, her full, firm cheeks against his need.

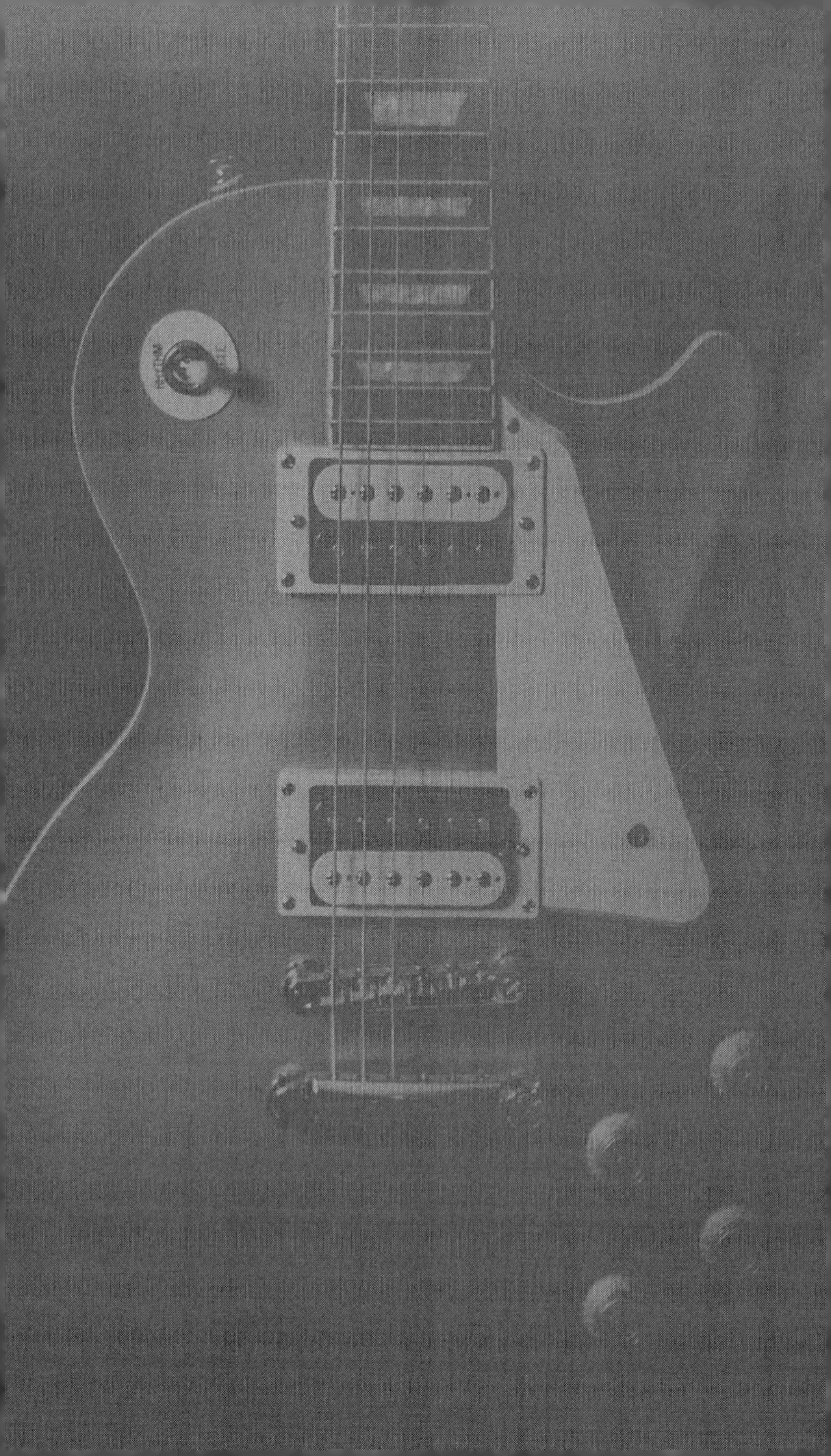

CHAPTER 18

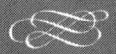

Skylar teetered on the edge of a shiver. Though she tried to stifle a moan, she wasn't successful. A feeling of satisfaction settled over him.

"Feel good, baby?"

"Mmm."

Dash loved the guttural sound that came from deep within her throat. She responded beautifully to his touch. It never occurred to him that his calloused digits could give such pleasure. The skin on his fingertips was thick from years of wielding a guitar. Now he strummed Sky's body as skillfully as he did his strings. Her muscles obeyed his commands. As he continued to ply and press her flesh, he fisted her hair, catching her cheek in his hand. She turned toward him, and he claimed her lips. Their tongues tangled in a sensual dance. He slipped his hand between her legs, making her jump. She gasped.

"Just let go, Sky. Let me love you." Her back arched as the connection sent a jolt through her. He nuzzled her neck, kissing, licking, and sucking her body into submission as his fingers moved to the hidden place. As he dipped his fingers inside the soft folds, his desire ramped up.

As her body responded, each clench increased his girth. Dash turned her around, moving with her until her back hit the wall. Nudging her thighs open with his knee, he imprisoned her hands above her head. His arousal was painful, hard, and throbbing with a life of its own. He parted her folds, driving his erection between the tender flesh to ramp up her pleasure and his own.

This intimate connection evaporated his thoughts as he spiraled into nothing but physical pleasure. The feelings he had for Skylar defied description. Nothing he'd experienced with any other woman had ever hit him so hard. All that mattered to him was dying that small, orgasmic death. His erection begged for relief. As an involuntary shudder raised her on tiptoe, he continued to stroke her sensitive bundle of nerves. She opened her eyes and he fell into her blue orbs. The silver particles within the hue flashed with a spark that made him shudder.

He could become addicted to this raw power. Making love to Sky was a completely new experience. He'd always believed sex was nothing more than a mechanized act. Even his fantasies at his own hands had never conjured the force energizing his insides. Fuck. Come. Done. While that might have been true in the past, the act lacked finesse. Not this.

As he watched her surrender to her pleasure, something inside of him changed. A switch flipped. This woman —this beautiful, complicated woman—was changing his perception of what lovemaking should be. He wanted to make her feel like a goddess. If she would let him love her completely, then maybe he could be loved simply for being himself. There was something magical about being with her. The two of them together were a rich orchestration of a beautiful song.

He ached to be inside of her. Take her. Fill her. Drive himself into her until there was nothing left of them but shards of pleasure. This was connection, real and fierce. The animal raging inside of him thirsted to devour her.

Dash nudged her opening with his tip. It took all his effort to control his entrance. He hooked his hands around the back of her thighs and lifted her. Cock to core, he pushed until he felt the hollow space. His eyes locked with hers, the anticipation of her release now too much to bear. He pulled his hips back and launched into her with a powerful thrust. Sky gasped as he filled her. He stilled to allow her to adjust to his size as pain and pleasure intermingled. Skylar held fast to his shoulders. As he prepared to thrust again, a loud banging noise came from the living room. Sky's fingernails dug into his flesh, both of them as still as statues.

"Dash! Where the fuck are you?"

* * *

Fucking Ian!

"Let me down. Let me down!" Terror colored her whispered command, and he immediately released her, and she scrambled to hide herself as soon as her feet hit the floor. She turned off the water, the bathroom door opening wide as the intruder pushed in. Dash tossed a towel from the rack to Skylar as her eyes flew open. She grabbed it, wrapping it around herself and clutching the spot where the ends met, and turned into the corner. She buried her face like a child in timeout, her nose pressed into the tile while he turned his back to shield her.

"Hey, man. Are you in the sho—"

Dash flew out of the shower before Ian could finish the question, and the heavily fogged door closed behind him. A rush of air cut through the steamy mist just as Ian walked in.

Ian peered over his friend's shoulder. "What the fuck's going on, man?" Ian's voice dropped as he caught a glimpse of Sky and noted Dash's semi-erect cock. A lecherous smile inched its way across his lips.

"Get out, Ian." Dash bellowed the demand, the acoustics causing the sound to bounce off every wall.

Ian's brow raised. Undeterred by his friend's visible rage, he refused to move. Instead, a mischievous gleam entered his eyes. "Say, sweetness, what do you say I get naked, and you, me, and Dash can have a go?"

In an instant, the violence in Dash's eyes was potent with rage. Now torn between leaving Skylar naked and alone or beating the shit out of Ian, he decided to take care of Ian first. His hands balled into fists, his fingertips tight, digging into his palms. One mere instant would decide which direction this scene was going to go. "I said, get the fuck out, Ian! Now!"

Instead of running, he walked. "Your loss, buddy. There's something to be said for double penetration." He carelessly tossed the comment over his shoulder as Dash followed him out into the living room. Ian plopped into a chair, sprawling back like he owned the place. Dash reached for him, grabbing him by the shirt, pulling him up until they were nearly nose to nose.

"Why are you here?" The words were seethed with anger, oozing bitterly through clenched teeth.

Ian gingerly placed one hand around Dash's wrist, pulling at his friend's grip. "Easy now." He slowly reached into his pocket and pulled out a joint. Sliding the rolled paper beneath his nose, he sniffed as the ragged edges caught on the scruff above his lip. He waggled his brows. "I thought that, maybe, you'd be up for a little partying?" He canted his head in the direction of the bathroom. "I don't mind sharing if you don't." Ian laughed. The low, gravelly, sinister sound escaped just before Dash's knuckles collided with his face. Ian's neck snapped back as blood erupted from his nose.

"Get the fuck out of my house."

Ian gave Dash a shove, sending him backward and breaking his hold. He swiped his face with the back of his hand, his eyes widening as he smeared the blood. "What the fuck is wrong with you? She's just a girl!"

"Don't talk about her. You don't know her. She's not some skank whore." Dash closed the distance between them and grabbed Ian by the throat. "Now get the fuck out and don't come back."

The smaller man tried to pry Dash's one hand from his throat with both of his own. He struggled for air until Dash released him, flinging hard enough that Ian's back hit the door.

Ian sputtered a cough. "You're fucking crazy! She's just a chick, and I'm your friend." He coughed again. "You're an asshole, you know that? I'm your fucking singer. You could've damaged my throat, you fucker!"

"Get. The. Fuck. Out!" Dash's monotone was white noise, permeating the room, filling every space with a benign hum. This wasn't the first time Ian had pulled this shit, but it would be the last.

Ian shrugged and stiffened his spine, narrowing his eyes at Dash as he inched his hand around the doorknob. "You could've killed me, motherfucker." He shook his head in disbelief, quietly muttering to himself under his breath. "And all over some pussy."

"NOW, MOTHERFUCKER!" Dash bellowed the words, the rage coming from deep down in his gut.

"You are fucking crazy, man." Ian opened the door, looking over his shoulder.

"And you don't know when to quit." He shoved Ian over the threshold.

Oblivious to the fact he was still naked, he followed Ian outside as he stumbled to regain his footing. He was so lost in his anger, crimson filtered his eyes, the fury within them unmistakable. "Stay away from me and stay away from Abigail! She's off-limits."

He went back into the house and slammed the door. Hinges rattled, and a picture behind the door tilted. At the same time, Ian continued to run his mouth loud enough to be heard through the barrier.

"You're nuts. And who the fuck is Abigail?"

CHAPTER 19

Dash headed to where he'd left Skylar. A tremor shook his hands. Heavy footsteps slapped against the floor as anger still weighed heavily upon him. He snatched a towel and wrapped it around his waist as he pushed the door open.

"Are you okay?"

She eyed him warily, her nod hesitant and exaggerated. There was something about the way she was acting that trembled his gut. A look of suspicion and doubt clouded her eyes, taking them from sky blue to smoke. It was as if some unseen presence had entered the space in his absence. Something other than Ian.

She took a half step back, definitely widening the distance between them. She threw her arms across her middle. She hugged herself tightly, her shoulders curling over as if she'd been sucker-punched. *Had Ian's smartass attitude affected her that much?*

"He's gone, Sky. I took care of it."

"I heard." Her tone was clipped.

Desperately wanting to go back in time, Dash

approached slowly and rubbed his hands up and down her arms. She stiffened, entirely unreceptive to his touch. Undeterred, he continued. There was no way Dash could have anticipated what had happened. Asshole Ian was always all over the place, and Dash wasn't his babysitter.

Dash wrapped her in his arms. Where fifteen minutes ago she was soft and open, now her entire posture was closed tightly. "I wish you'd try to relax." His tone was hushed as he gently tucked her head beneath his chin. Holding her close, he could only hope his words and actions were enough to erase the chaos Ian had caused. He wouldn't come back, of that Dash was sure. Ian wasn't stupid. He wouldn't risk getting punched again. Dash outweighed him by at least fifty pounds. Chances were he'd be sporting at least one black eye from the punch.

Minutes ticked by. Dash continued his soft caresses, but her body was strung tighter than his guitar. He cuffed the top of her arms and studied her face. "What's wrong?"

Sky averted her eyes beneath a mask of apprehension. One hand came up to pinch the fold of the towel that was holding it together, and she wiped away what he thought was a tear.

"Skylar, tell me what's wrong. I want to help."

Her eyes met his with a defiant glare. "Who's Abigail?"

"What?" The inquiry caught him off guard.

She pulled away from him as an angry flush inched from her neck to her cheeks. "Who's Abigail?"

The question hung before him. He had no idea what she was talking about. "Okay. I'll bite. Who's Abigail?"

"Oh, for fuck's sake! Abigail. You told Ian to stay away from her." Accusation steeled her tone.

Bewildered, he answered. "I don't know what you're talking about."

"Abigail. You know? Ab-i-gail?" Her volume increased

as she looked at him with querulous eyes. "My name is Skylar. I'd like to know who Abigail is. You told Ian to stay away from her. Who is she? Old girlfriend? Another girlfriend? Who?"

Dash quickly ran through his memory, but for the life of him, he couldn't recall saying that name. "I don't know anyone named Abigail."

Her struggle for composure was visible as her body trembled with pent-up rage. She bent down to retrieve her clothes and then pushed him aside to storm past. Incredulity shook her head. "I don't believe you."

Dash followed close behind her. "I don't know what else to say. It's the truth. I don't know any Abigail." The words clawed from his throat as he stared at her through exasperated eyes.

Skylar held her jeans as she froze, her feet rooted in place. A brow arched as she narrowed her eyes. "You must think I'm a fool. You don't think I can put two and two together?"

He threw up his hands. "I'm not questioning your fucking math skills, just your reason!"

Disbelief and anger widened her eyes, then, just as quickly she dismissed him. She muttered to herself as she stepped into her pants. Wrath fell off her in waves as she yanked them up and fastened them. She turned away from him as she hooked her bra and pulled her shirt over her head. Realizing she'd left her socks and boots in the bathroom, she ignored him as she brushed past.

Dash stalked after her, watching as she tried to slam down the lid of the toilet seat. He almost laughed at her impatient aggravation as it drifted down. Biting the inside of his cheek as she plopped her ass down on the lid, he leaned against the doorframe. "This is ridiculous."

She shoved her feet into her socks and shoes, refusing

to look at him. "Why did I know you'd say that?" When she was finished, she pushed past him. "Men are assholes."

"And women are unreasonable." His lighthearted tone was an attempt to lighten the situation. It backfired.

Skylar spun around, rage shaking her body. Fury fueled her blood. The cute blush he loved was now bright red, trailing down to her neck. The expression teetering on her face told him she was at a murderous tipping point. Suddenly Dash felt the delicate balance between life and death in her eyes. Instinct had him back up a step.

"No!" she bellowed. "You don't get to say that to me. It isn't unreasonable to react when the man you're about to have sex with spits out another woman's name! You don't get to act like I'm being unreasonable when you say someone else's name when you've just been inside of me. You don't know anyone named Abigail? Maybe you don't, but I'll just bet there's a whole list of names in your head— or maybe they don't even have names. What the hell do I know? It doesn't matter. I'm sure, to you and Ian, they were all faceless twats and only good for one thing—but, get this straight, I'm not one of them. And I never will be."

She grabbed her jacket, the sound of snapping leather heavy in the air. Skylar pushed past him, knocking into his shoulder as she stormed out. "Now get out of my way."

CHAPTER 20

Skylar didn't utter another word to him as she left. There was no purpose. She was done.

How could Dash so carelessly destroy their relationship? She was confident the things she'd said had damaged it further, but she would never take them back—just like he could never take back the name Abigail.

Even though she'd, pretty much, accused him of seeing her as just another fuck, at the moment, she couldn't have cared less. She walked and walked until she reached a place where she could grab an Uber. At least Dash couldn't follow her naked. She hadn't paid attention to anything except the urge to run once she'd left his house. Then she opened the app and requested a car, receiving a response that it was only two minutes away. She just wanted to go home.

She tied the sleeves of her jacket around her waist and leaned against the building she's stopped at. The brick at her back was as rigid as her resolve. The distance between them had given her a chance to simmer down, though she was still visibly shaken. She nearly gagged on the memory of her fight with Dash. Confrontation was not something that came naturally to her. Some people had tender hearts, and she was definitely one of them.

Looking back, it amazed her how far anger had pushed her out of her comfort zone. Something had snapped inside of her. Somewhere between Ian's assumption she could be shared, and Dash's slip-up referring to her as Abigail, she'd reached a breaking point. At least with the other assholes she'd dated, she'd known where she stood. Those guys were convenient and even those kinds of relationships dictated a certain amount of care, but they weren't love. *Love? Shit!* Was that what she felt for Dash? If so, that was a problem.

She closed her eyes. Though she could never take back her acidic words, she wasn't sure she wanted to. Words cut, or at least they could do irreparable damage. The things they'd said to each other today stripped whatever it was she and Dash had built. *Damn him!* The two of them had been doing just fine. Their relationship was on its way to being something both passionate and tender. Certainly, it had never been cruel—but today? Well, today they'd ruined it. What a joke.

All at once, it felt like a wound had opened. Her heart squeezed in her chest, the pain a dull ache. She longed for what used to be. After so much time wasted chasing relationships with no purpose, Skylar felt the cut of betrayal. Jagged and deep, it was as real as a bloody gash.

A black sedan approached, and Skylar checked the app for the license number of the Uber. It was her ride. He pulled up to the curb, and she got in, anxious to go home. The whole trip there she just stared out the window. Cars, houses, and landscapes whizzed by. As they passed a pretty blue house with black shutters, a rush of air escaped with an exasperated huff. During their many conversations, they'd talked about the things they liked. The places they thought of settling down. The kind of houses they wanted. All the things that made them, well, *them.*

A tear escaped. Sky made no attempt to wipe it away. As it trailed down her face further and further, she just felt sadder and sadder. The distance between their hopes and dreams had been here, measured today, and her heart and head felt the disconnect. She was sick to her stomach. Love was a fairytale. The man who'd brought her so much joy now brought sadness. She might as well face the fact that it —love—was never going to happen for her. To hell with Dash. No one would ever make her feel the way he had, she was sure of that. What she was equally convinced of was that she didn't need him. Her happiness had to be an inside job.

* * *

Sky cracked her eyelids open. Though they were swollen and scratchy, she looked at the clock. Once home, she'd collapsed onto her bed. After allowing herself a good cry, she'd fallen asleep. Several hours had passed, and now time bled back into conscious thought, and she had a headache.

She rolled out of bed. The hardwood floor chilled her bare feet, causing a shudder to rock her body. She crossed one arm over the other, rubbing the exposed parts to ward off a chill that had settled on her. Muscles and bones protested, joining her head to torment her.

She went into the bathroom and stood in front of the mirror. The reflection looking back at her was a woman vastly different from the one there this morning. That girl had been perky and glowing. This one was pitiful. Her face was pale, the color was absent from her lips, and her eyes were black, smudged with the residue of mascara. She swallowed the emotion that threatened her once again.

"You need to suck it up, buttercup." She should have given herself an order and toughened up. Instead, she crooned the words. Her already bruised heart needed a little tenderness, even if she had to be the one to give it.

She turned on the cold water and cupped it with both hands. Her anger now abated, all she felt was drained. Splashing her face several times, she washed away the salty residue of her tears. Picking up her brush, she slowly ran it through her hair and then twisted it up into a messy bun.

"Don't look so sad, girl. You did what you had to do." As she patted her face with a soft, fluffy towel, a twinge of pride pierced her heart. She'd said her piece without reservation, something that was very unlike her. No matter the cost, today she'd stood her ground. Spoken her mind. It was a given she'd be second-guessing herself. She'd plague herself with questions about whether she'd handled the disagreement well, though she knew in her heart she had. She would heal from the heartbreak. It would only take time.

"Always believe something good is about to happen, because today could be the day." She traced her finger down the edge of her mirrored reflection, remembering something she'd learned at a conference given by a writer she admired. She had to believe in herself. Pick herself up and dust herself off. No more doubts.

She attempted a smile, and her eyes reclaimed a tiny glimmer. "You'll be okay," she whispered on a tremble. "Promise."

She went down the stairs and into the kitchen. The first thing she had to do was take something for her aching body and head. A sliver of light pierced the seam of the curtains. After she swallowed a couple of Advil and downed a glass of water, she went to the window and peeked outside. The streetlamp cast an eerie glow through a foggy mist. Fells Point was usually abuzz with bar-hoppers, but tonight the streets seemed spooky and empty. The only thing that disturbed the scene was her grumbling stomach and a loud purr. She looked down at Hemmingway. "Sorry, buddy. I'll get your dinner."

As she went over to the refrigerator and opened the door, her stomach again growled. Spying some leftover soup in the back, she grabbed the half-filled container. The door drifted closed as Sky removed the lid and sniffed. Satisfied she wasn't going to poison herself with spoiled food, she stuck the container in the microwave and dished out some cat food for Hemi. He hurried to the bowl as she set it on the floor. She pulled out a chair from beneath the table, sat down, and lightly ran her foot down Hemi's back. A sigh escaped as she rubbed the back of her neck to make the ache go away. She only wished she could do the same to her heart.

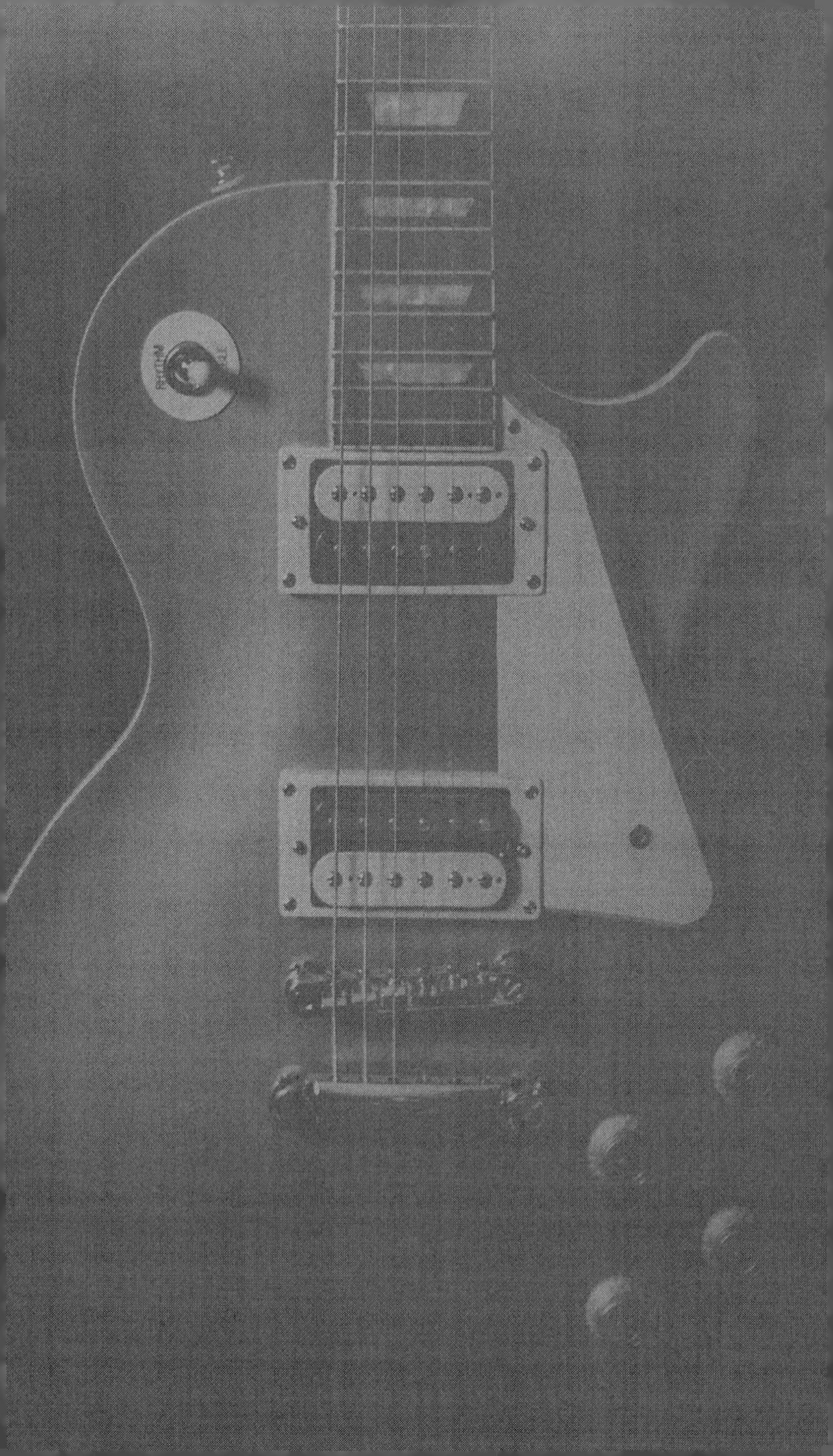

CHAPTER 21

Sky plopped down on the sofa and turned on the television. Soup in one hand and the remote in the other, she flipped through the channels. Nothing held any appeal, each show droning on with topics that were of little interest. If she could get something in her stomach without throwing it up, she might be able to go back to sleep without a headache. The pain reliever did little, but, then again, she'd cried enough to be dehydrated. Food and rest would help her body, if not her outlook. Two rounds of *Jeopardy* and a semi-full belly later, a wave of exhaustion rolled over her.

She slid her butt to the edge of the cushion and took a long stretch. When she sat up, she tossed the remote onto the coffee table. It landed next to her cell. She didn't know how long it had been there because she didn't remember setting it down. She picked it up. A gazillion notifications dotted the screen. She pressed to open her text messages and saw a list. All were from Dash.

"Sky, open the door."

"Sky, we need to talk."

"Please, Sky. Open the door."

"Dammit, Skylar. Stop being so stubborn. Open the door."

"Fine. I can wait here all night. You have to come out sometime."

"I'm not leaving."

What the hell? Her heart betrayed her by skipping a beat. She set the empty container on the table as she headed toward the door. Her hand trembled as she turned the knob. When she opened it a crack, she jumped back a step. Dash caught himself just before falling inside. He'd been sitting on the doorsill with his back leaning against the door. He lifted his eyes to meet hers.

"'Bout time." His tone was empty, the lack of inflection matching the vacant look in his eyes.

"How long have you been here?"

"Long enough for the fog to soak me through."

Skylar looked out at the damp, thick air and found it heavy with a chill. Spring and summer in Maryland always sported unpredictable temperatures. This night was no different. The low seventies during the day could mean fifty degrees at night. Dash stood up and brushed the wet film off his jeans and leather jacket. Not waiting for an invitation, he stepped over the threshold and brushed by her as he entered the house. She followed him with her eyes, slowly pushing the door closed.

He wasted no time moving toward the living room. She watched him as he removed his jacket, turned it to the inside, and threw it on a nearby chair. He plopped down on the sofa and looked up at her, his eyes glimmering with remorse. "We need to talk."

Sky sucked in a breath. "I don't think there's anything more to say, do you?" She bit back the words that danced on her tongue, but her eyes never left Dash's. He struggled with his composure. She noted the tremble in his hands and the hint of restrained emotion in his eyes. If the saying was true, and the eyes indeed were the windows to the soul, then Dash was tortured. She saw heartbreak reflected in his usually warm brown orbs. At the moment, they were hollow and lackluster. As much as Sky hated to see anyone in pain, she couldn't look away from him. An invisible connection commanded her to see every exposed part.

Dash ran a hand over his face and back through his damp hair as he cleared his throat. Though she tried to lock down her emotions the moment she'd seen him at the door, Sky's heart had rebelled. His pain penetrated her. She felt pity. The expression on his face was so broken it stripped her bare, tearing away all her resolve. Any attempts to steel herself failed miserably. It was official; she was a wuss.

"I only have one question," he begged. "Do you love me?"

"No." She blurted out her answer in a rush, then paused. She closed her eyes, shaking her head, and hated herself for saying the next word on her lips. "Yes." The whispered truth followed the lie. Though she desperately wanted to protect her heart, the fact burned her tongue. She wasn't a liar. Telling him the truth made her vulnerable, and though she couldn't decide if she'd made a mistake in telling him, she would be able to live with herself. She had no idea what he would think of it because he hadn't confessed to loving her.

The answer came quickly enough. Relief washed over his expression. His shoulders loosened. The tense lines on his handsome face softened. A breath escaped his lips in a rush. He cocked his head as a smile hooked the corners of his mouth. A split-second later, Dash sprang to his feet and stepped quickly over the coffee table that divided them. He crushed her as he wrapped her in his arms. Skylar could barely catch a breath before his lips came crashing down on hers. Hard and fierce, oxygen rushed from her lungs as he forced his tongue inside, tangling hers in a passionate dance.

For a moment, Skylar froze, but Dash shattered the ice with passion. Her head fell back as a tremble raced through her insides. Was it love or lust that made her shake? She should have pushed him away but couldn't. She was mad, and this was crazy.

Dash pulled her to him, his warm chest pressing against her breast. So tight was his hold, she could feel the racing beat of his heart. No matter how she felt about him, one nagging thought stood between her and the man she loved.

Abigail.

Who was she, and how could she possibly compete with her or the other women who made it their mission to sleep with the band? Why would he want a wavy-haired bookworm over someone with perky tits and a willing body? In his position, Dash could have any woman he wanted, so why would he want her?

As if he read her thoughts, he looked into her eyes. "There is no one else. There never will be. I love you, Sky. I don't know what it is about you, but when you left, I felt like you'd ripped out my heart."

His confession brought a tender smile to her lips. Emotion choked her. Tears spilled from her watery blue eyes. Any attempt at indifference crumbled beneath his words. *He loved her.*

Dash's face was a study of regret and relief. "I don't understand what's happening, but I love you and can tell by the look in your eyes that you love me too. Please, Skylar, don't push me away."

Like a stormy wind, Dash's sincerity scattered her

tortured thoughts. Her head was spinning with "what if" thoughts, but as she looked into his eyes, all she could see looking back at her was his love.

Sky bit her bottom lip, unsure of how to respond. She'd already admitted the truth about how she felt. If she were to be completely honest with herself and Dash, she'd realize she'd lashed out because of supposition, not fact. Though the sound of another woman's name falling from Dash's tongue had profoundly cracked something inside her, the fissure had been sealed as Dash held her in his arms. They could make this right.

Both of them had to work to repair the damage of their hurtful words. Dash was doing what he loved, and as long as he was out on the road performing, women would be everywhere he played, even when she couldn't be. Now was the time for both of them to rely on trusting each other.

She threaded her arms through his, wrapping them around his trim waist. He stroked her hair, caressed her cheek, and then pinched her chin between his fingers, tipping her head up so she couldn't escape his eyes. His gaze quelled any remaining, anxious thoughts. "I want you. I love you."

"I love you, too. I do. It's just hard when I know what goes on backstage."

"It's not as hard as you think. You just have to give us a chance. I love you, and you love me. That's what matters. Give this—us—a chance. Let go of any preconceived notions you might have about guys in a band."

A grimace wired her lips. "That's a little hard to do when you have someone like Ian screwing anything he can."

"I'll handle Ian. You handle me."

And then, suddenly, she saw his transparency. For the

first time she truly saw him and not the guy up on stage. He was more than determined by the look in his eyes. Suddenly, her twisted vision cleared. Hearing his truth put fresh breath into her lungs. Her love for him eclipsed her reservations. If she'd been paying attention to his words and not her angered presumptions, she'd have seen it. It had been right there all along. Red-rimmed and shadowed, his eyes bore the same soul-wounding hurt mirrored in her own. Worry lines bruised the corners of his brown depths. While Dash Barrows might be a rock god to some, to her, he was a simple man. Someone who felt the depth of love and pain just as she did. She'd reacted poorly, but his confession of love humbled her, sinking her fears so deep they disappeared into murky depths.

A rush of air stroked her back as Dash lifted her into his arms. She had no more concerns about the day's earlier events. There was no need for questions. No need for more apologies. As Dash held her tightly in his arms and carried her toward the bedroom, all doubt faded away.

He gently released her once inside the room. Her toes barely hit the floor when he pulled her against him. With tender fingertips, he traced her face. She closed her eyes as he placed gentle kisses on it, his breath whispering over her cheeks. His hand slid down to her hip, and he tugged her against him, closing any distance that remained. The evidence of his desire pressed hard against her lower belly, setting butterflies to flight as they fluttered in the spaces between her ribs.

When she opened her eyes, Dash caught her gaze. The passion in his eyes was unmistakable. Skylar's thoughts turned carnal as he led her to the bed. With eager hands, he undressed her and then himself, leaving her breathless. He ran his hands over every inch of her within his reach, his touch leaving her wanting.

He pulled her shirt over her head and undid her jeans. As her clothes fell to the floor, he undid her bra and slid it from her shoulders. She kicked her jeans aside as he pushed her panties down her hips. Dash didn't wait for her to undress him. He shucked off his clothes and kicked them away, the bedroom floor now a minefield of garments.

Sky rubbed her cheek against his, his day's stubble burning her skin as his face moved downward. Her head fell obligingly to the side as he nuzzled the sensitive place where her neck and shoulder met. His kisses left a burning trail as he lowered his chin to her breast. He licked the stiff peaks, issuing sweet torture as he sucked and nibbled the tender buds. Skylar's breaths increased, her gasps intensifying his response as he gently pulled her nipple between his teeth. Her knees weakened, threatening to drop her to the floor, but Dash held fast. She had no doubt he wouldn't stop until he was satisfied.

Hard and powerful, his excitement was evident. A satisfied growl escaped his throat, the primal sound rattling her insides as she reached out to touch him. She wrapped her fingers around his length. A violent tremor shook his knees as a moan escaped his lips.

Dash guided her footsteps to the edge of the bed, laying her down on the soft tangle of bedding. He laid down beside her, dipping his eager fingers between her legs to circle the tender bundle of nerves with a fresh rush of her juices. A startled whimper released from her lips as he continued his loving assault. His fingers stroked out a beautiful song, bringing sparks with its heat. He pulled his hand away as he retrieved a condom, then repositioned himself and covered her body with his. "Sky, look at me."

Her dark lashes fluttered against her cheeks as she opened her eyes, locking her gaze with his. He nudged her thighs apart with his knee. His touch was desperate as he breached her entrance with the tip of his cock. Her startled cry escaped on a gasp as Dash plunged fast and deep. The strokes were measured and teasing, driving them both toward a pinnacle of pleasure. The strokes quickened as he possessed her. He pushed her to the edge of desire. Sky was a willing prisoner to his lust as he claimed her. No words were necessary as she read the love in his eyes. The glint of tears stung the corners of hers, the undeniable pleasure intense and overwhelming.

Dash read her desire, the sensuality of the message more beautiful than words could say. Violent yet tender. Demanding and giving. His pace increased, the primal instinct possessing his hips. Her lips parted as a moan fell from them. His body spoke a language that hers understood, suffocating her heart. His thrusts gave and demanded in equal measure, coaxing her to come with him. His rhythm was set at sweet agony, and she savored the beat. She moved with him, her orgasm rippling into a tide. Lust bubbled her blood as he drove himself in a frenzied pace. Sweat misted her skin. He thrust harder and harder, taking her inch by inch with a driving force. He shifted up, his bone colliding with her clit until ripples of pleasure consumed them both. He reared back, the last blistering thrusts removing all ghosts of hurtful thoughts. He continued the beastly pace, driving them both until he exploded with a roar and her vision was nothing but starlight.

CHAPTER 22

*D*ash pulled at the blanket, inching it up over Skylar's shoulder as she sleepily snuggled into his side. Seeing her like that gave him a strange sort of satisfaction. She fit there. Every curve and edge of hers molded to his. His emotions swirled like a coming storm. What he felt for her was something he'd never felt for any other woman, and the prospect of losing her had settled something he'd been mulling over for weeks. It was a crazy notion, and he couldn't explain it, but it was now or never.

As he looked down at the beauty lying in his arms, all he could hear in the silence was the steady sound of her breaths. He ran his thumb over her shoulder as he attempted to rouse her from a semi-sleep. "Sky?"

Her dark lashes fluttered against her pale skin. As she half-opened her eyes, a smile broke on her lips. "Hmm?"

"Can you wake up and look at me for a minute? I want to ask you something."

She tilted her chin up and fixed her blue eyes on him. Reaching her hand to his face, she caressed his cheek. The love she'd so carefully guarded was now visible in her expression.

"Marry me."

Her eyes popped open, and she sprang up on her elbow. Her expression was a mix of confusion and disbelief. "What did you say?"

"Marry me." He relaxed against the pillows. There was so much more to say, but he was giving her a minute to wrap her head around the question.

Sky pinched the sheet between her fingers as she rose to a sitting position, pulling up the covers that had fallen to her waist and exposed her breasts. Her former sleepy and satisfied expression quickly shifted as skepticism sliced with steely knives. Her eyes seared him with uncertainty. "Why?"

His confidence tilted, unbalancing the words he'd planned to say and leaving him with only one. "Because."

She cocked her head. "That's not a reason." Her brow furrowed.

How could he define the unexplainable? Though he attempted a confident smile, he was still nervous as hell. Not because he didn't think she'd marry him, but because he was asking her to share a life without boundaries. Every little thing they did would be publicized and he was well aware of her desire for privacy. He thought asking her was the craziest thing he'd ever done, but he couldn't shake the feeling that having Skylar as his wife would be the most perfect thing he'd ever do in his lifetime.

He looked down at her hand, brushing it with his fingers. "See, there's this thing—this connection between you and me—that I can't explain. I felt it the first time I kissed you and when I thought I'd lost you . . . when you walked out—" He couldn't finish. The feelings were too fresh. He swallowed the emotion that rattled his voice and the lump in his throat that had been there since she'd walked out. It was a dance of unfamiliar steps for him. Something he'd never have imagined doing in a million years. Why couldn't she have simply said yes? Instead, doubt pierced him. His body reacted. His mouth went dry, his tongue felt like he'd been snacking on wallpaper paste. He wondered if Skylar could hear his racing heart.

He cleared his throat. "I didn't mean to hurt you. I would never do that on purpose. Ever."

Sky blinked, capturing unshed tears. If her efforts were to hide her thoughts and feelings, they'd gone awry. He didn't have to convince her his heart wasn't careless. He could see in her eyes that she believed him. Except for his one, royal fuckup, their connection was stable.

"I know." She looked past him. Sliding her tongue over dry lips, capturing the bottom one between her teeth as she composed her thoughts. When she looked at him again, her eyes failed to reclaim their glimmer.

"I know I screwed things up. I never meant to. And I know I'm repeating myself, but whatever came out of my mouth was not what was in my head. There's no other woman but you. I fucked up, and I'm sure it won't be the last time I fuck up about something, but the most important thing for you to know is my future is with you. I love you, Sky, and I don't want to do this life without you."

His truth stripped her expression to the point he could no longer read it. What he was hoping was that she would launch herself into his arms, kiss him, and answer yes to his question. But that didn't happen, and the moments spent waiting for an answer were killing him.

Sky took a deep breath. The steel in her spine softened to a more forgiving posture. Lying her head on the pillow, she turned to her side and studied his face. He felt a hopeless prick stab his heart. "I believe you."

Her words were as soft and warm as melted butter. In her eyes was a vulnerability that burned into his soul. Yes, he'd wounded her, and, yes, she had every right to be skeptical, but he hoped she could see the truth despite her reservations. "Then marry me."

She gently shook her head. "I can't.

"Can't?" If she were any other woman, she would have taken advantage of the situation. He studied her. Both of them were tentative because of a wounding mistake, but she had to see he was making himself just as vulnerable as she felt. Too many people would have used him and capitalized on his proposal. What she didn't realize was that to share his life with her, she would have to help him build a life outside of the spotlight. He was subject to the same thoughts and feelings as any man in love—and he was in love with her.

"You'll change your mind." He was as determined as she was cautious. Sky wasn't a woman to play games. There was no manipulation in her eyes, and he knew full well she didn't care about what he had in the bank. If she had her way, they would go about the rest of their lives in obscurity. They would live somewhere remote. Probably a big, old farmhouse on a thousand acres with a wrap-around porch and inspiring scenery, with Dash playing the guitar while she penned her stories. But he wasn't going to give her fodder for a story of love gained and lost. It might take some time to convince her to build a life with him, but he'd do it. Then he would ask her again. Next time she would say yes.

CHAPTER 23

The next few weeks passed without incident. Sky didn't mention a word about his denied proposal and Dash set about rebuilding her confidence in him and their future. As Dash stood backstage with Skylar, they both looked out at the crowd. His arm casually draped around her shoulders as he placed a kiss on her head. She responded by inching closer to him, snaking her arm around his waist, and hooking a thumb through a loop on his jeans.

Surrounded by the haze of a semi-sheer mist of fog, the light show pulsed streaks of purple, blue, and white to the heart-pounding beat. Thousands danced to the rhythms of the opening act. Some in the crowd jumped up and down, some swayed their bodies like snakes, grinding side to side in a figure-eight motion. Sky looked up at him, her baby blues interrupting his thoughts. She, too, was compelled by the music, her body gently rocking against his. Instantly, his mind took him back to the memory of that first date when he watched her from backstage. He remembered hoping that his absence would be forgiven once she discovered who he was and that he was with the band. Though that was months ago, he felt like he'd known Skylar forever—and forever was his goal.

Energy revved the air in the arena as electricity infused sparks into the atmosphere. There was something unique about seeing a live performance. Whether it was a sporting event, play, or rock concert, nothing could ever compare to seeing something up close and in person. The feeling clamped down on your insides, compelling you to let go of your everyday world and join the fun. Tonight was no exception. It was a Boundless Hearts performance that would cap off their twelve-city tour. The fact that he and Sky were going to take a much-needed vacation once this show was done added to his excitement.

There was a distinct feeling in the air tonight. As the haze of pot smoke mixed with machine-generated fog, the energy and love of classic rock brought the masses. Music seduced them. Dash couldn't think of a better line of work. For a few hours, he helped people abandon their everyday lives and rely on the band to take them on a ride outside of themselves. Their audience was so diverse. Young people were discovering the music of previous generations, and those of the older set connected with their style while revisiting the musical style of their youth. And he got to be part of that. There was nothing like it.

Just as the band finished their last song, Dash kissed Skylar.

"You look like you're anxious to get on stage." She bumped against his hip.

Dash flexed his fingers, itching to grab his guitar and play some mind-bending sound.

"After tonight, it's just you and me for a while, babe." He pressed another kiss to her lips. When he drew back, he sank into her gaze. The past few weeks had only deepened their bond. Though most would think his life exciting, without her in it, his days were nondescript. He made no secret of telling her how much meeting her had flipped the script on his future. Skylar's love for him bled joy into his solitary life. Through their many conversations, he'd impressed on her that while many people believed success brought happiness, the stage didn't buy happiness any more than a number one book on the Wall Street Journal and New York Times. Despite what the public believed, the media as a whole filled people's heads with bullshit, making mortal men into demigods. They based their reports on half-truths, some hype, some sprinkled with just enough facts to spin stories, whether good or bad, for sales. When he thought of the rock stars of his youth, his stomach sank. Now that he lived a similar life, he felt pity for them. Though when he'd started playing in public, he wanted to emulate them, he quickly learned the painful truth. Most of his idols had barely made it through their younger years with their lives, clinging to their health and relationships with drug-laced fingers, while others succumbed to alcohol. Many died, leaving behind wives and children. Rare were those musicians who'd managed to balance both well, but those who'd survived had one thing in common: they'd realized their frailties and had gotten their priorities straight. Health and family first. Now, that was his goal. He could create a sweet life with Sky while living out his passion. Loving her gave him purpose. He refused to sink into the self-imposed trap that had befallen so many others. He knew exactly what he wanted, and she was standing right next to him.

A large screen descended from high above the stage, and images of Boundless Hearts filled the white space. Tracks of their hits played through the sound system along with audio bites of individual band members. They were pieces of conversations that had been recorded during various interviews. A grin caught the corners of Dash's mouth when he heard a clip of his own voice.

"Yeah, man, it's great when the fans come out and have a good time, but it's not real, you know? Real life is where the lyrics are made, we just add the music."

Skylar listened as intently as he did, her expression showed that she agreed with his comment wholeheartedly. Unfortunately, the sweet look on her face quickly soured once Ian approached.

"Hey, maaaaaannnn." He dragged out the word as he sauntered up, pushing for a place between the two of them. He hooked one arm over each of their shoulders. "How are my favorite lovebirds?"

Ian's tone sounded more sordid than interested, which pissed off Dash. He clamped down on Ian's wrist and wrangled out of his hold. Once he was free, he removed Ian's hand from Sky's shoulder as well. With a laser-focused stare, he gave the man a warning. As heat crept around the collar of his tee shirt, the other man held up both hands in surrender. The sight of Ian touching his woman didn't sit well with him. Dash knew damn well Skylar didn't like it either. Ian looked between the two, suddenly aware his presence wasn't wanted.

"No harm, no foul, man." Ian backed off, but the damage was done. The atmosphere had changed once he'd entered the space. Tension thickened the air. Ian knew the cause because Dash had confronted him privately. Dash had still harbored resentment from the day that Ian had walked in on them, but he knew that changes had to be made. He held out his hand.

"Give me your key to my house, Ian." Dash was glad that Sky was nearby to witness.

Ian shook off his surprised look and reached for the

ring hooked on his belt loop. He looked between Skylar and Dash, opened it, removing one of three keys without even looking at it. He placed it in Dash's hand. "You're doing this now? Right before we go on? Are you seriously that pissed off at me?"

Without a word, Dash took the key and slipped it into the pocket of his jeans.

"Aren't you going to answer me?" Ian's question was insistent.

Dash maintained his silence, instead letting the action speak for itself. He'd ignored Ian's scum-sucking attitude in the past, but he wouldn't dismiss it anymore.

"Man," Ian smirked, "I get it. You got feelings for this chick, but haven't you ever heard the saying 'bros before ho's'?"

Ian was lucky they were about to perform. Knowing that they had a show to finish kept him from getting punched again, and it wouldn't do for the press to get wind of the bad blood flowing between them. Dash simply turned away from him, leaving Ian to wallow in convicting and doubtful thoughts.

Dash made up his mind then and there. This was the end of it. He wouldn't give Ian the chance to get between him and Skylar again. Though he somewhat disguised his feelings, he was acutely more aware of Ian's disgusting behavior. *Was it me or Ian who changed?*

Dash was torn. He felt like he'd failed a friend. If he'd paid more attention to his self-destructive habits, maybe he could have intervened. A part of him believed Ian was just having fun, while the other knew Ian was on a course of self-destruction. Dash denied any responsibility for the man Ian had become. He wasn't the man's babysitter; he was a friend. Although Ian was an asshole and always had been, the two men had grown in different directions. Ian had no morals while Dash had a clear vision of right and wrong. While he could dismiss the actions of a hormone-raged kid, he couldn't extend that same courtesy to a grown man. He had everything at his disposal to live long enough to enjoy his life but was headed toward self-destruction. Maybe he and the other guys had looked the other way too many times, but the time had come for Ian to face his own demons and exorcise them accordingly. It wasn't anyone else's job.

Dash shook off the guilt, instead focusing on the woman beside him. He could work with Ian, even joke around with him while on the job to keep the peace, but if he interfered in his personal life again it would be the end of both.

CHAPTER 24

"The clarity of that new sound system was killer! It really kicked ass!"

As Boundless Hearts exited the stage, the volume of Ian's voice rivaled the roar of the crowd. He was so loud that, backstage, he could be heard well above anyone else.

Skylar watched as Ian slapped a friendly arm around Dash's shoulder. Although Ian thought he and Dash were back to an "old buddy, old pal" kind of relationship, Dash no longer felt the same toward him. Since the day that he'd barged into Dash's house, it had become apparent that he didn't care for her. For Dash, that was a problem. As far as her opinion of Ian, the internet added insult to injury. The stories of Ian's reputation with women nearly crashed her hard drive when she did a Google search on him.

A scowl crossed Dash's lips at Ian's touch, but the moment his eyes connected with Sky's, his gaze had a possessive glint. She thought it wise to stay out of Dash and Ian's rippled friendship. She suffered no delusions she and Ian would ever share anything more than a superficial relationship. But as Dash came toward her, all those hesitant thoughts and feelings melted away. His outstretched arm was an invitation. She happily took it and leaned into him. Being in Dash's embrace was her favorite place to be.

A feeling of serenity washed over her. She'd come to rely on the peaceful feelings being with him gave to her. Some days the emotions were a little different than others. At times they were soft waves, and at others, they crashed through her skin to penetrate muscle and bone.

"We're going to do one more encore." Dash's voice slipped through the noise. She nodded. "Then, what do you say we take off for the weekend?"

"Take off? Don't you want to hang out with the band? I thought I heard them say they were celebrating. You know, last performance and all?"

"I'd rather just take off with you." His eyes twinkled with mischief, pulling her mouth into a smile.

"Where to?"

"I don't know." He shrugged. "Just away. With you."

How she loved his spontaneity. His freedom. She scrabbled together some unvoiced questions. Where? When? How long?

"Stop thinking so much." Dash's eyebrows tugged together as he read her thoughts. "We're just going to be spontaneous."

"But—" He halted her protest with a quick kiss. The chant of the crowd for the band to come back was in full force. As the rest of the guys approached her and Dash, Ian came up beside her.

"Skylar." He noted her presence with a nod of his head and a cocky grin. Lifting a bottle to his mouth, he took a long swig of water—or, at least, she thought it was water. Her muscles tensed as his eyes caught hers. "Staying for the after party?"

She never had the chance to answer him as Dash

grabbed his arm, and along with the other two men, rushed them back onto the stage. The roar of the crowd as they burst from the sidelines was deafening. Thankfully, she was saved from Ian's niggling. The last thing she wanted to do was to be in his company, but as she watched him on stage, she understood his appeal.

The audience was there for a good time, and Ian gave it to them. She watched him dance across the stage. His movements were seductive. Playful. Unpredictable. Though she was hesitant to give him credit for anything, she had to admit he was quite the showman. He could sing; everyone loved his smoky, raspy sound. Even she wasn't immune. Though she suspected it was vodka or tequila in his bottle, it didn't matter. His performance was flawless.

* * *

THE ENCORE WAS FINISHED, as was this part of the tour. Other than meetings and a benefit concert, Sky was excited to have Dash all to herself, if only for a little while.

The crew followed the band's exit, going onto the stage to break down the set. As Sky looked out, she could see that the crowd quickly thinned. Ian and the other guys had headed backstage, while Dash stayed with her.

He lightly pinched her chin, lifting it to look into her eyes. The man had just enjoyed the adoration of a vast crowd, yet she had all his attention. His gaze never drifted, enchanting her with his beautiful brown eyes. He inhaled deeply, then exhaled a long sigh. It suddenly occurred to her that she'd been holding her own breath. But then, she always seemed to have a limited supply of oxygen whenever Dash looked at her with such longing.

"I'll be back in a few minutes. I'm going to go get our stuff from the dressing room, and I'll meet you back here."

He pressed his lips to hers as she nodded. The idea of spending a few days alone with him brought a smile to her face. As he disappeared, she reflected on the past few months. Although she'd only been with him on the road for the last two performances, it was the first time she'd traveled with the band. The good thing about her job was that she could work from anywhere. Though she and Dash always had their own hotel room, the time spent on the band's bus was trying. She and Ian were like oil and water. He perceived her as a threat to his friendship with Dash, but she knew the truth. The discord in Ian and Dash's friendship wasn't her at all. She was just the scapegoat.

While Ian was content to party away all his free time, Dash had other interests. She could see that she and Dash were the band's first experience with one of them having a serious relationship. Except for their time spent in rehearsal or performing, the other guys seemed content with casual hookups. There were no wives, and she was the only girlfriend. Tonight, they wanted to celebrate. She couldn't begrudge their desire but left the decision to Dash as to whether he wanted to join in. The tour's hard work had everyone on edge. The party would allow them all to blow off some steam. They could indulge as much as they wanted because they could sleep it off tomorrow. Apparently, Dash had other plans.

* * *

SKY WATCHED the stage crew break everything down, wholly lost in reflection. Preoccupied with thoughts of Dash and where they were going from there, her track of time was detoured. A frown tugged her brows as she glanced at her watch. It had been nearly an hour since Dash had left her there, and he still wasn't back.

She couldn't shake the feeling in her gut that something was going on. He would never have left her hanging like that. She only hoped he hadn't gotten into it with Ian.

She headed down the hall in the direction Dash had taken. Roadies had completely broken down lighting fixtures, trusses, and sound equipment. They were now pushing wheeled cases outside to a waiting truck. She hadn't realized that they, too, were almost finished. Once they joined in, the party would be in full swing. To her, that meant one thing. Dash had gotten caught up in the festivities.

Sky's heels made an angry clip-clop sound as she walked through the hallway and toward the sound of voices. A thin stripe of anger stiffened her spine, its effects leeching through her insides.

She didn't begrudge Dash a celebration with his friends, it was that he'd left her backstage to wait for him. She was well aware that part of the reason the band and crew lagged behind at a venue was to give ample time for the autograph seekers to go home. When they were out and about, the guys never seemed to mind giving autographs, but after playing several cities, the guys were tired. All they wanted to do was hang out together for a while and then go home.

She stared at the floor. The tiles were marred with black lines. She could only imagine the number of people who frequented these halls, leaving their mark by way of shoe scuffs. She couldn't help but wonder how many of the greats had traveled the same path she now walked. Hendrix? The Beatles? The Rolling Stones? Probably too many to count.

The sound of music increased as Skylar approached the door. So did the smell of marijuana. It permeated the air. She opened the door, the muffled sounds and smells within the room now amplified. She could barely hear herself think, and breathing without getting high would be a challenge, but she had to find Dash.

She looked around the room but saw no sign of him. People huddled in groups of two or three. Her eyes narrowed as she took in the scene. In two separate corners were private parties. One girl to five guys. All she noticed were the hands, none kept to themselves. One woman gave her a disparaging look. Sky averted her eyes. All she wanted to do was get Dash and get out of there. There was no need to engage with someone drunk, high, or both. An altercation was the last thing she needed.

The next group of people she passed made her skin crawl. Their activities were a little more sinister. All the men had their backs to Sky, oblivious to her presence. With busy hands, they cupped, tweaked, or sucked the woman's breasts. While one played with curls of hair, another had a hand down her unzipped pants. With thin and tightened lips, she moved past them. Disgust churned her stomach. Her eyes narrowed as she walked past the scene.

A closed door near the back of the room grabbed her attention. As she made her way there, a scene to her right made her pause. There were times, as a writer, she found truth to be stranger than fiction. There, pressed face first against the wall with her legs widely spread, was a woman. She was naked from her waist to the top of her thigh-high boots. Her long, platinum-colored hair jiggled against the back of her shirt as the man behind her delivered hard thrusts. Sky caught a glimpse of his tattoo; the head of a serpent meandered down his back. For a moment, she was transfixed. The head rested at the top of a round cheek, exposing evil, yellow eyes, fangs, and a forked tongue. The slithering beast seemed to move with each thrust, the detailing of its body expanding and contracting. The man's dark hair hung down the middle of his back, his ponytail swaying back and forth as he moved.

Neither he nor the woman seemed to care where they were or who was watching. A mix of emotions caused Sky's fingernails to dig into her palms. Stunned for the moment, she tried to look away, but couldn't. Maybe she was as depraved as them. What did she expect? It was a night for celebration. Deafening music, rivers of alcohol, a sea of drugs—all were welcome tonight. But something inside of her felt dirty. She shouldn't be in this room. Shouldn't be watching acts that should have been private. She hated Dash at the moment for putting her in this position, while at the same time a pang of guilt cramped her stomach. Skylar closed her eyes for a moment, shaking off her feelings and focusing on the task at hand. Finding Dash.

Finally, she reached the worn, green door. As she knocked, chips of old paint clung to her knuckles. She brushed them off her hand as she waited, but there was no answer. She knocked harder. Again, no response. Pressing her ear against the door, she heard a man's voice. It took a moment to determine, but he sounded like Dash.

Skylar balled her hand into a fist and pounded the bunched flesh against the wood. When no one responded again, she turned the handle. Tentatively, she opened the door and entered.

"Hello?" Her tone was soft and light. It certainly was no competition for the harsh sounds of the bass. The speakers had been manipulated to emphasize the sound. Her insides rumbled and vibrated, and, as she walked forward, she noted that a few people were in the back of the room. It was thicker with pot than the hall outside. Her eyes burned and watered, making it difficult to differentiate who was who.

She took careful steps through the room as she investigated the scene, looking from side to side as she searched for Dash. Lines of leftover dust from snorted cocaine made a white snowflake pattern on the glass tabletop in the center of three empty chairs. Off to the side were two guys sitting on the floor. She couldn't remember their names, and couldn't see them well in the near dark, but she vaguely remembered seeing them with the road crew. Two steps closer, and she nearly tripped from shock. One man sat with his back against the wall. His jeans were open, his cock unhindered, with a woman's manicured fingers wrapped around it. She stroked up and down, eliciting sounds of pleasure from the man. He looked up, locking eyes with Skylar's widened ones. "What can I do for you, sweet thing?" His voice was as deep as a dark pit, the question sounding filthy and suggestive.

Not waiting for an answer, he gave Sky an indifferent shrug. With a nod of his head, the woman took his dick in her mouth. He placed a hand on the back of her head as it bobbed up and down. A sinister grin widened his face, hooking one corner up into a sneer. "She's trying to set a record. I'm trying to help her."

Skylar looked at the man, entirely shocked by his cavalier attitude. Disgust narrowed her eyes. "Where's Dash?"

He jutted his head in the direction behind him. "Takin' a piss."

As if on cue, the door opened. Dash looked at her as he fastened his belt, his eyes vacant.

"I waited for you." Impatience sharpened her tone.

His smile was lecherous as he took her in. "If I'd seen you, I wouldn't have passed you by." *Passed her by? What the hell?*

Sky's mouth fell open. Confused and speechless, she stared at him as he stuffed a hand down his pants to adjust himself. The intensity in his gaze burned through her, and, suddenly, the room started spinning. Her thoughts scrambled as she tried to make sense of this twisted scene.

"What the hell happened to you? You told me to wait for you, and you never came back."

Dash leaned into her. He ran his index finger through her hair and pinched a lock with his thumb. He flicked the curl against her throat as he knitted his brow. "Sweetheart, we can go anywhere you want."

Her thoughts raced as her heart beat out a warning. Sky closed what little distance there was between them, her muscles twitching beneath her rage. Dash had just spoken to her in the same way she'd heard these guys talk to sluts. Possessed by the anger of a thousand wrongs, her arm buzzed. Her blood bubbled and boiled. Muscles tightened. Fury ignited. Before she realized what was happening, her hand sailed through the air, a loud smack connecting with his face.

The room went deadly silent as everyone stilled in shock.

"You don't talk to me like that. Ever!" Red colored her cheeks, loathing radiating from her eyes.

Dash's eyes were vacant as he rubbed his cheek. It took a moment, but then he looked around the room as if he didn't know what was going on. He stopped when his gaze met hers.

"Skylar?"

Instantly, she knew something was wrong. She pinned him with a stare, but his expression was puzzled at best. She had no time to address it. At the same time a million questions swirled in her head, a disruption behind her caught her attention.

She jumped out of the way of the man who, a moment ago, had been getting a blow job. The woman he was with fell back gagging as he jumped up. He looked down at his pants, and Skylar's gaze fell to his hands.

Grabbing the material at both sides of his zipper, he stared at the thick and slimy white coating. His nostrils flared. His neck and face turned red. He looked down at the woman, his expression thick with disgust. As he swiped both hands over his middle, he moved his shirt and wiped the sticky substance from his bare skin. "You stupid, fuckin' bitch!" He spat the words, his voice angered and raised. He tore his gaze from the woman, looking around the room. Those guys close to him were laughing, but there was no amusement in his eyes. His jaw tightened and ticked as he filled everyone in on what had just happened.

"Damn cunt threw up on me! I'm wearin' everybody's jiz!"

CHAPTER 25

Once in the rental car, Dash's expression was pained. Neither of them said a word when they left. Though confused, Skylar tried to wrap her head around what had happened. The mayhem created at the disgusting display had sent Sky scrambling to gather their things and get out of there. At the same time, everyone else laughed and bantered, involving themselves in what would forever be known as the "up-chuck incident."

She couldn't make sense of much. In the last hour, she'd seen things that had left a bad taste in her mouth. A few of the women in the room had gagged and laughed at the same time. There were also those rare people that had offered assistance, grabbing napkins and passing them to the semen-soaked man, but Skylar had had something else on her mind. Dash.

The odd behavior followed by the blank stare. The loss of time. The sudden recollection of who she was and where he was and then him trying to shrug everything off. Something had happened in there that gave her a bad feeling in her gut. For a few, brief moments, Dash had been lost. Though he wouldn't admit it to her, she'd read it in his eyes.

The road ahead had few vehicles, giving them a leisurely ride and time to talk. It was the perfect opportunity to gain some clarity. She looked over at Dash, placing a hand on his knee. "So, what happened, babe? Why did you leave me waiting all that time?"

"I honestly don't know." He shrugged. "I don't even remember hanging around. I went back to get the stuff and then planned to leave. Next thing I knew, I was taking a piss and eyeing up a pretty woman." His smile was weak. Reaching out, he grazed her arm with a light hand. "Sorry, babe. Maybe I've had too much shit on my mind. The only thing I can think of is that I sat down and crashed. One of those "power nap" things." He yawned. "I'm tired as hell. I feel like I could sleep for a week."

She wasn't sure what to do. Should she bring up the blank stare? The empty gaze? The hollow expression?

Though the incident had dug in deep and sprouted roots, there were questions to weed and answers to pull out. She didn't know if she should press for clarity now or wait for a better time, when Dash had gotten some sleep and regained focus. The last two weeks on the road had been grueling. Maybe he did have a lot on his mind with the tour, upcoming meetings, his strained relationship with Ian, and their relationship. His appearance had suffered. As she looked at his handsome face, she noted the addition of a few more worry lines on his brow and wrinkles at the corners of his eyes. Also, he confessed that he hadn't been eating or sleeping right. That could be the crux of the problem. If she pressed, she might not get the responses she was looking for. Her heart demanded answers, but her head dictated she find a rational way to get them. If she waited, an opportunity for clarity would present itself in due time.

Resigned, she shrugged. She wasn't happy about what had happened, but it wouldn't do any good to overthink the incident. There could be a million reasons, and though she didn't like it one bit, a little patience wouldn't hurt. Besides, she needed to give her overactive imagination a vacation. There was no need to "borrow trouble," as her friend Lydia would say. That's one thing she and Dash didn't need any more of—trouble. Pressing the issue could only breed more of it.

"Are you pissed at me?"

Skylar stole her gaze from him to look out the window. "Maybe. No. Oh, I don't know." She gave him a quick glance. "I don't think so."

He gave her a questioning look.

"I probably overreacted, but, then, I did wait almost an hour for you." She turned, shifting in her seat, and mustered a weak smile. "I knew there would be lots of people more than willing to celebrate with you—if you know what I mean."

Dash placed a reassuring hand on her knee. "You know better than that."

A sarcastic chuckle puffed from her chest. "I do, but I'm still a girl in love with a guy who is adored by thousands. Even you know that some of the women in that room would be willing to cross any moral line without a single thought."

"I get that, but they would have to have a willing partner." He rubbed his hand up and down her thigh and patted her knee. "I'm not that guy, babe. You have nothing to worry about."

Sky let his words sink in just long enough for her shoulders to relax. *Let it go, girl.* It was time for a change and Skylar decided to change subjects. There was a topic Sky wanted to discuss before the next part of the band's tour, Ian. Sky wanted to know more about him. What was that saying? Keep your friends close and your enemies closer? "Okay. On to something else. Talk to me about Ian."

Dash let out a long sigh and settled back into his seat. He ran his thumb underneath the seat belt lying across his chest. "I'm not sure we have enough time. Ian's a topic that could take days." He huffed out a sigh. He eyed her with a mix of humor and wariness. "What do you want to know?"

She mulled over her many questions. Where should she start? Ian was a puzzle. One thing she did want to know was the origin of their friendship. She knew very little about Ian, but what was more interesting to her was the dynamic that he and Dash shared. Their personalities were yin and yang. Different but connected. Ian mattered to Dash, and if she and Dash were talking a long-term relationship, it might be in her best interest to learn enough about him that might make her care a little about him too.

"Ian's . . . odd."

She smiled at his hesitation and the way he scrunched his face when giving his one-word description of his friend. She was sure he could read the "you don't say" expression on her face when she glanced over at him.

"We met in high school. Freshman year. He was kind of the class clown, you know? Funny, yeah, but outrageously so. You either loved him or hated him."

"Doesn't seem much has changed!" Her blurted words caused them both to laugh.

"One thing was for sure, you could always count on Ian to do something to get attention." He paused, looking over at Sky with a sardonic grin. "We met in detention."

Skylar lifted her eyes to the heavens, shaking her head in disbelief. "Why am I not surprised?"

Dash sighed while arching a brow. "I wasn't the kind of kid that found myself there often, but once I started hanging around with Ian, we became regular visitors. After a while, our teacher only showed up long enough to take attendance; he didn't want to be there any more than we did. Once he left the room, Ian launched into conversations about his drug connections. He was quite the opportunist. He even set up a private corner in the back of the classroom for girls who wanted to perfect their blow job techniques."

Shock rounded her eyes. "You're kidding, right?"

Dash laughed as he put up his hands. "Swear on my grandmother. There was a rolling chalkboard with adjustable legs. Ian put it as low as it would go and made a makeshift sex closet using the board as a privacy screen. Behind it was a chair for the guys. He used jackets to cushion the girl's knees."

Of course, he did.

Dash, visibly amused by his adolescent recollection, continued. "For an hour and a half every day we were in there. Ian never stopped talking. His list of willing girls was impressive, and guys started pulling all kinds of shit in school just so they'd get detention." He shrugged. "I mean, really, what high school boy wouldn't want what Ian advertised." He gave Skylar a look, admiration clearly in his eyes. "He was quite the entrepreneur. Supply and demand, babe. Ian was a high school legend. Still is to this day."

"Maybe, but it's a little extreme."

"To a sixteen-year-old boy? Hell, no, it wasn't extreme! It was worth the risk to get your rocks off. Growing boys. Active glands. What can I say?" Dash's face screwed up a little. "It was all good until I told him to fuck off in front of the whole class."

"Oh my God. Why did you do that?"

His look was matter-of-fact. "Ian was an asshole, and I was fifteen. He'd been trying to get this one girl to join in on the backroom debauchery. Her name was Halo and, I assure you, she was not an angel. Rumor had it she had no gag reflex and she sucked like a Hoover." He paused, looking over at her as pieces of a memory pinned his thoughts. "This sounds worse now that I'm older." He shook his head. "Anyway, Ian hooked me up with her. I was out of detention, trying to get my grades up, and I didn't want to go back there. You know?" He winked at her. "I wanted to graduate, not spend my life in high school." Dash's expression went blank. "I don't know why, but I kind of had a crush on her, and I thought she really liked me too. I found out the hard way that she wasn't interested in a one-on-one relationship." As Skylar stole a quick glance at him, she saw pain veil his expression.

"You mean you saw her with another guy?"

He nodded. "Several." He paused. "Anyway, once I wasn't there, Ian didn't want to be either. He stopped getting in trouble and didn't have to go to detention anymore. I think he felt terrible he'd exposed the girl for what she was, and he started following me around. I played the guitar and a buddy of mine asked me to play in a band he was putting together. We were about ten sessions into our rehearsals in Tommy's garage and Ian came along just to watch us practice. The guy playing bass guitar, Charlie, had a sore throat that night. We played a few songs without anyone singing, but when we got to "Kashmir" by Led Zepplin, Ian, just goofing around, turned into Robert Plant." Dash shrugged, his hands opening in a surprised manner. "He shocked everybody. None of us knew that boy could sing. We'd been hanging out for months, but that was the first time he came to band practice with me. We played a couple more songs, and Ian, just bullshittin', let his inner rock star take the stage. Really, he was just playing around, but it was brilliant. Something came over Ian when he sang. Before the night was over, he had taken over the persona of David Lee Roth, Steven Tyler, and Roger Daltrey." The memory washed pleasantly over his face, his eyes a warm glow as he reminisced. "It was . . . amazing."

And there it was. The pregnant pause indicating that the twist of the story was about to be revealed. "What happened?" she asked, a hush to her tone.

Dash shoved his back against the seat, his lips a tight grimace. "Drugs. Alcohol. I would say women, but he was always a ladies' man. High school girls were just the tip of the iceberg. They were nothing compared to all the women over the last fifteen years. Add tons of money and easy access, and you come to where we are now. None of us ever know what's up with Ian. We try to keep him grounded, but we aren't his babysitters either."

"But you two are still close. Ian had a key to your house."

"Yeah. We are, and we're not. I can take just so much of him. We all have our limits. Every once in a while, he believes his own hype and his ego blows up so big it's hard to reel him in. The other guys might fool around a little, but if you notice, they don't hang around too long at Ian's after-show parties. It gets old after a while." He turned to her. "Know what I mean?"

If she didn't understand completely, she now had a damn good idea. Sky pictured all the articles that had popped up in her Google search. Ian had no trouble keeping himself in the top ten search results, that was for damn sure, but some of the other stories she read were just sad. Musicians, many of them family men, leaving wives or girlfriends, after meeting someone while on tour. Families were destroyed and nobody seemed to blink an eye. It was a tough life. A hollow existence. If you, somehow, happened to be one of the lucky ones and managed to keep your marriage and family intact while on the road making music, you were rare.

She exhaled a heavy sigh. "Yeah, I think I do."

CHAPTER 26

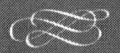

The sun slowly drifted down in the sky, its evening descent painting the crystal waters in shades not found at the high point of the day. Dash had lied to her. He had no intention of jumping on a bike and taking off. He had a plan. A surprise. A vacation in Key West.

Ripples of water lulled Skylar into a deep state of relaxation, their delicate sounds were soothing her soul. The brilliant azure waves lapped against the side of the boat. As it gently swayed back and forth, the sun's rays transformed the blue color to liquid gold. She followed a lone seagull as he flew above her, looking for a late afternoon snack. It was a gentle reminder to never take the little things for granted, no matter how insignificant you might think they are.

She leaned back against the cushions, her body bearing the evidence of a two-week tan. Dash had dropped anchor for the night in a secluded fingerling cove, thick with mangroves. There was very little to worry about when surrounded by all that beauty. She wondered how he'd pulled it all off when he had been so busy with the band, but she wasn't complaining. With very little effort, she could get used to this kind of life. Coffee on the water while watching the sunrise. Fishing from late morning into early evening. A delicious supper made from the fresh catch. Add in a bottle of wine, and it was absolute heaven.

The ride back from their fishing spot was nothing less than exhilarating. Dash revved the engine, the fiberglass bottom of the boat skipping over the water. It was just enough of a thrill to make her tummy flip. Once he'd spied a place to moor the vessel, he steered into a comfortable position and dropped anchor.

Skylar closed her eyes, sinking into the near silence. The only sounds out on the water were that of nature. Dash's Sea Ray Sundancer was a luxury cruiser. It had everything they needed to completely disconnect from the world and decompress. She'd turned on some music, keeping the volume low, though there wasn't another boat anywhere in sight. With coffee in hand, she swayed to the tunes of Clapton, Stevie Ray Vaughn, and B.B. King.

Weekends found Key West peppered with many kinds of boats and all sorts of people. The combination of water and high temperatures coated her skin in a thin sheen of moist heat. Though technically part of Florida, there was something distinctly different about Key West. Inhibitions fell away, alcohol freely flowed, and even the staunchest personality unshackled. There was nowhere else in the United States like the Conch Republic, as the locals called it, and she and Dash were soaking in every minute of freedom it offered.

"Hey, baby?"

The sound of Dash's voice brought a smile to her lips. "Yes?"

"Do you have coffee up there?"

"Yes."

"I'll be right up."

Happiness welled up inside of her. The timing of this getaway was exactly what they'd needed. Since Dash had a break and she'd finished the second draft of her current novel, this small amount of downtime afforded them the perfect opportunity to get away. Winters in Maryland were fickle, the weather as moody and unpredictable as the love life of a teenage girl. In the time they'd been there, they'd not only spent time out on the boat, but they'd partied together, just the two of them. They'd hopped from bar to bar, and, though there'd been many other patrons, they'd only had eyes for each other, as if no one else existed. Sky liked living in their little, invisible bubble, just the two of them. Free of tour dates and book deadlines, not to mention Ian's antics, they were using this time to take their relationship to a whole new level. It was heaven. Pure heaven.

As Dash came topside, a rush of pleasure coursed through her, interrupting her thoughts. He looked over at her as she reclined. The warm breeze caressed her skin just as the look in his eye warmed her heart. Giving her a devilish grin, he stripped off his shorts. Modesty wasn't his strong suit. With a mischievous look in his eye, he placed his foot on the cushion near her knee in a blatant copy of the Captain Morgan pose.

She skated an index finger up the back of his calf, scraping ever so gently with her fingernail. Desire bubbled her blood. She slid her sunglasses an inch down her nose,

peered over the top, and fixed her eyes on his semi-erect appendage. Slowly she dragged her eyes upward, noting that the sun-kissed glow on his skin was a shade or two darker than hers. Dash's naked body was a thing of beauty. It was no wonder he was desired by women all over the world. Sky took mental inventory, appreciating the view as her eyes traveled to the pronounced V that flowed into his pelvic area. What was it about that area that made women salivate?

Skylar was no exception. A well-developed man was a work of art. She gave him a sultry look, her blue eyes meeting his sparkling brown ones.

Although early, it was already in the high 80s. Dash's tight abs formed an impressive six-pack, and droplets of heat-driven sweat glistened in the crevices of his tanned skin. Her playful mind kicked in, urging her to forget the early hour, lick the salty sweat from his skin, and chase it down with a shot of Tequila.

"See something you like?" His tone was playful and suggestive.

She arched a brow. "Maybe."

A hearty chuckle was all she received before he shocked her. A quick step up, and then he launched himself over the side of the boat. She yelped. Graceful, he wasn't. His cannonball exploded when his ass hit the surface, the water splashing high enough to give her a good dousing.

"Dash!"

She sprang upright from the jolt of cold water. Running one hand and then the other down her arms, she wiped away the unexpected droplets. Though they cooled her skin, she blotted away the remaining beads with a nearby towel as Dash took a short swim around the boat. Before long, he hopped up on the swim platform and made his way back to her. He shook his head like a dog, flicking more water as he stood above her.

"Stop! You're getting me all wet!"

He grabbed a towel and dried his hair, leaving the rest of his body to the elements. "You're not sugar. You won't melt." He laughed, straddling her. Caged between his thighs, the remaining drops on his skin trailed down to hers.

"You're getting me all wet. Didn't you hear me the first time I said it?" She reached out to his muscular thighs and floated her palms on his skin.

"That's the goal." His tone was suggestive, and a rush of desire moistened her bikini bottom.

Dash stretched out, laying his body on top of hers to prevent her from escaping. "Besides, what kind of husband would I be if I didn't make you wet?"

Husband? She gave him a wayward look. "We aren't married."

"We will be." His measured tone gave way to a low growl. The sound incited all sorts of images, but the statement earned him a playful eye roll. Dash tucked his lips beneath her chin, heating her skin with kisses. She shivered as his cold body pressed against her sun-heated one.

"You're so cold." Sky giggled, squirming beneath him.

His entire body imprisoned her. He gave her pelvis a gentle thrust. "Mm-hmm, and you're so hot." His rich baritone dropped to a sultry bass, the sound traveling deep inside her. Skylar shivered again, but this time it wasn't from a chill. "You're so bad," she said.

"Yes, I am, but I'll make it good for you."

He kissed her long and hard, the way she'd grown to love. His passion stoked hers, the enthusiasm ratcheting both his desire and hers. He ground his erection against her, the only thing separating them was her thin, white bathing suit bottom. Blood rushed to his cock, and within seconds he'd grown rock hard. With the stiff member digging into them both, Dash hooked his thumbs inside the band and slid the garment over her hips, down her legs, and off until it lay on the deck. He parted Skylar's thighs with his knee, forcing her legs to open to him.

Sky's eyes flew open as she gasped. She snapped her head left and right. "Dash, we're out in the open. Someone might see us." Her plea fell on deaf ears.

"There's no one around, baby." He kissed her again to silence further protests.

Though she weakly protested, the idea that someone could come upon them and witness their lovemaking sent a jolt of excitement through her. Still, she wanted it on record that she'd made an attempt at modesty. "Really, Dash. A boat could come near us at any minute."

"Shh." Dash, undeterred by her protests, continued to tease and tantalize.

Skylar sucked in a breath as he moved off her and leaned on his side, his fingers trailing along the inside of her thigh until they disappeared between her folds.

She moaned as his fingertips grazed the sensitive area. The sound sent a fresh supply of blood to his already turgid member. Dash nudged her thighs wider as he dipped inside. A rush of wetness mixed with her heat, her body begging him to continue.

Skylar's hips swayed as she writhed with pleasure. Dash removed his hand just long enough to position himself between her legs. As his tip breached her entrance, she moaned. She thrust her hips upward to take him in, but Dash moved back, letting her know he controlled their pace. With a free hand, he untied the strings securing her top, tossing it aside once it was free.

Dash teased her, running his tongue along her mouth. Her lips parted, allowing him entrance. Naked and out in the open, Sky's modesty had ruled her initial thoughts, but when Dash kissed her like this, she let go. It was as if he read her body. At the exact moment she submitted totally, he invaded her with both tongue and cock. Her back arched, the coordinated move causing her to gasp. A wave of pleasure washed over her with the initial thrust, but as he pulled back, the retreating drag of his smooth cock hitting every nerve doubled the pleasure. Her body responded, gripping him with each move of his hips.

"Oh, God." Skylar's moans were a prayer as her body begged for release. She lost herself in the feelings. A touch of danger lingered, caused by their exhibitionism, but it added to her excitement. The fear of being discovered created just enough trepidation to turn her on.

She craved Dash, her body begged him to possess her completely. Lust had settled into her marrow, turning Dash into both conqueror and slave.

Over and over, he pushed her body beyond any pleasure she'd ever experienced. Driving. Claiming. They were blind to anything other than satisfaction. Skylar cried out as she approached her climax. Dash responded to the sound, thrusting harder, driving deeper. With one final thrust, her cries ignited an explosion. Dash took them both over the edge, Skylar shattering as he emptied himself inside her.

* * *

DASH RESTED his head on Sky as the sun beamed down on them. She played with his hair, inching the pads of her fingers over his scalp as she massaged his head. "Tell me about your family."

He lifted his eyes to hers. "What do you want to know?"

"I don't know." She shrugged. "I don't really know anything about them. You've mentioned them in passing, but not much."

His expression shadowed. "My mom and dad were great people. I couldn't have asked for better parents. They were working class. Dad was a postal worker. Mom was a teacher. I'm an only child, so I'm sure you can guess that their world revolved around me. They came to every baseball game." He sat up and stretched his neck muscles. A tender spark lit his eyes. "They had two folding chairs, the woven kind. They packed them and a little umbrella that clipped onto the arm of the chair. They always packed a little cooler with a couple of sweet teas for Mom, ginger ale for my dad, and four bottles of water for me. My parents were the biggest cheerleaders in the world. They'd yell at the umpire if there was a bad call and screamed when anyone on my team made a home run." Sad laughter slipped from his lips. "They were great people. Embarrassing at times, but great."

"How did you come to play guitar?"

"I don't remember not having a guitar. I think I was five when my mom got one for me. My grandparents were gone before I was born, but my mom said that my grandfather played the fiddle and my grandmother played piano. My parents said I was a natural. I just picked it up and played. I've been playing for as long as I can remember."

"Sounds like they were awesome. How did they die?"

His face tipped up until he met her eyes. "My dad died of a heart attack just after my first gig. Mom outlived him by ten years. Cancer took her. She did take treatments, and went into remission twice, but it came back with a vengeance the third time. She got to a point where she felt like the treatments were doing more harm than good." His brows pinched with pain. "She was so sick. She told me she didn't want to do it anymore and asked me if I'd be mad at her if she stopped. I told her hell no. After that, I took her to Florida. It was winter in Maryland. Mom always loved being by the ocean. I found a house down there on the beach. I'd wrap a blanket around her if she was chilly, but she loved it there. She passed sitting in her chair, looking out at the Gulf."

"I didn't mean to make you sad."

"You didn't. It's been a while since I've thought about them. If anything, you did me a favor."

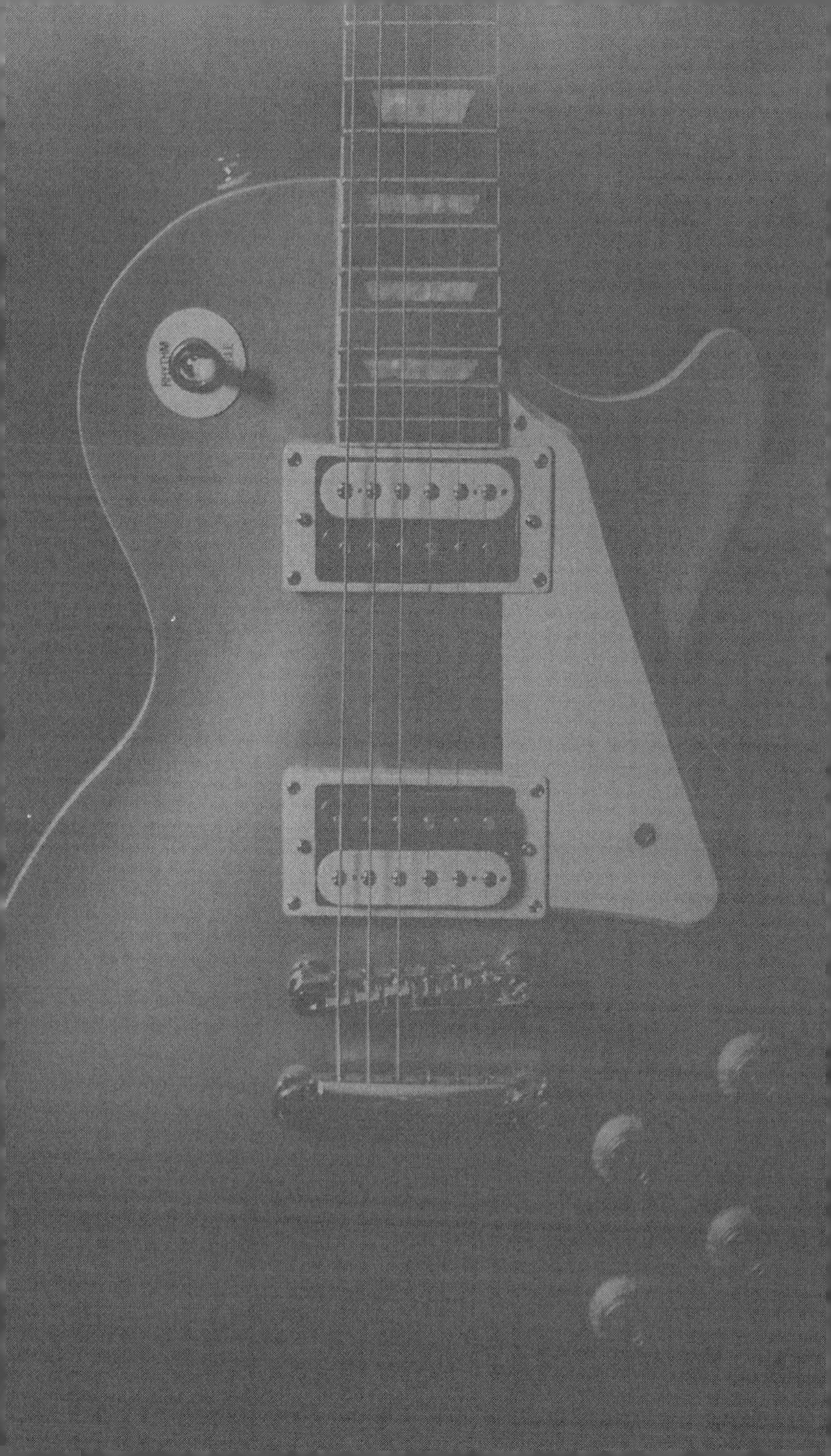

CHAPTER 27

There was something magical about a dark sky with a million stars. After another day spent on the water, they were far from the light pollution of the city. Sky lost herself as she stared into space. Her thoughts floated, drifting her in and out of dreamy views.

"Happy?" Dash pressed his hand to the curve of her hip and gave it a gentle squeeze.

"Unbelievably." She ran her fingers through his hair. "I am getting chilled. I think I got a little sunburned."

"I should have put you on top. You'd look cute with a smart, red ass."

She swatted his shoulder. "I'll just bet you'd like that. Unlike you who stands for his job, I have to sit. The last thing I want to do is try to concentrate on a storyline with a stinging, itchy bottom."

Dash laughed as he rose to his feet. He extended a hand to Sky. They watched the sunset and sat talking into the night. "You want a glass of wine?"

"Sure." Sky wrapped her arms around herself. Goosebumps pebbled her skin. The combination of night air and sunburn were responsible for the chill. Though the night was still warm, her slightly toasted skin was sensitive.

As Dash poured the wine, Sky went down below to grab something to wrap around her shoulders. It was such a beautiful night. She ran a brush through her hair, flipped it through a ponytail holder, and returned to where she'd left Dash. There she found him sitting in the captain's chair. She came up behind him, wrapped her arms around his neck, and placed a kiss on his head. This had been such a nice break from the everyday grind. Her heart was light, her spirit playful. "Whatcha doin', hot stuff?"

Dash didn't respond. Sky pressed her mouth closer to his ear. "Dash?" He didn't move. A chill ran through her as, suddenly, she sensed something was wrong. She dropped her arms, walking around the side of him until she could see his face. "Dash. What's wrong?"

He didn't turn to look at her. In fact, he didn't do anything. She snapped her fingers in front of his eyes, but Dash's face was devoid of expression. Instantly, fear gripped her insides. She placed her fingers beneath his chin, pinching ever so slightly to raise his head. His eyes met hers, but in them was a befuddled cloud. He was lost.

*** * * ***

THIS WAS no time to panic. After several attempts to bring him back from whatever black hole he'd slipped into, Skylar took his hands. Dash appeared to be locked inside his own thoughts, unable to make a connection. She pulled and he stood up. Walking backward she led him down two steps to the cabin below. He followed her direction but wasn't engaged. He sat down when the back of his legs hit the bed, and Skylar gently pushed him until he laid down.

He closed his eyes, and she covered him with a light blanket.

Terror isn't something that can be controlled. The moment that fear takes root it floods the body with adrenaline. It hitches a ride through your bloodstream and sets every system on high alert.

Skylar sat on the other side of the bed, watching Dash as he rested. Peaceful sleep smoothed the lines of his face, in direct contrast to what she was experiencing. She was in the midst of the worst panic attack imaginable. She didn't know what to do.

She swiped away helpless tears. Why hadn't she learned how to operate the boat? She should have insisted Dash show her what all the gears and gadgets were for, but she'd been having too much fun. Her mind was filled with guilty thoughts. Her ignorance could be their undoing.

Skylar wrestled with her fear, slowly inhaling some deep, calming breaths. It took everything she had to slow her mind and rationally examine their situation. She leaned over and pressed a kiss to Dash's cheek. The best thing she could do was to leave him to sleep through whatever it was that had snatched him from her.

She went above and took a seat nearest the cabin door. That way, she could hear Dash if he woke up. Her stomach churned, the sick feeling rising in her throat. She replayed the last half-hour. What had happened in the few minutes she'd gone down below? And what was she going to do now? They were stuck in the middle of the sea, at night, with no one around them. She couldn't get a cell signal and didn't know how to use the radio to call for help. She also couldn't get them back to the marina. She didn't know the first thing about driving a boat. *Drive a boat?* Was *drive* even the proper term when talking about the movements of boats?

Looking over, she saw Dash had poured the wine. She picked up the glass and downed it. There was nothing she could do then except calm her racing thoughts and come up with a plan.

She leaned her head back and rested her neck on the soft, beige leather. The sky was so dark and the stars so bright. This evening could have been another magical one but had turned grave. She couldn't let her guard down. Two things required her attention, getting the boat to shore and hoping that whatever had happened to Dash could wait until she could get him medical care. The blank stare. The non-responsiveness. Had he had a ministroke?

Though she'd begun to put some order to her thoughts, exhaustion overtook her body. The sun always had a draining effect after a day spent in it, and swimming, fishing, and lovemaking had compounded the impact. She was dead tired.

Breathe, two, three, four, five. Out, two, three, four, five. Count. Slow. Calm. Down.

Skylar repeated the mantra as she concentrated on the variety of night sounds. It wouldn't do either one of them any good if she couldn't keep her head about her.

A rustling noise caught her attention. She flew down the steps, but Dash was fine. He'd kicked off the covers and turned on his side. Sky exhaled a sigh as she reached for a blanket. Laying down across from him, she fluffed out another sheet and put it over herself. Her eyelids were heavy, and her body weary. She closed her eyes, reaching out her hand and placing it against his back. As fear gave way to exhaustion, she prayed.

* * *

Skylar blinked.

The sound of a flock of birds overhead broke the silence of the morning. A few more blinks and her eyes opened a little further. The night sky had brightened, the smokey blue color of breaking morning joined by shades of pink and yellow. She shivered, drawing the blanket up to just below her chin. She pulled her knees up, tucking the cover tightly around her to ward off a chill.

Suddenly, her eyes flew open, and she bolted up. How could she have fallen asleep? She'd barely had time to think when she heard movement behind her.

"Hey." Dash came toward her, two cups of coffee in his hands. His steps were kind of a lazy stumble, but not one that wasn't normal for him before coffee. She took one from him, and he ran a hand through his tousled hair.

Her mind warred between wanting to attack him with questions or throw her arms around his neck and tell him how happy she was that he was okay. Instead, she took a sip of the brew and gathered her thoughts.

She wrapped both hands around the cup to steady them, peering at him over the rim. "How do you feel this morning?"

Dash gave a slight tip of his head and gave her a questioning look. "I'm not sure. I feel kinda groggy. I didn't think I drank that much yesterday, but I guess I did."

"You didn't." Her response was immediate and took him by surprise.

At first, his eyes rounded with a look of insult, but then they narrowed as armor. "Well, okay. Whatever it was, it knocked me out."

Sky's head demanded answers while her heart told her to calm down. Putting him on the defensive wasn't going to get them anywhere but into an argument. She slid her legs off the bed and placed them on the floor. "You scared me last night."

"Scared you?" A huff escaped him as he gave her a dismissive look. "Why the hell would it scare you that I fell asleep? I was tired. I passed out."

"You didn't pass out. You blanked out."

"Skylar . . ." He gave his head a shake, his eyes looking to the side.

"Blanked out is the only way to explain it, Dash." Her voice raised to an excited pitch, her hands animated as she spoke, to emphasize her feelings. "I went below to get dressed. When I came back, you were sitting in a chair staring at the wheel. Completely blank. You didn't move. You didn't speak. When I looked at you, it was as if you were looking right through me."

Dash didn't say anything for a few moments. It seemed he simply thought about what she said and then gave Sky an indifferent shrug. "Oh, well. I was probably more tired than I thought. Haven't you ever heard of people falling asleep with their eyes open?"

"No. I haven't, and I was terrified."

Dash sat beside her. "I'm sorry you were scared but, whatever it was, I feel fine now. Just a little slow starting the day." He paused another minute, then pushed aside the incident. He stood, went to the doorway, and gave her a smile. "What do you say we go back and get some breakfast?" He didn't wait for an answer, simply disappeared above deck.

Skylar forced a weak smile.

CHAPTER 28

Bubbles breached the wet surface as the engine came to life. Next came the telltale whirring sound of the anchor being raised. They'd been out for hours yesterday, giving Skylar no clue as to exactly how far they were from land. Skylar came up behind Dash, placing a hand on his shoulder. He turned his head, watching her as she cataloged everything he did. Although he hoped that what happened to him last night was an isolated incident, he wanted Sky to listen, learn, and be prepared. Since he had no recollection of what she'd said happened last night, there was no way to promise it wouldn't happen again.

He patted Sky's hand and steered them away from their secluded spot and out into the open waters. In measured increments, he increased the speed of the boat. Sky stood behind him. He ramped up the motor just a bit more and then looked over at her. "You wanna try it?" Necessity dictated his voice be a shout as he wanted to be sure she heard him above the engines.

Sky's skin was peppered with droplets of salt spray, and

as the boat went across the water, more were added every minute. Her head bobbed up and down, her eyes dancing with delight and excitement. She accepted his invitation, coming inside of his outstretched arm to take the wheel. He took both hands off, giving her complete control.

"You've got this. Just steer straight ahead. Once we get to the marina, we'll pull back the throttle, and I'll show you what to do."

"What if I screw up?" Worry lines formed on her brow.

"You won't. I'm right here with you." Dash's gaze was tender. Wrapping an arm around her waist, he pulled her between his legs. He leaned back on his elbows. His heart squeezed in his chest. There was just something about watching Skylar that made him feel like he'd just won a million bucks.

* * *

SKY WAS PROVING to be a natural at boating. Once they reached the marina, Dash took control of the wheel. She was a quick study, though. At Dash's direction, she helped to secure them in the slip. He only had to tell her what to do once, and she did it.

Once the boat was secured, Sky threw on a pair of shorts, a shirt, and slipped into her flip-flops. Dash did the same, hopped up on the pier, and gave her a hand up. It was a short walk to the restaurant, and he was starving.

Hand in hand, they walked over to Caroline Street. The dress code at Pepe's was relaxed, but, then, most places in Key West were. Though it was very early in the morning, the place was packed. It looked like a hole in the wall; it was just a quirky little joint, seemingly slapped together with leftover odds and ends, but the food was excellent.

This made the third time they'd been there for breakfast since they'd arrived in the Keys. Thankfully, the line moved quickly.

Dash led Skylar by the hand as they were seated. The same white and black cat he'd seen on their previous visits lounged in the exact place it had been the other two times. If he didn't know better, he would have thought it wasn't real. People passed by where it lay, and it paid them no attention. He and Sky were no exception. He kind of wished it would have responded to Sky. He could tell by the look on her face that she missed Hemi and could use a little furball love.

As he looked over at her, he noticed her gaze fell to the floor. Her eyes seemed vacant, and she appeared to be lost in her thoughts. He was sure he knew what was bothering her. He was ready to move on from what had happened on the boat, but Skylar was far from dismissing it.

In truth, he was more than a little concerned himself. He knew Sky had no reason to lie to him, but he couldn't recall what had happened. He'd ignored what she called the "blanking out" incident. Like rocks in the little boy's hand, he'd skipped over the surface of the topic, and then let it drop. As he looked at Skylar, he could tell she wasn't ready to let it go. While the waitress poured them both a cup of coffee, he thought of how he'd respond if she resurrected the topic.

"You all decide what you want?" The woman with a long, blonde braid holding a half-empty coffee pot in her hand needed no pen or paper to remember an order. She appeared to have been part of the original serving crew, but it wasn't possible she was that old. Dash deferred his request, waving a hand in Skylar's direction and waited for her to order.

"Um . . . I'll just have scrambled eggs and bacon. Crispy." She handed the menu to the lady, then looked at Dash.

"Western omelet. Sausage on the side." He, too, passed over his menu. The woman nodded as she tucked both under her arm.

"Got it. Thanks, folks." She turned, disappearing into the back.

Skylar reached across the table, taking hold of his hand. "I need to talk to you about last night."

He thought he could get away with a playful tone and gave her a sly smile. "And I'd like to talk to you about last night too. Want a repeat?"

Skylar shook her head, his sudden playfulness pricking her serious mood. She rolled her eyes. "Not that part of last night—although that was great." A blush stole over her cheeks, pinkening them to a near-red flush as she sheepishly eyed the patrons around her. She lowered her voice. "After."

He blinked, knowing that he had to get ahold of this before Skylar made more out of it than it was. "I told you, I was just tired." He let go of her hand and leaned back in the chair. "You worry too much, Sky. Let it go."

"And you don't worry at all." Her response was quick. "What if it was something, Dash? Wouldn't you want to know?" A red tide of worry crept up her neck and flooded her cheeks. "I thought you were having a stroke."

He took in a quick breath and let it out with an amused huff. Dash knew how important it was to erase her fears if he hoped for the topic to die. "A stroke? That's crazy."

The comment bruised her expression. Her brow pinched, and her lips turned down. "It's not crazy. I'm concerned," she insisted.

His tone came off as harsh, and he was immediately

repentant. "I didn't mean it like that." He leaned forward, reaching for her hand. "Babe, look. I'm tired. More than tired. Sure, we're on vacation, but I jumped from playing dates to playing with you." He rubbed small circles on the top of her hand, pleasure lifting his lips into a smile. "It does catch up with me. The guts and the glory. Once I regulate my food and my sleep, I'll be fine. Really. You have to stop worrying so much."

The waitress approached with one plate in each hand. "Scrambled eggs and crisp bacon for you." She placed a plate in front of Skylar. "And Western omelet, sausage for you." The woman looked between the two of them. "Anything else I can get you, folks? More coffee?"

"Yeah, I'll take some more." Dash looked over at Skylar's cup. "She'll take some too."

The woman smiled. "Got it. I'll be back with the coffee and the check."

Dash waited until the woman had distanced herself from the table. He picked up his fork, cut off and pierced a piece of meat, and watched Skylar. In the time he took to put the bite in his mouth, chew, and swallow, Skylar did nothing but push the food around on her plate. He took in an exasperated breath. Tapping on Sky's plate with his fork, he got her attention. "Stop, Sky. I mean it. It was nothing."

She looked away, and he nudged her leg. Her jaw was set while determination burned in her eyes. "I can't help it. You aren't nothing to me."

"Prove it." He severed a piece of the omelet and popped it in his mouth.

A question was pinching her brow. "What? How?"

He pointed at her with the tines. "Marry me." His brow raised in challenge.

"Oh my God. Seriously? You're doing this now?" A side

pucker hooked her lip, while an exaggerated eye roll helped to define her feelings.

"Yes. Seriously. Marry me." He let the comment fall while he continued to eat and drink. She still stared. He smirked.

"Why?"

"Why get married?" He half ignored her. He liked this game. "Because that's what people do when they love each other, Skylar. Because that's usually part of the plan when you want to spend your life with someone. And, oh, I don't know, that's what I've been asking you to do for months." Suddenly, he locked eyes with her in a deadly serious look. "If you're really concerned about me, then prove it, dammit. Be there for me. Ride my ass about my health. Hold my hand as we grow old. Be my wife."

Skylar stared but refused to speak.

Dash put down his fork. "Look. It's simple when you think about it. Everybody needs someone in their corner. I have no one in mine. No family. You can be that someone, be my family."

"You're romantic, I'll say that." A lazy grin slid onto her lips.

"Actually," he challenged, "I am." He let out a huge sigh, splayed his hands on the table, and pushed up from his chair. As he came around the table, his focus was solely on Skylar; he never saw the server he crashed into. The tray sailed from the man's hands. Food flew, and plates crashed to the floor. Everyone in the restaurant froze. Dash hurried to grab hold of the man before he fell to the ground. "Shit!" He caught the guy and helped him regain his balance. "I'm really sorry, man." As the man straightened, he looked at the pile of broken dishes and food. Distressed, his brow tugged in the middle. He bent to pick up some of the pieces as someone came from the back room with a broom. From the corner of Dash's eye, he saw people pulling out their cell phones—and he knew what was coming.

"Stop!" He yelled with his hands in the air. He made a plea as he turned in a circle to address everyone within earshot. "Please! Put the phones away."

One by one, he watched as they laid their phones face down on the table or slipped them into handbags. Dash turned to the server he'd knocked down, lowering his voice.

"Sorry, man. I'll pay for all the damage." He gave the man's back a friendly slap, then looked out into the restaurant. "I'll pick up everybody's meal, and I'll take a picture with every person here who wants one if you'll give me this one moment without taking a picture."

Dash's gaze traveled the room, and, as he looked over at Skylar, he saw that she was doing the same. "Great. So, we're all in agreement, right? No pictures?"

A roomful of heads bobbed. Satisfied, Dash took Skylar's hand and dropped to one knee. Gasps and a flurry of shock dusted the room, and then silence fell. Teetering on the edge of excitement, Dash had the notice of everyone in the room, but his attention was only on Skylar. Her cheeks flushed as he caught her eyes with his.

"This isn't sudden, Sky. I know you're the one. I knew it the first time I saw you. I promise you a crazy life with no privacy and a man who is devoted to you and will love you forever."

Skylar, momentarily speechless, paused.

Dash added one last appeal. "I don't want to do life without you, Skylar Harrison, and I know you feel the same way." He reached up, grazing her cheek with his fingertips.

As if they were the only two people in the room, Skylar's eyes softened. A smile lifted her lips and cheeks, joy smoothing out every worry line as she answered with a nod and one, hushed word. "Yes."

CHAPTER 29

"What do you mean, you're married?" Disgust and anger etched foul lines on Ian's face at hearing Dash's news. "You got married to her? Shit." He turned to Skylar, his scowl cementing his disdain.

Immediately angered by Ian's tone, Dash stopped himself from reacting. It wouldn't take much to push him over the edge, but this was a benefit concert and they were a few minutes from going on stage. What he really wanted to do was drag Ian outside and school him on the proper response to someone's good news. Since that wasn't going to happen right now, he repeated the news. When he looked at Sky, love filled his eyes. "We're married, and we couldn't be happier."

An indifferent shrug shook Ian's shoulders, but his body language was a lie. His posture was a contradiction to the look in his eyes. "Good for you." His tone was flat. Clearly, he was agitated.

He glanced toward the stage, then pulled out his cigarettes. "Guess there's time for one more." His mutter was barely audible. He flipped the top open and dragged a cigarette out with his lips. Striking the flint of an old, silver lighter, he took in a lungful of smoke. When he exhaled, he blew the cloud of smoke in Skylar's face. Dash was immediately incensed.

"What the fuck, Ian?" He pulled Skylar back, waving away the nicotine haze as she coughed and tried to catch her breath.

Though the rest of Ian's face remained immobile, satisfaction tugged at the crinkled corners of his eyes.

"You really are an asshole, aren't you?" Sky coughed. "You need to grow up."

Ian gave her an indifferent shrug and took another drag.

Dash, familiar with Ian's antics, caught him before he exhaled another cloud toward Skylar and issued a warning. "Don't do it."

Ian dismissed the threat. "I wasn't doing anything. I congratulated you. What more do you want? I mean, hey, you're a big boy. As long as she doesn't Yoko Ono you, we're good."

"You can't help it, can you? You just don't know how to be civil. Sky's my wife. Get used to it."

"Oh, c'mon Dash. I'm just playing with her. If you take her on the road with us, she's sure as hell going to be putting up with a whole lot more than jokes and smokes."

Dash narrowed his eyes. Taking Skylar's hand, he gave it a reassuring squeeze. "Yeah. About that. I'm taking off for a while."

Disbelief rounded Ian's eyes while anger tightened his jaw. "What?" He stole another angry drag. "You can't do that, asshole. We have obligations. I got us hooked up for this benefit, then we're going back into the studio. The lawyers will have a field day suing your ass."

"You didn't do jack shit! Our fucking manager got us

hooked up for this gig. I wouldn't have come back from Key West if this wasn't for a good cause. When it's done, I'm taking off. Call it a fucking sabbatical." Dash turned to Skylar, shaking his head at Ian's self-centered attitude.

"A sabbatical?" Ian gave him a smartass look as he put invisible quotation marks in the air. "Who the fuck are you, man?" His brows pinched as he raised his voice. "You play guitar, asshole. You're not a college professor. We need to lay down some tracks. Strike while the iron is hot. We don't have time for you to be playing house. Get your head out of your ass, Dash." Ian emphasized his point with a disbelieving shake of his head. A snarl curled his lip as he muttered in a low tone. "You must be losing your fucking mind."

Dash looked back at Skylar; their gazes locked. "Don't pay attention to him. I'm taking some time with my wife. I can get looked at by a doc and get my shit together as far as my health. A couple of months will be useful for all of us."

Ian cocked his head as he watched the tender display. He stared down Skylar before looking at Dash. "And you're doing this, why? Because of that twat?" He slung the words as weapons, intending to wound her. Instead, he ignited Dash's temper, which he'd barely been holding in check.

"Watch your fucking mouth!" Instinctively protective, Dash took a step in front of Sky as if his body could shield her from the sting of hurtful words.

Ian sniggered at the display. He lifted the cigarette to his lips, the end so red hot and glowing that the stub nearly burned his fingers. His next motions were exaggerated and dramatically slow. "Do whatever you want, man. Ruin your fucking career, but I'm not letting you take the band down with you." He shrugged. "Personally, I don't give a shit, but if the shit hits the fan, I won't do a goddamn thing to protect you. I'll throw your backstabbing ass right under the bus." His face contorted into a sneer as he eyed Skylar. "And you can take this bitch with you." He choked out the last, bitter words.

Ian thought he'd had the last word, but Dash sprang back. His skin flushed red as the color crawled around his collar. "You are a petty, little man. Most days, you can barely pour yourself out of a goddamned bottle or get your dick out of some sleazy whore. Don't talk to me like I'm some little shit, and don't talk to my wife like she's one of your tramps."

Ian laughed. Vindictive and arrogant, he closed the distance between them and leaned in close to Dash's face. He launched spittle-laced words through clenched teeth. "You haven't figured it out yet, have you, Dash my boy? You guys may have started the band, but, like it or not, I'm the draw. The personality. I'm the fucking reason you have job security. Me and my God damned bottle? I keep us front and center in the media. Those stories sell the papers. It drives up ticket sales. I'm not as dispensable as you think. Guitar players are a dime a dozen." He poked a finger in Dash's chest. "You would do well to remember that."

The atmosphere shifted as fury filled Dash's eyes. He looked down to where Ian had placed his finger and when he lifted his eyes, his glare was deadly. With barely five minutes until they went on stage, Dash grabbed Ian by the shirt. Though there was barely space between them for a punch to be thrown, he pulled back his arm as his fingers curled into a fist.

"Dash, no!" He heard her, but, before Skylar could stop him, his knuckles made contact with Ian's jaw.

In a flash Skylar jumped in between them, rushing to grab onto his arm before he issued another blow. Their bandmates sprang to their feet, holding Dash back before he could hit Ian again.

Blood dripped from Ian's mouth. He staggered from the strike, wiping at his face with the back of his hand. Everyone around them froze. Thankfully, no one on the other side of the curtain could see what was going on backstage.

As Ian righted himself, he flicked his tongue over his lip to inspect the damage. He winced as it touched the split. The metallic taste of blood coated his tongue. He dragged a black gaze toward Dash, his expression as cold as death.

"You stupid motherfucker. I'll give you this one, asshole," he said, shaking off the incident. He straightened his spine before issuing a warning. "Touch me again, motherfucker. I'll have your ass arrested."

Dash's retort was equally torrid. The red ring around his neck matched the murder in his eyes. "Try it, asshole. You'll hit the ground before you dial the last number."

Bystanders stared. The stage crew froze. Boundless Hearts was going on any minute and backstage they were a shit show. The singer had a bloody mouth and the guitarist sported scraped and bruising knuckles. For a benefit concert there wasn't much goodwill in the air.

Dash straightened up as he took some calming breaths. Each band that was playing had thirty minutes. What that meant was lots of people and lots of flurry.

Dash put some distance between Ian and himself. After a few minutes, everyone went back to what they'd been doing before Dash had belted Ian. Hopefully, no one had snapped a picture, but Dash didn't care. He was going to talk to the guys. Some changes had to be made and one of them might be to replace Ian.

The other guys gathered around Dash. With a few friendly slaps on the back, the other members were satisfied he could keep himself in check while they got through the performance. Dash thanked them for jumping in before he turned to Sky.

A weak smile played at her lips, but concern was evident in her eyes. "Are you okay?

Even with all the shit that had just gone down, all she cared about was him. "I'm good, baby." Though her shoulders sagged with relief, it didn't take away the hesitancy in her eyes. Dash pulled her to his side. "I don't want you to worry. Ian thinks I'm a fool, but I would never make a decision without thinking it through. I've already talked to the other guys. We all agree that a few months spent brainstorming will be good for us. They all get it. We hit it real big, real fast. We need to reevaluate where we want to go from here." He jutted his chin in Ian's direction. "The only one I hadn't talked to was him."

Worry lines formed on her brow. "But what about a lawsuit? Ian said —"

Dash cut her off. "Fuck, Ian." His tone was as soft as his fingers caressing her cheek. "This isn't Van Halen, and he isn't David Lee Roth." He took her hand, raised it to his mouth, and kissed her diamond wedding ring. His lips curled into a smile, as did Skylar's. "If Ian doesn't watch himself, he's going to find himself out of the band. Roth was dispensable. So is he."

CHAPTER 30

Skyler stood backstage, watching her husband. The crowd went wild when they rushed onto the stage. All the songs they played went off without a hitch. After seeing Ian's reaction, she was glad they'd tried to keep their marriage secret from the public. After a meeting with Vince about her book, she'd flown out for this performance. Although the other guys were more than welcoming, after witnessing tonight's display, she was glad she wouldn't be in Ian's company for some time.

A happy smile filled her lips as they neared the end of the set. The air was thick with energy. If they held true to other performances, an encore would be in order. After that, they were out of there.

Among the thousands of people who filled the arena, her new, wifely status secured her to Dash—no matter what trouble Ian tried to cause. She'd often heard it said that every living thing vibrates with a different energy, and those things that are meant to be together will find a place to peacefully coexist. Even matter at rest has power. If those things were true, it certainly applied to Dash and her. Their love described precisely what happens between two people who are meant to be together. They are, somewhat, matter at rest until they find each other. And when that happens, the connection between them causes a cosmic shift. Something beautiful and wonderful and transforming. The magic between brilliant stars and the darkness of night that makes the contrast between the two so vastly different, surprising, and breathtaking. A perfect balance happens when two things, so completely opposite, complement one another. They continue that way until they are spent. Used up. Put to rest. It's that kind of energy that had led them to each other. That thing from which the cosmos was born.

From the moment Skylar had met Dash, something shifted in the space between them. In their own worlds, each was busy doing the thing that made them happy. And then something changed. Something in the universe had been waiting for her and Dash to find one another. Everything that was good, from that point, became better. Richer. Love filled in their lives with color and texture, and, ultimately, changed them into what was meant to be.

Skylar's eyes softened as she watched Dash perform. She loved seeing him play. He was in his element, lost in the music, his fingers connecting with the guitar strings, vibrating them just enough to make him one with the music. Though his fingers had calloused, and his neck muscles had grown tight, she knew there was nothing else he'd rather be doing. The same connection she felt spinning words into tales. His softer music cradled her soul. Nothing gave her more satisfaction than listening to him play while she plotted a story and she was looking forward to more of that.

Though they hadn't spent as much time together as

they would have liked since their trip to Key West, that moment on the beach when they'd connected as husband and wife had changed them. They had their whole lives ahead of them and were at the top of their games. The book and music charts reflected it.

Dash had said twenty-six was his lucky number, since that was the date of their marriage, and when he had, she'd scoffed. She didn't believe in luck, only hard work and determination. Still, as she stood mesmerized watching her husband, she had to surrender a small amount of logic to whatever events had brought them such good fortune. One of the band's songs—one that Dash wrote—held the number twenty-six spot on the Billboard chart, while her latest novel sat in the same position on the USA Today best sellers list. Crazy. Maybe there was something to luck after all.

Thunderous applause interrupted her thoughts. She'd been daydreaming, and now everyone was filing backstage. It was for just a few short minutes, just enough time to get a drink of water and wipe the sweat off their faces. Soon, they'd rush out for an encore. Then she and Dash would take off.

As he approached, she held out an ice-cold bottle of water. He gave her a sweet kiss, his lips causing hers to tingle.

"Thanks, babe." Dash took the bottle from her hand, quickly downing the contents. Tiny droplets escaped his lips and dribbled down his chin.

He used his sleeve as a napkin, evidence of his quenched thirst escaping his throat with an exaggerated ahhh. Skylar pushed his messy hair away from his damp forehead, the beaded line of perspiration curving along his hairline.

"You were wonderful." He beamed a smile at her

comment, and she wondered if he could read the worship in her gaze. One morning during coffee, she'd told him as much, and he'd replied by admitting he was equally in awe of her writing. She wasn't even aware he'd read her books.

"Gotta go." He leaned in to give her a quick kiss and give her backside an affectionate pat. With that, he was gone, having jogged back onstage with his bandmates.

Again, the crowd erupted. Sky smiled. As she watched Dash, she wondered how she'd gotten so lucky. Dash was as handsome as he was talented, and he was all hers. His faded blue jeans were ripped at the knees and as tight as breathing would allow. A fan of button-down shirts, he rolled his sleeves midway between wrist and elbow. The tail hung free for ease of movement when he played—he never tucked them into his pants. The rounded hemline skimmed his lower back, coming to rest at the top of his very toned ass. He wore a tee shirt beneath it, which was usually soaked and clinging to his six-pack abs by the end of the night. His black Frye boots hid beneath the bottom of his jeans, which lazily rested against the leather. He was an enigma. How could someone so famous be so genuine and humble?

Her gaze drifted from Dash out to the audience. Their joy was infectious. Some were dancing, some were swaying, just as she had during that first concert. She smiled, leaning her head against one of the tall, black cases. It was a great prop for her, just a short distance away from public view while empty, but soon would house the band's equipment.

This song was her favorite. "Lost and Lonely." It was a song he'd written just before they'd met. The song had a great guitar solo, which was her favorite part. Dash, with a lone guitar, filled the empty space with a haunting melody.

The sound of the crowd had quieted to a hum, and she closed her eyes. She savored the sound of Dash's talented fingers seducing the strings.

And then there was nothing.

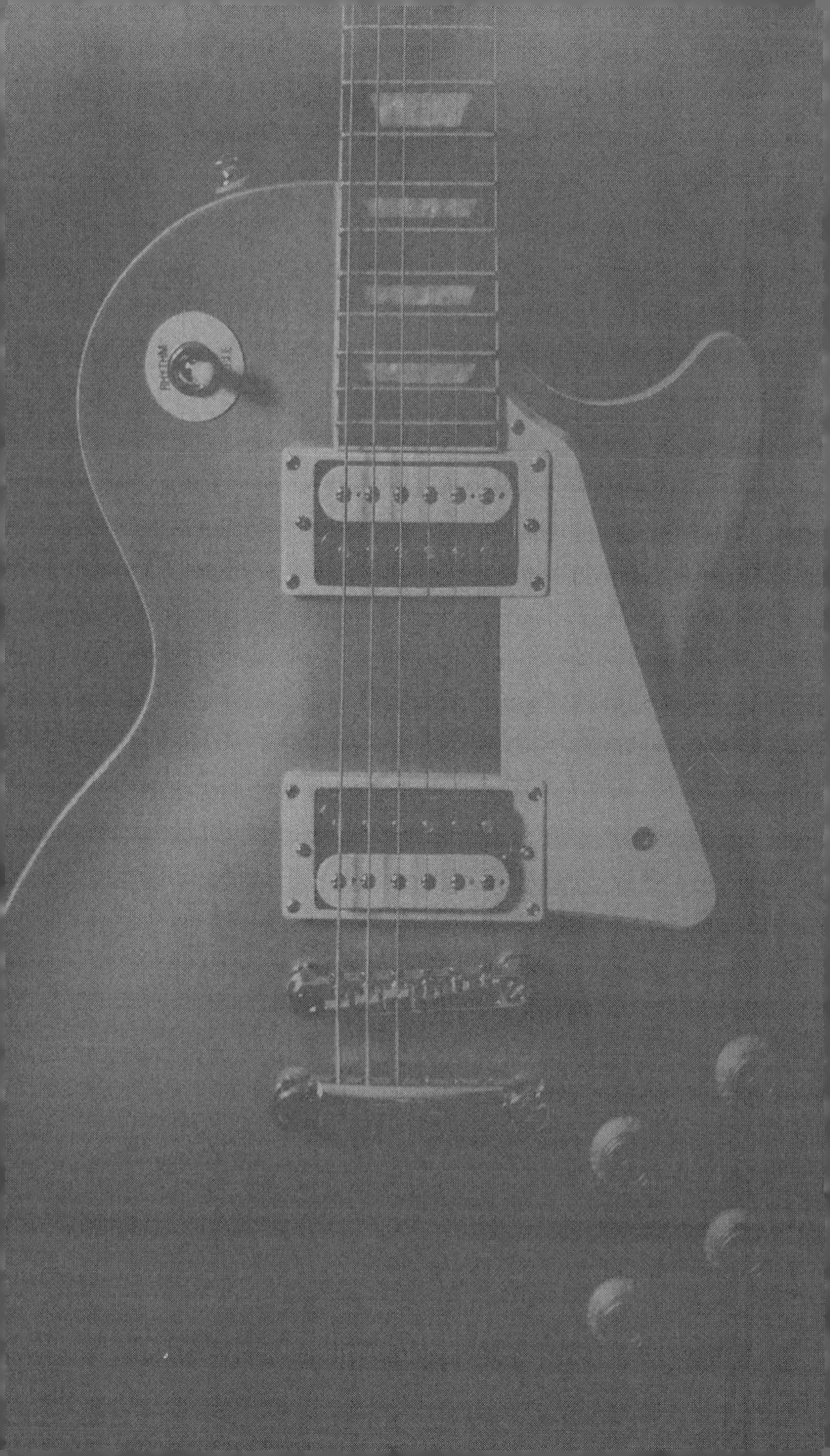

CHAPTER 31

Skylar opened her eyes only to see that Dash had stopped playing. Initially, the crowd thought it was a part of the song, but as a hush blanketed the room, all eyes were on the stage. Expressionless, Dash's face was as a blank canvas. Sky, equally bewildered, wondered if this was improvisation. Maybe a new twist on an old song.

She moved slightly, hoping to get a better view. Her eyes locked on Dash, her heart stuttering a beat. He was gone, his gaze completely vacant. The hand that, moments ago, had caressed his custom Paul Reed Smith guitar, had fallen limp to his side. His other lay motionless on the curve of the instrument. It was as if someone had turned a switch from on to off, disconnecting Dash from the power source. If she and the crowd were stunned, his bandmates were equally so. Ian was the first one to approach him.

"Dash. What the fuck?"

She could hear Ian, though his microphone was absent. It now sat atop a mike stand several feet away. Though Ian nudged Dash, he didn't move. Her heart danced a death march, its tune wrapping ghoulish fingers around her throat. The nightmarish memory of Dash and her on the water had gone from a private affair to one played out before thousands. Ian, whose face was shrouded with worry, continued trying to engage him. A pang of pity struck Sky's heart as she watched Ian's expression morph from arrogant to frightened.

Finally, Tommy and Charlie intervened. One of them disconnected Dash's guitar from the amplifier while the other took his arm. Both slowly guided him toward her. The once hushed crowd was now a sea of speculation, murmurs churning up in waves.

"Dash." Ian's expression fell as he walked with the other guys and continued to invoke the name of his friend. As they came near her, Ian shook Dash's arm. "C'mon, man. Talk to me." His tone was desperate.

It was like she was reliving a nightmare. Just like that night on the boat, Dash blindly followed where he was led. Skylar took his hand. He looked from face to face, any note of recognition totally absent. The road crew and some staff formed a circle around him. The next group to perform went by, all of them looking over at the scene before stepping out on stage. Sky was thankful for the diversion, all the while knowing that photos of her husband had already been posted on the internet. What was worse was that this benefit was in London, and the British press was notoriously rabid. Within hours, every corner of the world would be filled with images of Dash, and the public would be waiting to swarm him. Though calm on the outside, her heartbeat in her throat nearly choked her. Somehow, she had to get him out of there.

She looked into his eyes. "Come back to me," she whispered.

Giving his hand a reassuring squeeze, she ignored everyone and everything around them. His gaze met hers, and she felt a check in her spirit. Something clicked. Recollection unveiled his eyes as his thoughts registered. It was as if he'd paused for a time and tuned everything out, but now was back.

Dash breathed in a lungful of air, and Skylar swore she felt everyone near him do the same. He then let out a sigh of relief, his posture no longer stiff, but relaxed as a smile kissed his lips. Now he was the one who gave her hand a comforting squeeze as recognition completed its residency. His gaze was tender, full of love, and adoration. Skylar choked back a sob as he acknowledged her presence, uttering one word.

"Abigail."

* * *

HIS EYES SAID that he recognized her, but his lips spoke another name once again. He canted his head, his gaze soft like a puzzled puppy. "What's wrong, my dear?"

"What the actual fuck?" Ian's eyes rounded in fright and disbelief. His brows tugged as he looked at Sky. "Who the hell is Abigail? He said that when he threw me out of the house. At first, I thought that was your name."

Ian added another layer to the puzzle. If he didn't know who Abigail was, she had little chance of finding out her identity. She swallowed the hurt, knowing it was imperative to not only get Dash away from the public but away from there as well. There would be rumors flying because of the name faux pas. The press would soon know they were married. They would have a field day not only with his on-stage blackout, but if they got wind of this newest slipup it would add fuel to the fire. She looked around the room at the people near her. Two security men were a short distance away, standing sentry at either side of the stage entrance. Knowing they'd witnessed everything that happened, Sky waved. "Excuse me. Can you help me get him out of here?"

"Where are you going to, mum? There's a mob outside." Skylar was no more familiar with London than she was with half of the cities Dash played.

"I don't know." A helpless feeling weighed in her stomach.

"I can 'elp." One of the men approached her. "Whadda ya need, mum?" The man's cockney accent was thick, but his eyes were full of concern.

"Right now, I need a way to get out of here. I don't think our hotel is safe. Everyone is going to know he's there." She held fast to Dash's hand while everyone else concerned themselves with the music.

"I can do 'at fer ya." She watched as the hulk of a man used his thumb to hit something on his cell and put it up to his ear. He distanced himself from the group as he spoke in a low tone.

"What's wrong?" Her eyes went to Dash. It was as if another layer of recognition had washed over him. He looked from side to side, seemingly surprised. "What's going on?"

She searched his expression. "Dash?"

Spooked by several sets of eyes watching him, he jerked back like a slingshot. "What the hell's going on? Why are you guys staring at me?" He patted his body with anxious hands, looking down at himself as if he were the emperor in new clothes.

Skylar's heart hadn't slowed its pace, but she had to keep up her composed façade. "How are you feeling?"

"I feel fine," he answered. His eyes were full of questions. "Will somebody tell me what the fuck's going on?"

"You fucking checked out on us, man." Ian was back to

his cocky ways. He bounced a pointed index finger against his temple, his bottom lip swollen from their earlier altercation. "Stopped dead in the middle of your solo."

"You're lying." Dash's expression hardened. He looked around for confirmation of Ian's comment and found it in the eyes of everyone around him. Ignoring Ian, he sought Skylar, helplessness bleeding into his expression. No matter what, she had to keep it together.

"One of the guys is making arrangements to take us somewhere. There are too many people and too many unanswered questions."

"Where?"

"I'm not sure yet, but it will be better than being here."

Dash gave her a silent nod just as the security man approached.

"I've got a car waitin' fer ya, and a new place to stay. Me sista' does one of those Airbnb rental fings wif her carriage 'ouse. No one's usin' it right now. It'll be private."

"Thank you." Skylar was touched by the gentleman's care for their situation, issuing him an appreciative smile. She turned to her husband, careful not to let worry dig her fingernails through his hand. "Let's go, babe." She kept her tone calm, but fear clawed up her spine. "Once we get somewhere quiet, I'll tell you everything that happened. Promise. Then we can figure out what to do."

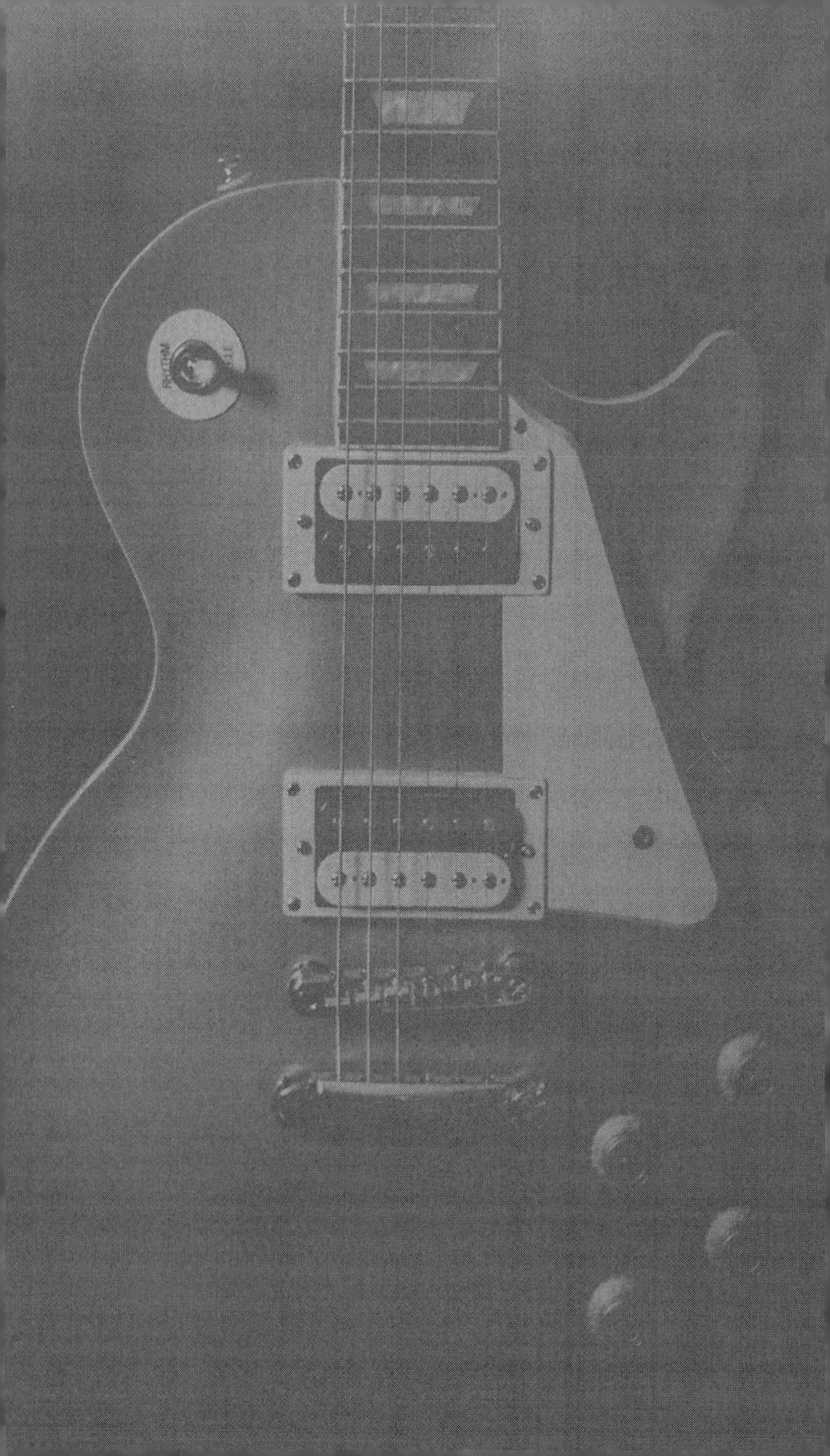

CHAPTER 32

Dash didn't remember much from the night before. For as much as he wanted to understand what had happened onstage, nothing made sense. He'd dismissed the previous occurrences as exhaustion or merely mixing up words. Until last night he hadn't given them much notice. Now other, smaller incidents came to mind. He felt like a kid playing connect the dots, all the while knowing the total picture wasn't going to be pretty.

"You were so tired when we got here that you fell into bed. Can you remember anything?" Looking at Skylar, he felt a pang of guilt. She hadn't signed on for this. He didn't know what "this" was, but it wasn't the way he'd planned to spend the first part of their marriage.

"I wish I could." He felt like he was sinking to unknown depths as he thought of smaller incidents. The latest one that came to mind had happened while he'd been brushing his teeth. Though he'd dismissed it at the time, the memory now seemed ominous. The alarm had gone off at 7:30. His typical morning routine was to brush his teeth, comb his hair, and shave. Although he recalled putting the toothbrush away and rinsing his mouth, the next thing he remembered was looking at himself in the mirror. Finishing the routine, he'd returned to the bedroom to get dressed. He'd been a little blindsided that the clock showed it was nearly nine-thirty.

Where had the time gone? He'd chalked it up to being lost in thought. Whose mind doesn't wander before coffee, but for nearly two hours? Though he'd dismissed it at the time, he couldn't any longer. What should have been a private problem was now a public circus.

Skylar sat quietly beside him. It was just the two of them. His eyes were locked on his hand, trying to hide yet another spasm. Were these things connected somehow?

"You know I love you, right?" Her tone was warm and tender. Her expression equally so. "Can you tell me what you remember?"

Anxious thoughts had him twisting inside as he gave her a hesitant look. "It isn't much. The last thing I remember was playing our encore on stage, but not much after. Things are kinda hazy."

Though Sky tried to hide her concern, he read the signs of worry. She held her bottom lip prisoner between her teeth. Her usually bright blue eyes had grown dim and unsettled.

"It was as if someone pulled the plug on you. You just stopped playing."

Dash dropped his head in his hands. Wiping them over his face and running them through his hair, distress filled his thoughts. He looked up at her through worried eyes. "And there's fallout, I suppose."

Sky nodded. "Yes. Vince has been sending me messages. It's all over the internet."

"Shit." Dash bent over, putting his elbows on his knees. He felt like he was physically carrying the weight of the situation on his back. "This isn't good, Sky. I wish I had answers, but I just don't." His voice trailed off as he straightened his spine. Worry creased his brow. "Is that it? Did I do anything else?"

"The guys led you off stage. A man named Caton helped us. We aren't at the hotel. We're at his sister's Airbnb."

He shook his head. "I don't remember him."

"There's something else. You called me Abigail again."

His heart broke as the sorrowful words tumbled from her lips. Why did he keep saying that name? He kept hurting his wife with the name of a person he didn't know. If it were possible, he would purge the name from his head.

Dash followed her expression. Though she was doing a great job maintaining her composure, anguish was evident in her eyes. And he was the guilty one who'd put it there. "I'm sorry, baby. I don't know what to say."

Sky stopped him, choosing to skate over her pain. "Dash, this isn't about a mixed-up name anymore. We can't ignore this. Your life isn't private. One YouTube video already has a few hundred thousand hits. Even if you could ignore it, I can't. I'm worried."

He stared at the floor.

"You need to see a doctor."

His head popped up. The word no sat on his lips, but the pain he saw in her eyes made him bite it back.

"Please," she begged. "If we get you to a doctor, your publicist can spin whatever happened for your benefit. Explanation is better than speculation. You'll be able to control the information. Honestly, publicity aside, wouldn't you feel better if you got checked out?"

A check in his gut made him pause. He hated doctors. His opinion of the medical profession as a whole was questionable. Too many stories of bullshit diagnoses were out there. The last thing he wanted was to be a statistic. He gripped his thighs to stop the trembling in his hands and knees. "I don't want to go to the doctor."

She nodded slowly, but he caught sight of the determination in her eyes. "Dash, rumors follow the videos. Forget all the good things you've been able to do with your music. This will shadow all the charities you support and the foundation you told me you wanted to start in your parent's names. You'll be chasing this nightmare forever. The tabloids will ride this for every penny they can get. You can't ignore it. Everything from drug addiction to a stroke will be reported in the press." She inhaled deeply and looked away. Shifting her weight, she turned to him with angry eyes. "If you won't do it for yourself, do it for me. I'm scared. Wouldn't it be better to find out what's causing these spells and be proactive?"

Skylar's shoulders slumped as she said her piece. *Damn it!* He hated seeing her like that. It broke his heart to think of the bullshit she'd have to put up with. If what happened only affected him, he would give it some time. One call to a lame-ass reporter for an exclusive and they'd be more than happy to run with whatever story he gave them. But this wasn't just about him now. He had a wife he adored, and, because of her status, she'd be dragged into anything that involved him.

"They know everything. Some reporter turned up our marriage license."

Skylar looked like she'd aged ten years overnight. They hadn't announced their marriage to the press, but the event last night had sent them digging. He wanted to talk to Charlie and Tommy to see how they were dealing with the fallout.

Though Skylar hadn't mentioned problems with Ian yet, he knew from past experience he would want to ride any story involving the band. He loved to talk, and when he was drunk, he did even more. If Dash was going to protect his reputation, he had to do what Sky suggested and take appropriate action. At least if he went to a doctor, he would be protected by privacy laws. No matter what they found out, he could control the information in the press. It might take a call to someone he trusted to report more of the truth than the tabloids would, and someone at *Rolling Stone* was sure to be interested.

Skylar patted his hand as she grabbed her phone. "Let me show you something."

She typed in something and pulled up a YouTube video. She said nothing as it played, instead letting the impact of the recording sink his stomach. There it was. He was lost in the song, playing his heart out, and then nothing.

Seeing it was so much different than having her tell him what had happened. He lifted his gaze, suddenly drowning in embarrassment and sorrow. He couldn't watch anymore as the rest of it played out, but he could hear it. First, the silence and then the murmuring that gradually increased in volume before it cut off at the end. He didn't need Ian to make this a shitshow. It already was.

"Now, there are over two million views. The last time I checked was a few hours ago." Skylar reached around her waist and stuck the phone in her back jeans pocket. She took his hand in hers. It was warm and comforting and, at the moment, it felt like a lifeline. "You don't have to listen to me, Dash, but I wish you would. Let me take you to the hospital, if not for your peace of mind, then for mine. Please."

It was a crossroads moment. Internally, Dash fought against what he knew needed to be done. The list of odd occurrences could no longer be ignored. Muscle twitches. A forgotten meeting with the band. Waking up in the middle of the night only to forget where he was. All those things had been easy to brush off as the imbalance of tour life. The public didn't see the toll it could have on a person. Being on the road and in the public eye was not for the faint of heart. Skylar might have willingly accepted him but expecting her to walk on eggshells every time she went to the grocery store wasn't fair. Her showing him the video was the slap in the face he needed. It was time to suck up his pride and do what was right—for both of them.

"Okay."

"Really?" Skylar lifted her eyes to his.

Resigned, he nodded.

CHAPTER 33

As Dash made calls to Charlie and Tommy, Skylar coordinated their departure from England. From what she overheard of his conversations, verbal pats on the back and good wishes were issued by Dash's bandmates. Once he was finished, she motioned to Caton. With the calm ease of a night whisper, the Englishman and three more security staff closed around them and ushered them to the car.

Skylar held onto Dash's hand. As they exited the building, their burly guardian angels hid them from prying eyes. The damp London air nipped the tender skin on her cheeks, hastening her steps. Dash's thin denim jacket didn't offer him much protection from the cold. Something about the whole situation had her on edge. It wasn't only about what had happened on stage. Something was terribly wrong. She could feel it in her gut. Call it woman's intuition, but an ominous weight had her stomach tied in knots. She could only hope her plan, which she'd thrown together overnight, could protect Dash from the damaging court of public opinion.

Neither she nor Dash said a word. Once securely in the back of the car, Caton got into the driver's seat. She caught his eye in the rearview mirror. He brought his fingers to the top of his head in a mock salute, giving her a smile that said everything would be all right. She hoped he was right.

Her mind raced. She looked over at Dash, who appeared to be lost, staring out the window. On closer inspection, she saw his eyes were closed. There was no way to tell if he was sleeping or if he'd blanked out again. She didn't try to rouse him awake or from his thoughts, and as they headed out of the city, he softly snored as his head fell to the side. He was asleep.

FEELING BEWILDERED AND HELPLESS, she stuffed down her emotions and swallowed back her tears. This was a hard one. Just hours ago, they were looking forward to days of casual conversation and endless lovemaking. *And now?* Now she just wanted answers.

She resettled herself in the seat. Caton was blessedly quiet, leaving her alone with her thoughts. Although Dash had once again called her Abigail, there was no mistaking the look in his eyes. It was Skylar that he'd seen. That tender look belonged to her and her alone, no matter what he called her. Something had short-circuited his brain and made him mix up words, but there was no mistaking the visual tether between the two of them. Dash clearly looked at her with love, no matter what kind of word salad he'd mixed. It was like he was existing in a ball of confusion, and what discouraged her the most was that none of it made any sense.

For the next twenty minutes, Skylar stirred a vat of speculative thoughts. They went nowhere, each more of a dead end than the one before. She played out possibilities, a ministroke, a brain infection, some weird meningitis, her mind created the most horrifying scenarios. Sometimes being a writer with a vivid imagination had its disadvantages.

The papers would print what they wanted, no matter where they were, so Caton had helped her arrange a private charter, using fictitious names for them on the flight manifest. She would have him home within twenty-four hours and being seen by someone who might be able to answer their questions.

Looking over at her sleeping husband, her bottom lip puckered. It wasn't the first time that she'd noticed the tremor in his hand. In his sleep, both that and his leg shook. She bit the inside of her cheek to quell her rising panic. It took a few minutes, but she was able to swallow her fears, albeit temporarily. She might have given in. Maybe even shed a tear or two, but that wouldn't do anyone any good. Once she knew what they were dealing with, she'd have a good cry, but not before.

The hum of tires on the road lulled her into a few minutes of rest. There weren't many other cars on the road, but then Caton had told her he was taking the back roads. Giant trees parted beneath the breeze, allowing the sun to filter through the smoked windows. As she looked out, the morning's cloudy sky had given way to patches of blue. Normally a scene such as this would invite her outside for a walk, but today the muscles in her neck and back tightened the closer they got to the airport. She could only pray the press wasn't waiting for them.

Her cell phone buzzed, vibrating in her lap. *Ian.*

"Yes?" She cupped her hand around her mouth and the phone. She was in no mood for his games.

"Where are you taking him?" Ian's voice was heavy with demand, making her jaw clench. She chose not to answer him, her silence speaking volumes while proving her to be an equal match for his aggression.

"Goddamn it, Skylar! Tell me!"

She felt her cheeks flush with anger. It took all she had to stay composed but, again, she gave him nothing. Ian was a child, always expecting to get what he wanted, on demand. To him, she was a nuisance, not that she cared what he thought. Thus far, he'd never behaved like an ordinary person, but his grandiose opinion of himself didn't hold any weight with her. She was Dash's wife, and thankfully so. Who knew who would have made medical decisions for him if they hadn't gotten married? His doctor, perhaps? At least she now had the legal right to insist on immediate care at one of the best facilities in the world: Johns Hopkins. No matter Ian's inflated ego, now that she and Dash were wed, he had no leverage to usurp her authority and manipulate people. That was probably the only benefit to their marriage being outed by reporters. The whole world knew.

Exhausted, Sky was about to hang up on Ian and dismiss the call but leave it to him to manage to get in one more dig.

"Don't play games with me, Skylar. You can't keep Dash away from us. I have ways of finding out where he is—oh, and just so you know, I'm not the only one who thinks there's something fishy about you snatching him away. You're too much of a bitch for a nice guy like him."

Her eyes flicked to Dash to make sure he was still asleep before she freed her tongue and unleashed it on Ian. It was time to cement her position. She had no time to deal with a man-child.

"Listen carefully to what I have to say because I want you to understand me clearly. Dash's well-being is not your burden. I'm getting him the help that he needs. I have that right and responsibility. I don't care what you think of me. I don't care what you think of what I do. *You* are not my concern, Dash is."

"I'm his best friend," he screamed.

"In your mind," she countered. "You think your friendship overrides your asinine behavior? Consider this to be advice as well as a threat. Grow up, Ian. Take some damn responsibility for your actions and your life. If you want to live your life in a haze, so be it. But if you try in any way to come near Dash when you're high or stoned, I'll have you arrested. Live your life the way you want to but stay out of ours."

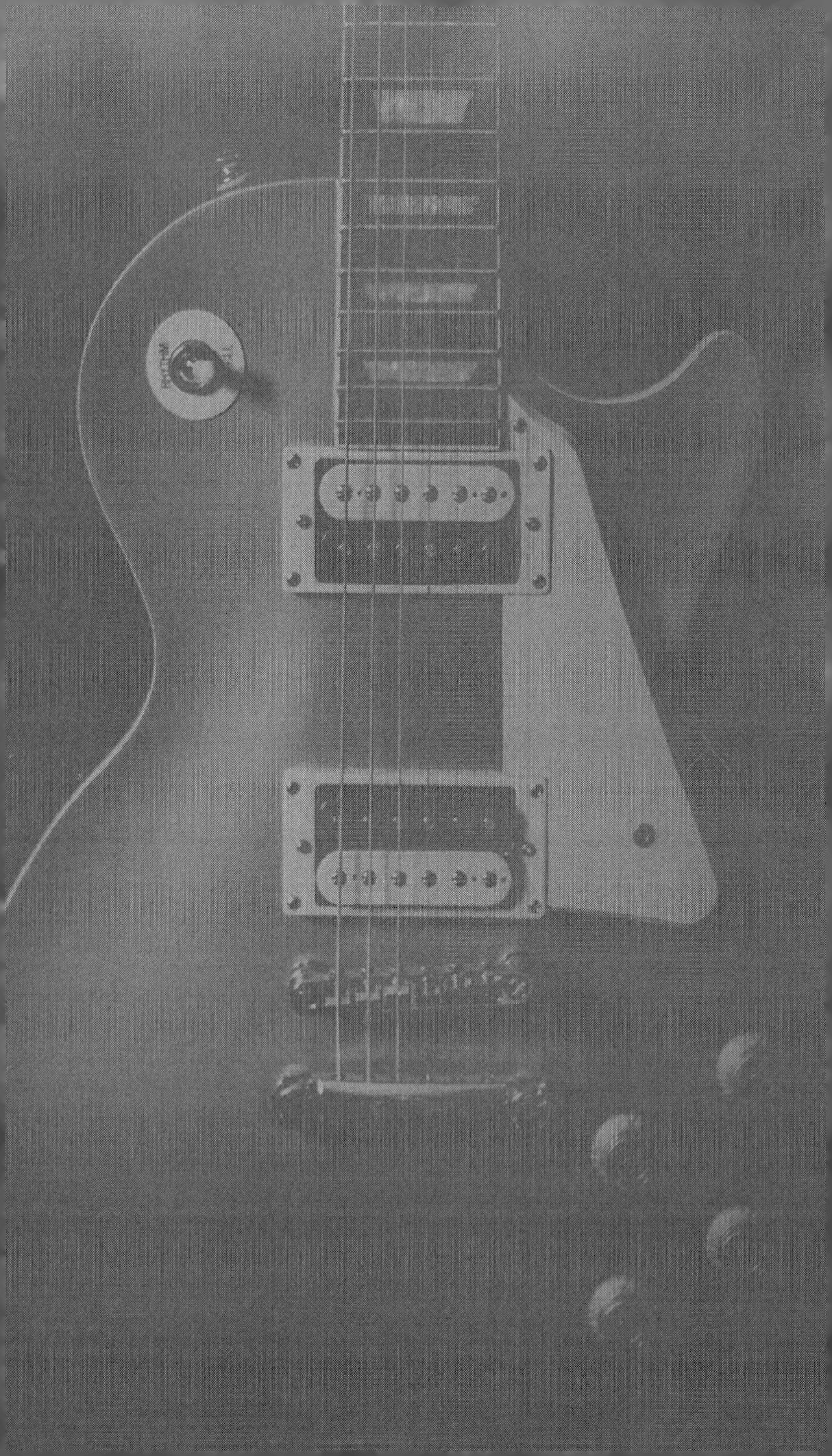

CHAPTER 34

Dash hated the sterility of hospitals. The bland walls, the smell of disinfectant and alcohol, and the uncertainty of his test results had put him on edge. At least the view from his window was interesting. There weren't too many places in the United States that had kept the cobblestone streets.

The weather today was as dreary as his mood. A chill held his body. Whether it was the actual temperature or fear, he couldn't determine. He'd been at Hopkins for a week. Skylar had never left his side. Though he'd asked her to climb into bed with him, she'd been sleeping in a chair bed the entire time. Hopefully, today was the day they'd get some answers, and by nightfall, they'd be home.

He looked over at Skylar. She was looking down at her phone, gauging the interest of the press. Luckily, some of the stories had died down. Seemed some Wall Street executive with ties to a Hollywood mogul had been caught in some kind of a sex trafficking scandal. News like that was far more interesting than a zoned-out rock star. Leave it to the fickle public to feed on tragedy.

With Skylar at his side, he'd been admitted to Hopkins under the name of a fictional character. It seemed like a good idea at the time, and it added just a little humor to the situation. He'd let Skylar pick the character. He was Gaston from Beauty and the Beast. Of course, she'd pick him. That whole fairytale revolved around a girl who loved books, who tamed a beast. Then, like all fairytales, they lived happily ever after. He could only hope for the same.

After seven days of speculation, numerous doctors, and a multitude of tests, they'd been promised answers. In that week, the tremors and muscle spasms had gotten worse. Skylar had noted a few episodes where he'd "disappeared," but they'd been brief. Fear ran icy fingers down his spine, given this latest development: slurred speech.

While he and Sky were talking, he felt a heavy weight fall on him. When she asked him what was wrong, he answered with a thick tongue. It was an effort to pronounce words clearly. Syllables stuck to his teeth, making his speech lazy. He wasn't the same person he'd been a month ago, and he hated it; he hated being so fucking helpless.

"We've got this." Skylar came up behind him and placed a reassuring hand around his waist. He turned around to face her, concern furrowing his brow.

"What if we don't? What if we can't? What if the thing that's wrong can't be fixed?" The questions tumbled from his lips, betraying his composure and exposing his fear.

A tender smile filled her lips, her words hushed and comforting. "Then we'll deal with it together."

"I don't want you to deal with it. This is one hell of a wedding present."

"*You* were my wedding present, and I think you're getting ahead of yourself. Let's wait and see what the doctor has to say. It may be something, and it may be nothing."

Dash nodded. He pulled the hoodie up over his head like he was a kid hiding inside a blanket fort. He could take Skylar with him and disappear from the world. He wrapped his arms around her and huffed out a breath as he held her tightly. If only it were that easy.

* * *

FROM THE MOMENT Dr. O'Hara entered the room, Dash and Sky gave him their full attention. He was the man who held all the answers, as well as their future, in his hands. He was kindhearted, tall, and good-looking with a sprinkling of gray at the temples of his ebony hair. He looked more like someone who should be modeling for the over-forty set of GQ. He had soft eyes. He also had a great bedside manner. Not someone with a God complex. Thankfully, he was able to strike a balance between clinical and kindness. As long as he knew what he was talking about, Dash didn't care about anything else. Skylar squeezed his hand, distracting him with her reassuring way.

"Good morning, Mr. Barrows. Mrs. Barrows." His voice was deep. Not as deep as Dash's, but the tone was rich, robust, and confident.

With a jutted chin, Dash returned the greeting. "Hey, Doc. You all have tested me from asshole to appetite. I don't think there's anything left inside of me you guys haven't poked, prodded, or x-rayed. I'm hoping you have some news."

The man nodded. Dash paid attention to his body language. He noted the corners of the doctor's eyes pinched. Noting the firm set of his jaw and the seriousness of his expression, Dash wasn't expecting good news. Skylar unconsciously tightened her grip. He brushed his thumb over the back of her hand, tugging just a little. It got her attention long enough for a quick, reassuring glance.

Dr. O'Hara scanned the room. "May I sit?" The man didn't wait for an answer. Instead, he wrapped a hand around the arm of one of the visitor's chairs and dragged it closer to both of them. "I do have news, Mr. Barrows. After all the tests and reviewing your family history, we looked for several things. We combined the results of the tests and your symptoms. I'm afraid it isn't good news. You have Alzheimer's disease."

Every muscle tightened. His breath had left his body with a sucker punch. He looked at Skylar and then back to the doctor, his mouth suddenly gone dry. "Alzheimer's? That's crazy. It's an old person's disease. I'm only thirty-three."

Nodding, Dr. O'Hara continued. "That's true. In most cases, the patients are older than you, but Alzheimer's is no respecter of age. Your symptoms were our first clue. Once we learned your family history, and that your grandfather had passed from complications of dementia, it wasn't hard to reach the conclusion.

It helped that your grandfather was seen in this hospital. Though hospital records from nineteen fifty-one to current day don't use the same terminology, we were able to use them as a basis for testing. You filled in the rest, and the medical tests support the diagnosis. When patients give us a history of odd occurrences, doctors have to play a guessing game. Still, there are certain medical parameters that we add to our equations. There are no signs that you've had a stroke, Mr. Barrows, which was the first thing we checked. When that possibility was eliminated, we searched for other clues to support a hypothesis. One area was strongly consistent with those in patients suffering from dementia. Your physical symptoms came into play. Am I correct that you reported to my staff that you'd experienced some of the symptoms more than three months ago?"

Dash's eyes averted to the side as he scanned his memory. "I guess." He gave a slight shrug. "I don't know. I've never had insomnia before, but I started having trouble sleeping about then. That's when the muscle spasms started too, but I just figured they were normal. There were twitches in my leg. Around then, too, I had some twitches in my face. My eyes. The corner of my mouth. I had them there, but I had them in my arms and legs too."

He looked at Skylar. He could tell she was nervous. With her head canted, she'd hung on the doctor's every word as she raked her fingers through her soft brown hair. "What about the one in your hand? That's the one that seems to bother you the most."

Apparently, Sky had been running through a mental checklist, repeating anything unusual that he'd mentioned to her.

"Right." It was the symptom that had affected him the most, the cramping in his hand. How could he have forgotten to mention it? "I have them in my hand. I'll be rehearsing, and suddenly, my hand jerks, then cramps. I can't control it or knead it out. But it's a muscle thing. Not a brain thing. At least, that's what I thought. I wouldn't think there was a connection."

Dr. O'Hara acknowledged the information with a nod. "There are so many things that we don't know, but for those that we do, we try to give you the best information that we can. You're correct; you are not the normal patient that we see for Alzheimer's. Even early-onset Alzheimer's patients are, typically, older than you, but it isn't unheard of for someone in your age group to be afflicted. Unfortunately, from your history of symptoms, it appears that the progression is more rapid than most."

Dash's insides shook, suddenly making him nauseous. His hair stood on edge from the back of his neck to the top of his head. If what the doctor said was right, he didn't know where to go from there. Alzheimer's was a death sentence.

Whipping thoughts tortured him with the precision of a metal-tipped cat-o-nine tails. This disease had no cure. His promising future in music and the life he looked forward to with Skylar had just gone up in smoke. All their hopes and dreams had burned to ash in ten minutes, leaving nothing. The quality of his life would deteriorate and, according to the doctor, much faster than Dash was prepared for. Nothing was certain. People thought money could buy anything, but no one could buy their way out of a death sentence.

Dash splayed his hands on his knees, gripping tightly to settle his trembling. "So, what do I do now? Just wait for the inevitable?"

"No. There are things that you can do. We'll go over your treatment plan. We can discuss how it's working at your appointments and make adjustments, if necessary. For now, why don't we get you out of here and back home? I'm sure you'd feel much better sleeping in your own bed. I'll send in your nurse. She can go over your discharge instructions. She'll also give you a date for a follow-up visit with me at my office." The chair legs scraped against the floor as he stood. "We'll do everything we can, Mr. Barrows. For now, go home and enjoy your life. Enjoy your wife. You're newlyweds, right?"

Dash looked over at Skylar. She wore a weak smile. "Yes. A little more than a month."

"Congratulations." He extended his hand for a friendly shake. When Dash returned the gesture, the shaking in his hand was evident. The doctor closed his other hand over Dash's to steady the tremble. "We'll talk soon."

Though Dr. O'Hara had tried to deliver the news as gently as possible, nothing had prepared Dash for the brick wall that had just come crashing down on him. The diagnosis was crushing.

Once the doctor crossed the threshold, Dash lost it. He dropped Skylar's hand, covered his face, and let his head fall to his chest as he choked back a sob. Questions plagued him. How long before he forgot how to play his music? When would he forget the names of the guys he'd worked with for so long? Would he wake up one morning and suddenly forget everything? What about Skylar? Would he forget her too? The thoughts were unbearable.

Though he tried, he couldn't hold back the dam of emotion threatening to break through the walls of his inner strength. Sorrow breached his control and, though he felt like he was drowning, he had to hold on. There were things he had to do. Details to work out. Though he didn't understand all that was ahead of him, he had to make plans for after he was gone. Though he had dreamed of growing old with his wife, he had to face the fact that the life he wanted would never come to pass. He had to man up, get his shit together, and get on the phone with his attorney. It was important to him that Skylar be taken care of after he was gone, even if she was successful on her own. There was so much he'd planned to do with her. This news meant . . . what? He was fucked. Fucked.

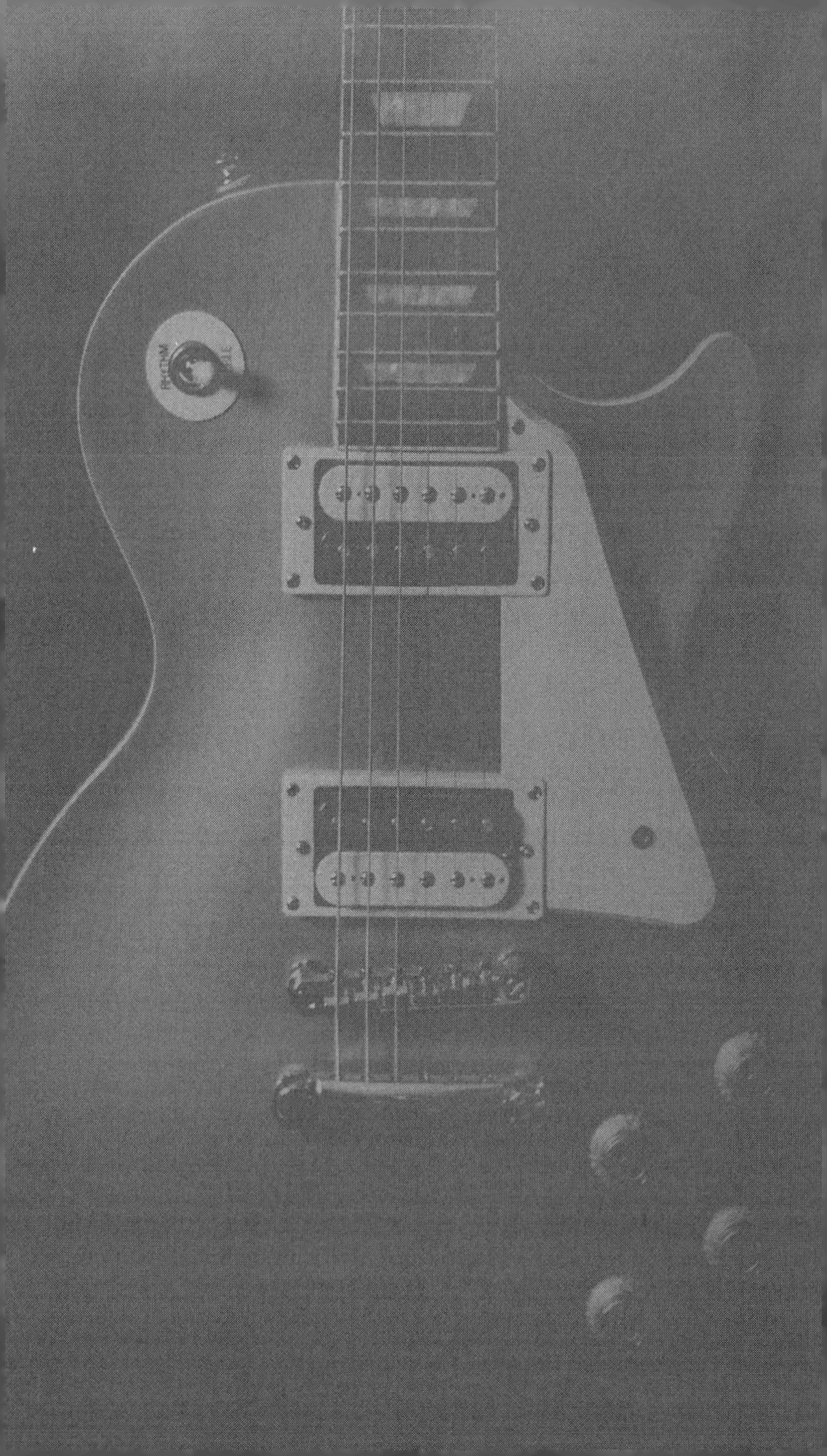

CHAPTER 35

Skylar wrapped her arms around Dash, swallowing the flood of emotions that threatened to take her under. "It's okay. It's okay." Her voice was hushed. The words that used to console were completely hollow because it would never again be *okay*.

She shook off her feelings. She had to be strong for Dash and could only hope she could mask her anguish, for his sake—and hers.

Dash tried to get ahold of himself and hide his momentary breakdown. Skylar watched as he swallowed the impending threat of tears. Suddenly, he straightened. He lifted his chin, cleared his throat, and sniffed back fear. All he could muster was a weak smile. "I'm good. I just need some time to wrap my head around this."

She patted his hand. "How about I leave you alone for a few minutes. I forgot to ask the doctor a question about your appointment." Though she'd lied about the content, she did have one thing that she needed to clarify.

"Yeah." The sadness in his eyes almost rooted her to the

spot. "I'm just gonna wait for someone to come in and tell me I can get out of here."

She kissed him, a tender smile pinking her lips. "I'll be right back."

Though leaving Dash by himself tore at her heart, there was one thing that nagged at her. Looking down the empty hallway, she walked to the nurses' station. A tremendous amount of activity was taking place at the central hub of C-wing, but one woman sat quietly behind the desk.

Dressed in a blue shirt and a matching jacket, her eyes lifted from her computer screen to Skylar. "May I help you?"

"Yes. Is Dr. O'Hara still around? I have a question to ask him about my husband."

"Yes." The woman swiveled in the office chair, craned her neck, and pointed down the hallway. "There's a small office down there. He's finished his rounds and is in there updating patient charts. I'm sure he won't mind the interruption."

"Thank you."

"You're welcome. A nurse will be in to see your husband in a few minutes with discharge instructions. Is there anything else?

"No," Sky answered. "I just need to see the doctor. Thanks again." She took off in the direction of the office, her legs still wobbly noodles from the avalanche that had just knocked her down. She stuck her head in the doorway of the room where Dr. O'Hara was dictating. "May I interrupt you?"

"Sure. What can I help you with?" The doctor placed the portable Dictaphone down on the desktop.

Sky took a seat in the one lonely chair. "My husband has been calling me by someone else's name. It's not an affair, it's something else. I mean, he actually looks at me like I'm me, but the name mix-up . . ." She paused, giving her stomach a moment to cease its flip-flops. She took a deep breath and swallowed a clog of fear. "Could this be related to his diagnosis?"

Dr. O'Hara nodded. "Yes. Certain things are everyday occurrences in patients with Alzheimer's. Mixed-up words and names are one of them." As the doctor leaned back in his chair, it squeaked, protesting his large stature.

Sky's life with Dash had been good and bad, Skylar tried to find a balance. When Dash was himself their relationship was magic. At one time she thought that Abbie was a rival. But now she wondered if she was a memory or a figment of his imagination? What she realized was that Dash was losing his grip on reality. "Could he be hallucinating?"

Dr. O'Hara studied her for a moment, paused, and then pressed his lips together. Leaning forward, he rested his elbows on the desk and steepled his fingers. "I know this was the last thing you were expecting, and I'm sorry about that. There are two types of Alzheimer's that we believe could be the culprit in your husband's case, and neither of them are good. But then, a diagnosis of Alzheimer's is never good. All we can do is provide you both with the tools for the best quality of life, however long that might be. I think there's a difference between mixing up someone's name and believing that you are someone else. Which one do you think it is?"

Skylar reflected a moment. No, it wasn't a slip of the tongue. The way Dash looked at her. The way he smiled. He was wholly convinced she was someone other than who she was.

"There was no confusion in his eyes, Dr. O'Hara. He saw me as someone else. When he is completely lucid, Abigail is someone he insists he doesn't know. And I'm not the only one disturbed by this mix-up. Dash is too. When he is addressing me as Abigail, he responds differently. His tone is different. He talks like Abigail is someone familiar but that she is me. He isn't apprehensive or startled at all when he approaches me as her. In fact, he looks relieved to see me—except he sees me as her."

Surprise made Dr. O'Hara lean back. As he nodded, a look somewhat like pity crossed his eyes for a brief moment. Though he tried to hide it, Sky felt it was confirmation that Dash's condition might be further along than initially thought.

"Mrs. Barrows, there are delusions, and then there are hallucinations. What you're describing sounds like more of a delusion. A delusion is, more or less, a false belief, Dash believing that you are someone else. A hallucination would be seeing something that wasn't there, like a chair or a person, that no one else could see."

Worry made an ant-like sensation crawl over her skin. "Will it get worse? Will he really forget who I am? I've never known anyone with Alzheimer's, but I've heard the stories."

Dr. O'Hara's brows tugged together. "Although no two patients are the same, the one thing they have in common is that they forget the people they love. I know that news is hard to hear. If your husband believes you are someone else, he may communicate that way." He threaded his fingers together as he folded his hands and rested them against the desk. "I'm going to be honest with you, Mrs. Barrows. Although there is no concrete evidence until biopsy or autopsy, I believe your husband is suffering from a form of Alzheimer's known as Cruetzfeld-Jakob disease. His rapid deterioration is consistent with the progression of symptoms your husband is suffering. If we are correct, he has a few months at best. If the two of you have plans to do something, now would be the time. It might be helpful for us to treat him if you would keep a journal and note anything concerning. I'll see him for appointments, but you'll be with him all the time. We can go over things that you note, changes that will help us to stay apprised of his condition. But, as far as everyday life with just the two of you, enjoy each other. There's a reason for the saying, 'there's no time like the present.'"

Tears stung her eyes as she looked away. "We were going to move to the Eastern Shore. Make a home. Grow old together." Skylar's voice trailed off. She couldn't look at the man until the threat of tears passed.

"Then do it, Mrs. Barrows. Your husband said in his medical history he has no other living relatives. He will have to trust you to make decisions for him once he's unable to do so for himself. I know that it's hard to hear, but now's the time for the two of you to be talking about things that don't get talked about. It's never easy, especially in a case like this. Death is the one thing that is certain in this life, yet it's the one thing we all are least prepared for."

Skylar looked down at the floor. Dr. O'Hara had just handed her an ominous weight, and she felt the heavy mantle of Dash's care fall on her shoulders. She didn't know what she'd expected, but it wasn't dementia. Though she knew the doctor was trying to be helpful, at that moment, it was hard to accept. The word "death" had a way of shaking the core of even the strongest person.

* * *

When Skylar reentered the room, she found Dash sitting in a chair. His eyes were red-rimmed, his neck mildly flushed. He'd broken down in her absence, of that she was sure. She approached him with an understanding glint in her eye. As she placed a kiss to the top of his head, her nose was tickled by errant strands of hair.

"I don't know what to do." Dash lifted his gaze to meet her eyes, and she saw the evidence of his despair. His brown eyes were nearly black beneath the tragedy, and the rims were a darker red than she'd first noticed. He was utterly lost. Crushed. Grief-stricken. He took her hand in his. "I don't know if I want you here for this, Sky."

Instantly offended, indignation sent a rod down her spine. Did he think he could just send her away? That wasn't going to happen. She'd never even considered it an option. Her words were clipped. "While I appreciate you saying that, I don't need you to make my decisions for me."

He shook his head back and forth, a rogue teardrop escaping to dot his jeans.

He rubbed it away with an open hand. "Don't you get it? We're married, but I don't want you to feel like you're obligated to do anything. I'll make arrangements to go into one of those homes. You don't have to go through any of this. It's your easy out."

His words were a controlled and quiet scream, yet instead of feeling sorry for him, anger rose within her. "Stop. I don't want to hear it. I get to decide what I want to do, and I want to stay with you. Better or worse, got it?"

She nearly lost her composure as he looked up at her with pain-filled eyes. Anguish crumbled his semblance of control. "But this is so much worse than 'worse.' This . . . this isn't living with better or worse because this won't be living at all. I'm going to forget everything. Everyone. Anything I've ever loved. I'm the last of my family. Once I'm gone, there will be nothing left except a tragic story of a successful man who lost it all because his brain became Swiss cheese."

"I'm your family." Her jaw was set as she let her statement sink in. Hoping and praying Dash would understand what she was about to say, she prepared her words so the meaning would cut through his destructive thoughts. "I want you to listen to me." She gently lifted his chin, assuring he was looking into her eyes. Though her heart twisted painfully in her chest, she had to make him understand her marriage to him was not an opportunity but a commitment. "I married you, and there are a million reasons why, but the most important one is because I love you. Not your money. Not your fame. Not because you're good-looking and make my panties melt." The last comment brought such a brief, but happy, smile to his lips that her heart buckled. "The minute I said 'I do' I'd already committed my heart to you for the rest of my life, and yours. No matter what you say, I'm not leaving you. I'm staying."

As Dash studied her face, her love for him filtered through every cell. She was confident he could feel it too. It flowed through her blood. Gave her joy. Skylar was determined that no matter who he saw her as when he looked at her, he would always find in her eyes the thing that mattered most. Love.

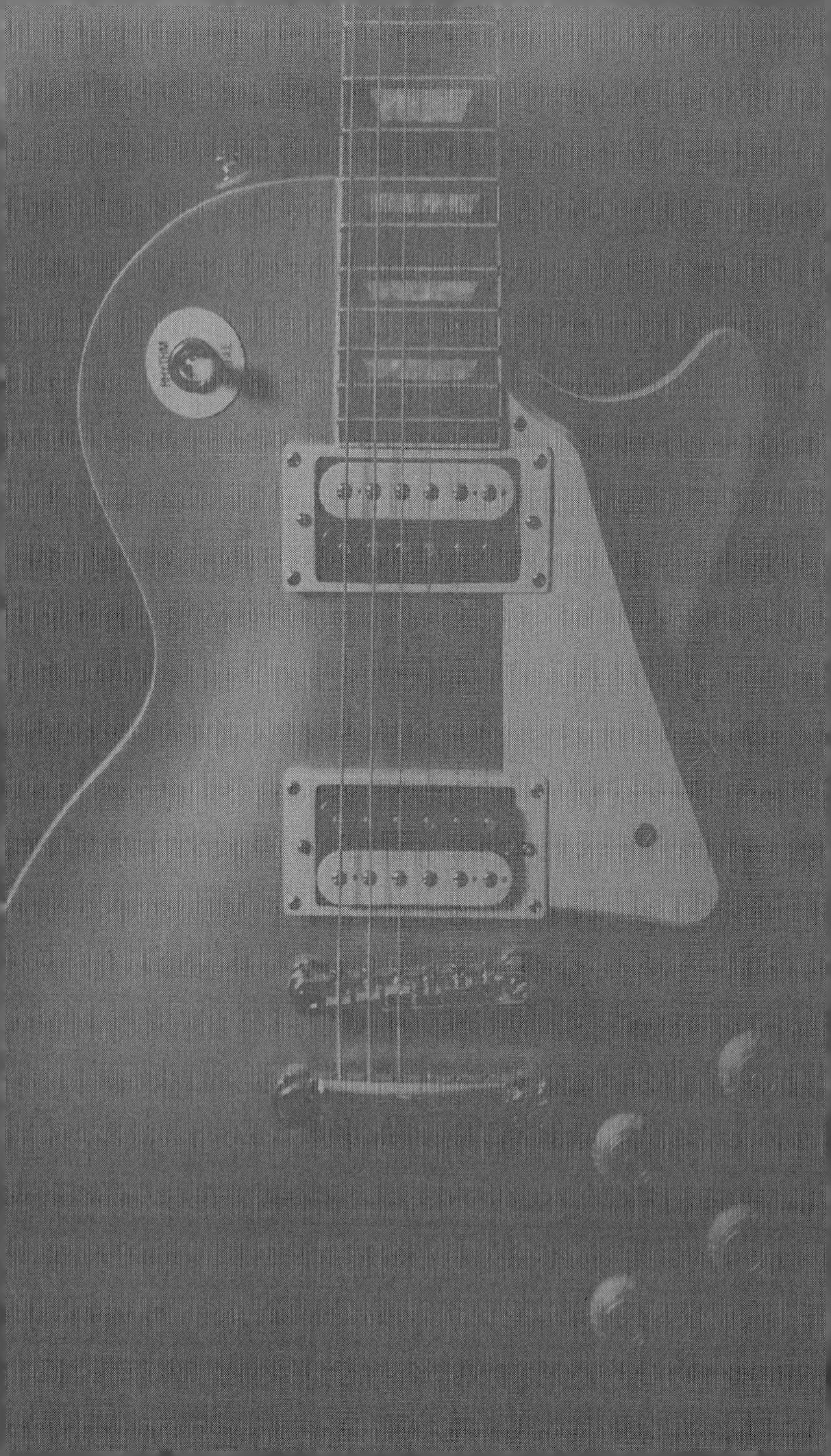

CHAPTER 36

Skylar paused, taking a deep breath. It had taken her several weeks to put her plan into motion, but, eventually, everything had fallen into place.

With Dash's blessing, she'd accomplished all she'd set out to do. Her first task had been to get Dash home from the hospital and make him comfortable. As the grim prognosis settled into their bones, they were determined to put as many of their plans as possible on the fast track. Dash's condition had deteriorated rapidly since the London incident. His tremors had increased as had his vacant periods. He also tired more easily. With the assistance of his doctors, Skylar had been able to secure competent medical professionals to assist them in their everyday lives.

He wanted a home. Not his. Not hers. Theirs. They picked their house from an internet ad. She secured packers and movers and had Vince supervise the transition. It amazed her what one could do if they had enough money. The only things it couldn't buy were health and more time.

Though it didn't seem so crucial until his diagnosis, she

and Dash had added each other to all their accounts. With one phone call, Dash's attorney had added her name to the titles of all his possessions and had drawn up a will for each of them. It seemed like overkill, but Dash had insisted. He had no living family—until now—and was a little OCD about tying up loose ends.

On the day they'd received his diagnosis, when she'd left Dash to find the doctor, Dash had phoned his lawyer. He'd granted her power of attorney as well as made her his legal guardian, should the need arise. She'd been too busy seeing to the details of their living arrangements and didn't learn of the changes until she had to sign the documents. Her primary concern was Dash and his care. Her secondary was hiding her heartbreak.

Their new home was on the Eastern Shore of Maryland. The sparkling water of the Chesapeake Bay was the view from one side of the house, while the other greeted them with a tree-lined entrance and English gardens. A large fountain sat in the middle of a circular driveway, obstructing any visitor's view of their beautiful home until they'd nearly reached the front door. She'd never dreamed she'd share a home like this with her husband. For that matter, she never imagined she'd have a husband. It certainly hadn't been on her to-do list, but she'd always be thankful for the chance meeting that had turned into a love story. For however long they had together, it would be their home.

"Good morning."

She smiled as she heard Dash approach her on the patio. She was confident his nurse was somewhere close by. Though he'd insisted he didn't need one, Skylar had assured him her time was better spent elsewhere. It was best that someone else monitor his medications and his condition. None of this was what they saw for their future together, and she preferred to spend her time in the way most newlyweds did, by holding his hand and having conversations about mindless drivel. She wanted those things to be her memories when Dash was no longer able to communicate, not medicine dosing.

Sky patiently waited until he took a seat beside her. When she'd left him that morning, he'd been sleeping. She'd alerted the nurse she'd be outside with her morning coffee, and the woman had busied herself in a nearby office until he woke. It wasn't so much that she worried he wasn't physically capable of maneuvering by himself, but he'd had a few periods where he hadn't known where he was. Skylar and his nurse thought it best that he had someone with him, without it feeling overbearing. There were four of them in the house at all times: her, Dash, a nurse, and a bodyguard. Since Caton had proven to be such an asset in London, she'd offered him the job, and he'd accepted.

Sky poured some fresh black coffee for Dash from the carafe she'd brought outside. The heady aroma wafted as it hit the porcelain cup. She looked over at him, hoping her warm smile and some relaxed conversation would be enough to break away from the cloud that always hovered above them.

"Bare feet, huh?"

"You know me, babe. Barefoot's how I roll."

He chuckled. She loved the sound and would take whatever humor she could muster from him these days. "Where'd you learn that? MTV?"

"I get around." Her eyes lit up to see him wearing a happy expression. As the mental vacancy spells had increased, each day became more unpredictable. She kept her sanity by focusing on the moment.

"You're beautiful, you know that? I'm a lucky man."

She swallowed. Reaching across the small table separating their chairs, she briefly took Dash's hand. He would need both to steady the cup. There were times when seeing and feeling the spasms when she held his hand pained her heart. But she held tightly to him as much and as often as she could. In truth, she never wanted to let go. It was a strange sort of existence, knowing that time was limited. Every touch, every kiss, every laugh—was committed to memory. She not only knew the end was coming, she knew that it was closing in.

"I've been thinking."

"Oh, no. Now we're in trouble." She peered over the top of her cup as she took a sip of her coffee. Today the gold flecks hidden within his brown eyes sparkled with delight. He tugged at her hand.

"Are you going to let me speak?" His eyes fixed on hers, an amused smile playing at his lips.

"Yes. Please continue." She smiled a mischievous grin as satisfaction rolled across his expression.

"I want to start a foundation. A way for kids to be able to study music or learn to make musical instruments. Something to pay it forward for what music has given to me. What do you think?"

He stared at her, trying to read the answer in her eyes. Leave it to Dash to dream up such an undertaking. Although his intent was noble, he didn't have the strength to carry out what starting a foundation would require.

"I think it's a beautiful idea, but—"

"I know, I know. It's huge," he interjected. "And whether you say the words, I know you think it's too much for me. So, I guess what I'm really asking is if you'll do it for me after I'm gone." His eyes never left hers. She could tell he read every emotion she tried to hide. "Let's face it, Sky, I'll probably be dead before the year is through. I'd like to leave behind something more than a widow. I would like my life to have had a purpose. Before you, music was my love. When I'm gone, I want both you and the music to be cared for." Resignation filled his tone.

Sky looked away, fearful he might see the emotions that threatened to burst through the walls of her resistance, she chose to look out at the water instead of picturing Dash's funeral. "Can we talk about something else, please? I feel like I should have a drink in my hand for this conversation."

The corners of her mouth turned down, the thought of Dash's death souring her stomach. Though she wasn't denying the truth of the inevitable, she simply wanted to enjoy a beautiful morning on the Bay without death crashing the party. The serenity of the scene quelled the emotional storm within. Before long, mornings like these would only be a memory. It would be up to her to refresh Dash's recollections when they started to fade, reminding him of what beauty was found in colors, sounds, and fragrances.

Guilt washed over her. She had no right to be selfish or hesitant about his request. Dash was trying to do something good. She wiped away an errant tear and turned back to him.

"Sorry. I just don't want to talk about this stuff today." She whispered the words as she looked deeply into his eyes. That same unique pull she had when she'd looked into his eyes for the first time tugged at her heart. She had to look away from him before she crumbled completely. Regardless of how long they had together, loving Dash added sweetness to her life. Though they had experienced only a small bite of living together, it was an addictive taste that, each day, left her begging for more.

"Don't be. I've already put too much on you." A remorseful look clouded his face.

When she turned to look at him, he was looking away, defeat weighing him down as he slumped in his seat. She sat her cup on the table and pushed out of her chair. She went to her husband, taking a place on his lap. Snaking her arms under his, she pulled her legs up and tucked her body into his.

"I'm selfish, I know. I don't want to think about after you're gone, but I know we have to talk about it while we can." She choked out the words on a sob, but quickly snapped it back. All she could manage was a whisper. "I hate this."

CHAPTER 37

The comment was so quiet Dash almost didn't hear it. Emotion welled up inside of him. Until this moment, he'd been more concerned for her than for himself.

Fury rose up within him, and, for the first time, he allowed himself to fully feel the injustice of their situation. He would have raged if he were alone. If the beast that was bleeding his mind dry affected only him, he would have torn this place apart. He would have busted every stick of furniture and broken every piece of glass if for nothing else than to release the storm within him and purge himself of his hateful feelings.

But he couldn't.

He'd vowed to the woman beside him that he'd love, cherish, and protect her. And the horror of it was that he would fail miserably on the last one. He was helpless in so many ways, but the one that mattered the most was his inability to shield his wife from the thief that was coming. The bastard disease would eventually take him and tear her apart. The irony of it all was that he had an unfair advantage. He would be blissfully ignorant of the pain he was causing her, while she stood helplessly beside him.

He tightened an arm around her, suddenly feeling exhausted. Closing his eyes so he couldn't see her pain, he felt himself drifting away.

"Remember what I told you, Sky. Our life will never be measured in years, but in moments."

CHAPTER 38

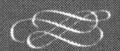

"He looks good." Vince poked his head into Skylar's office, then walked in and took a seat. He looked around the room, satisfied with the job he'd done to help make Dash and Sky's house the way she liked it. They'd been friends for so long that he knew her taste well. "The house looks like it suits you, and Dash said that if you're happy, he's happy."

"Packers and movers, as you well know. Thank you for all of your help with the move. It's amazing how quickly things can get done—for a price, of course. We wouldn't be here without you." She smiled at the thought as Vince seated himself by the desk.

Vince acknowledged her comment with a smile and a nod, then jutted his chin toward the laptop on her desk. "New storyline, I hope."

She shook her head. "Sorry, but no. Research." She lowered the top, closing down the screen. Sitting back, she crossed her arms over her chest. "Dash wants to start a foundation. I was hunting and pecking through the topic on Google."

"He's a good man, Sky. I just left him with the nurse. We had a good talk. He was there for a while—and then he wasn't."

Skylar felt a tug on her heart. The first part of his comment was thoughtful. The second part reminded her of how much more she lost every day. "He is that." She stood. "Let's get something to drink."

She pulled the office door closed behind her and wrapped a loving arm around Vince's waist as he settled his hand on her opposite shoulder. As they crossed the living room, they peered out the French doors. Vince had left Dash on the patio with his nurse, where he sat looking out at the water. His eyes were vacant.

She wondered how it was possible for her to hold both love and hate inside the same thought. There were things and people that she didn't like, but hate was such a strong word. It conjured up thoughts of murderers and abusers, yet it was a feeling with which she was becoming familiar. One minute she would be having a heart-to-heart talk with Dash on a topic for which they both shared a passion. And then he would disappear; another sweet element of their relationship stolen. Something that had the potential to become a treasured memory erased. Cut from Dash's mind with a steely knife while leaving her with the scars. Today was no different.

The visit from Vince had brightened Dash's spirits. She'd watched from the doorway as they'd talked football, which players were their favorites, and the possibility of the Baltimore Ravens going to the Superbowl. All had been going well, then, without warning, Dash had vanished behind a veil of failed thoughts. The monster had wounded them again, leaving yet another bloodstain.

Vince spoke in a gentle whisper, his voice low enough that Dash wouldn't be able to hear him should he suddenly come back from the darkness. "I'm going to be honest, in the beginning, I didn't want you to date Dash—especially not after I found out who he was. I mean, when we first met him, I thought he was a nice guy. Then I Googled him. I suppose I had a preconceived notion about musicians. I thought he'd hurt you and I wanted to keep you safe."

Skylar frowned, her eyes now locked on Vince as her expression bore a hint of arrogance. "A little prejudiced, don't you think? Dash's friends from the band have called to see how he was doing, offering us any help we need."

"I'm very protective of you. I make no apologies for that. You're a nice girl, Skylar. Organized. You live a squeaky-clean life. You have a place for everything and everything in its place. Nothing of that speaks remotely to the life of—or what I thought was the life of—a musician. The only images in my head were of loose women, drugs, and alcohol. I couldn't picture you fitting in with any of that."

Curiosity raised her brow. "And now you've changed your mind?"

"About that lifestyle?" He answered her question with a question. "No. I'm happy to say that Dash is the exception, as are you. Both of you are remarkable people, and I think you balance each other well. What is that they say? Opposites attract."

Skylar smiled, turning her attention back to the quiet man staring out at the Chesapeake. Being near the water seemed to soothe him. The tremors and spasms had grown worse, but in his eyes was peace. She could only hope she was part of the reason for that. It was her desire that their life together, however brief it might be, provided some sweetness to his days. Hers, however, was becoming void of the flavor. Every time he slipped away, she grew more bitter.

She swallowed a sob, the remaining shudder chilling her. The man who made her want to be a better person and take life less seriously sat in silence. It was her prayer that somewhere in the blank space, a note or two of their life together would remain for him to hold onto. She bit the inside of her cheek to keep from crying in front of her friend. It seemed so unfair. Hour by hour, Dash's mind was being picked apart. All the brilliance locked inside of him had become a feast for vultures, stealing his memories away, only leaving behind scraps of a man hungry for life.

* * *

THE EXCITEMENT of the day had taken its toll on Dash. It was hard to imagine that a little more than a month ago, he was performing before stadium-sized crowds, and now one visitor exhausted him.

Sky took a seat beside her husband. His eyes were tired, the lids lazily drooping as he struggled to stay alert. There was no doubt in Skylar's mind they'd made the right decision to sequester themselves. She promised Dash he wouldn't die in a hospital, and she intended to keep that promise. Though she tried not to let it get to her, the responsibility weighed heavily on her. Coordinating their life by herself, while trying to spend every one of Dash's coherent moments with him, had left her bone tired. His periods of not communicating were longer, and the lack of muscle control left him weak.

"Why don't we go inside? Take a rest." Her tone was soft. She wasn't sure if he was with her.

"A rest?" He canted his head, puzzled. Though he seemed to be cognizant of most or some of what she was saying, Dash's comprehension skills had been severely affected. At first, she'd remained silent while he'd searched for words and definitions, but then frustration had taken over. It pained her to see him search his thoughts and reach for the proper response. Things that had been so familiar were lost to him. She'd found a way around his residual frustration and anger by merely adding clarification when he asked a question.

"Yes." She smiled as she watched his eyes. It was like someone had opened the shutters and let the light pour in. "A rest in bed. You'll be more comfortable, and it will do you good. You'll have more energy after you give your body and mind time to recharge."

"Right." He brought her hand to his lips, kissing it in that princely way that always made her feel cherished. "I'm here, Sky. I understood you the first time. We're just approaching dusk. I'd rather stay out here enjoying a beautiful sunset with my wife."

He was here! She had no idea how long this episode of clarity would last. Still, she would treasure it all the while, knowing that whatever they did tonight would be a memory for her tomorrow. Her smile widened as her heart leaped. "We can do whatever you'd like."

Dash again kissed the back of her hand while watching a sailboat crossing the vista. "The last I remember, you hadn't spoken to the press. Has that changed?"

"No. We have a good security system here, and Caton has been keeping everything in check."

"Caton?" He raised his eyes, searching his memory, then looked back at her with a smile. "Caton! I remember him." He paused, pleased with the small victory. "Okay. You might not want to talk to them, but you have to. They might not be visible, but they're out there. Probably hiding in bushes and trees. It's better if you control the story. Once this gets out, there will be a shit storm of paparazzi, and they'll be hunting for photos."

A sigh escaped her. This was the third time Dash had brought up the same subject, though he didn't remember bringing it up at all. She'd been doing everything possible to maintain their privacy, but it had become increasingly difficult.

"I know you're right. They have a small amount of information. Some outlets reported that the incident was due to exhaustion. Still, the jury is out in the court of public opinion. They'll keep digging until they get what they want."

"That's partly true. Even when the press gets what they want, they put their own spin on it. That's the downside of fame." Dash shrugged. Still holding Skylar's hand, he tugged it. "Come sit on my lap."

A gentle breeze fluttered the curtains at the doorway. They billowed softly as she rose from her seat. Honoring his request, she carefully took a seat and placed her arms around him. She would take as many quiet times like that as she could get. As the bright sky faded into hues of blues, pinks, and yellows, Dash's body relaxed. He pulled her legs up across the top of his thighs and cradled her in his arms. She leaned into his chest and spoke quietly. "Tell me what's on your mind."

"I'm afraid." His tone was flat, yet calm, as the words rushed out. She lifted her head to find him looking out at the bay waters. They, too, were tranquil, peaceful, and blue, reflecting his current mood.

"Of?" she asked.

"Yes." Her brows popped up. The answer seemed inappropriate, but he chuckled. "Of everything, pretty much. Of what's to come. Of losing you. Of losing me." He paused. "If I haven't already, I want to say thank you."

Confusion knit her brows. "For what?"

"For loving me the way that you do. Before you, I'd

heard of love, but really had no understanding of how it could affect a person. You've defined it for me—just like you do with some of the words I'm forgetting. I don't know what I'd do without you. You've taken care of everything, and you've never flinched." He hugged her. You're my anchor, Abbie."

Abbie.

Again, the interchange of names. Dash had been using both her name and Abigail's for several weeks. Surprisingly, it no longer bothered her. After talking to Dr. O'Hara, the mix-up had lost its power to hurt her. She'd grown accustomed to it. Where she used to feel a threat when he swapped them, she answered to the names Abigail and Abbie as well as she did to her own.

"You're welcome, but thanks aren't necessary." She snuggled closer, placing her head on his shoulder. Inhaling deeply, she took in his fragrance. His hair smelled of a mix of shampoo and brine; the waters of the Chesapeake clung to the strands. The aroma was distinct, a blend of fresh water from the rivers and sea salt from the ocean. Though most thought a brackish water breeze would be unpleasant, living on the Bay proved that to be untrue. Dash spent as much time outside as possible, his fragrance also hinting of the outdoors. Since living there, they'd only experienced a few rainy days where he had to be confined. That first day he was unpleasant to the point of combative, but, as luck would have it, there was a covered veranda off the master bedroom. Though the gentle breeze and serene waters had morphed into stronger winds and whitecapped waves, Dash's temperament had calmed once he was outside. That was another facet of Alzheimer's—mood swings. The changes in his demeanor couldn't have been predicted any more than the uncertainty of their future.

Sky closed her eyes, savoring everything about him

from his scent to his body heat. It was unbearable for her to think of the day when she would no longer be able to do this. A day when all she would have left were memories of days like these. It didn't matter to her that in his confusion, he intermingled names, mixed up words, and muddled past events. She'd learned to sit quietly while he spoke, all the while knowing that one day it would be a strain on her mind to recall the sound of his voice. The quiet terms of endearment. The soft whispers while lovemaking. Those were hers and hers alone. Her heart would break when he was gone, and all she would have were recordings of him to remind her of how he sang and played his guitar. But the tender moments they shared—she tucked those into her heart. They would have to suffice for the rest of her life. It wasn't enough. She wanted more.

She gently swiped away a tear, knowing that in time there would be hundreds more to drown in. Watching her husband deteriorate before her eyes was as much an emotional death to her as it would eventually be a physical one for him.

"A penny for your thoughts, Abigail."

"I was just thinking about how much I love you." Skylar pushed away from her disturbing thoughts. All they brought were sorrow. If she were to survive this, she would have to stay in the present and simply concentrate on these sweet moments as they occurred.

Dash leaned his head back against the wood. A considerable yawn consumed him while amusing her.

"Now, you really are acting like an old man." Skylar's eyes twinkled as she teased him.

Dash playfully waggled his brows. "Then maybe you should put me to bed and tuck me in."

She slid her legs from his, placing her bare feet on the cool patio tile. Despite their situation, it had been a magical day. Though the pull of sadness had a solid grip on both of them, she was determined to fight the bad things and cherish the good ones.

She stood, moving in front of him, and offered him her outstretched hands. "C'mon, you old fart. Let's go."

He grabbed hold of them, a merry gleam sparkling in his eyes. As he stood, the nurse appeared. "Let me help you with him, Mrs. Barrows."

The nurse looped an arm through one of his to assist him, as the tremor in his leg caused him to lose his balance at times. As Sky went to do the same with the other arm, the doorbell rang. Both she and the nurse exchanged questioning looks. She hadn't been expecting anyone other than Vince today.

"Why don't you go lie down? I'll be there in a minute." Dash nodded, following the nurse's lead. Skylar waited until the bedroom door closed behind him before going to answer the front door. Whoever was there was now pounding impatiently.

Placing her eye against the peephole, she let out a sigh. It wasn't enough that she was exhausted, and her nerves were worn thin. Now she had to deal with Ian.

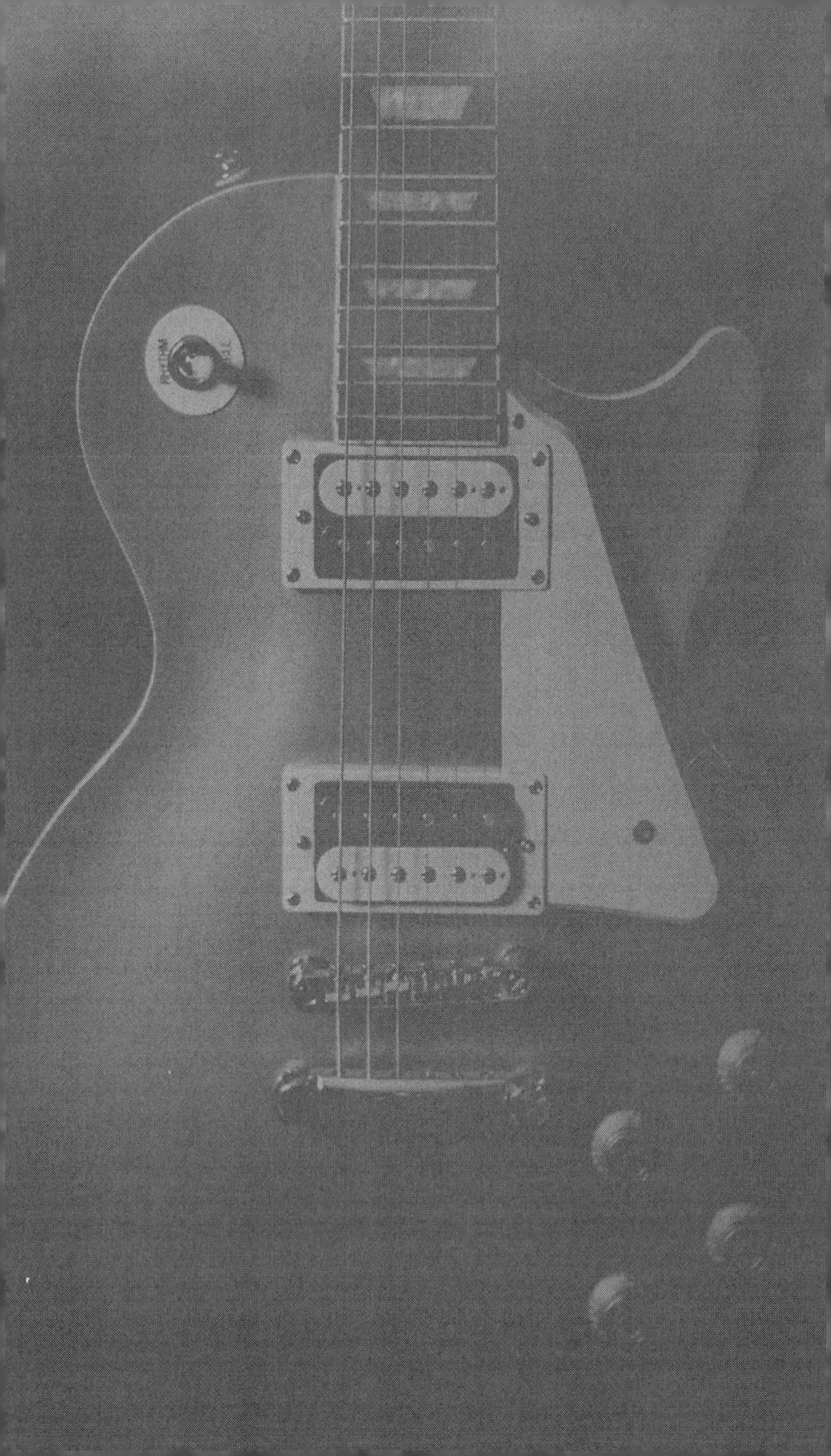

CHAPTER 39

Skylar stared at the floor, inhaling a deep breath. Hopefully, Dash wouldn't be able to hear anything from inside their room. The last thing she wanted was for him to know Ian was there. It wouldn't do anything but upset him. Still, Ian was Dash's friend, and though she owed him no loyalty, what was happening to her and Dash would also alter his future and the future of the group. Though she wasn't ready to have any discussions regarding the band, addressing Ian was an immediate issue. He was persistent, she would give him that. He'd phoned her more than a dozen times and called Dash's cell even more. It had been too much to deal with at the time, so she'd turned off his phone. All of it was hard enough on her without having to deal with Ian's possible threats and slurs about her actions and character.

"Open the damn door, Skylar! I know you're in there." Ian's shouts penetrated the wood. She could only hope his rough voice and harsh tone weren't indications he was drunk or high.

"Do you want me to take care of him, missus?" Caton came up behind her. She'd barely heard him approach, she was so preoccupied with her thoughts but was glad he was nearby. Ian would never have slipped by security, but she had added the guys in the group to the list of people who could get past the gate that secured their property. Now Ian was at the door, but he posed no threat. Caton would see to that.

Caton had traveled with them from London after Skylar had asked for his help a second time while there—to get them to the airport as inconspicuously as possible. He'd had everything arranged within hours, taking the burden off her so she could focus on her husband. That was what mattered to her. He was the only one of the security staff that lived with them. Although he supervised a team of three other men, he took one of the bedrooms in the house and was ready any time she needed him. It eased her mind to know that he was there.

"I'd like it if you would stay close by." Her voice was heavy with sorrow. "If I let Ian stay, I'm going to tell him what's going on. He's unpredictable and if he gets out of hand, I'd appreciate you removing him from the house so he doesn't upset Dash."

The burly man nodded, stepping a few paces behind her but close enough so that he could intervene if necessary. He took a military stance, legs apart and hands behind his back. Skylar turned her attention back to the door, closing her eyes for a moment to center herself and mentally prepare for the firestorm she was certain awaited her.

"Skylar!" I said, "open the door!"

Just as he finished shouting the demand, she swung open the door. "Hello, Ian." Her tone resembled a hiss over barbed wire. Soul shivering and menacing. Hopefully, Ian detected the chill in her voice. "Do you think you could keep it down? Dash is resting."

"Fuck that." He pushed past her. "I've known him since high school. You've known him for what? Five minutes? If you're here, I'm here." He went past the foyer, his head turning left and right as he looked around the room. He stalked toward her, his eyes ablaze with anger. "Where the fuck is he?"

Caton, who'd positioned himself against the wall, stepped forward. He walked right up to Ian, bumping his chest with his. He towered over the skinny singer by nearly a foot and outweighed him by at least sixty pounds. Ian's eyes flew open, having hit a brick wall made of flesh and bone, but the rage was still evident in his eyes. Skylar intervened before the smaller man was injured.

"Ian, this is Caton. I'd like to talk to you, but if you aren't up for a quiet, rational conversation, I'll have him escort you out."

Ian's eyes narrowed as he gave Sky a sideways glance and then returned his gaze to the monster of a man before him.

Skylar gave Ian's arm a gentle touch. "If you can put all your attitude and bullshit aside, Ian, I really would like to talk to you."

Ian looked into her eyes. She could only hope the sincerity he saw there was what caused him to let down his guard. His posture relaxed as his attitude deflated. He nodded, though his eyes still shot hateful, warning daggers at Caton. Sky chuckled inside. Caton would flatten him if she just said the word.

"Thanks, Caton. I think I've got it from here."

He kept his feet planted firmly in front of Ian but

turned his face to Skylar. "I'll be in the next room if you need me, missus."

"Thank you." She followed Caton with her eyes as he went into the kitchen, then turned to Ian. "Let's go into the den." She didn't wait for Ian to agree or disagree, she just walked, hoping she would be able to find the right words to say. What she had to tell Ian wasn't going to be easy, no matter her personal feelings.

* * *

THE DEN WAS LIT by a table lamp, the soft light lending itself to a quiet atmosphere. Both a combination of office and library, the back wall was lined with books, mostly the classics. She took a seat in one of two fireside chairs, and Ian took the other. He wasted no time, attacking her verbally as soon as she'd settled back in her chair.

"So, first you marry my boy behind my back, then you steal him away from the concert, and land his ass in the hospital? It took me a while to find you, but I told you I would. What did you do to him, Skylar? Fuck him up in the head?"

If only it were that simple.

"Ian, I don't want to fight with you. If you love your friend, you'll let me speak."

"Fine." Ian sounded like a petulant child. "Tell me what the hell's going on."

Again, Sky closed her eyes, centering herself. Knowing she needed to protect her energy, she didn't want to rush through the conversation, no matter how deep a barb Ian became under her skin.

"Do you remember when Dash called me Abigail?"

"What the hell! It's no big thing," he scoffed. "I get chicks' names mixed up all the time."

Sky ignored his comment, knowing that recalling the events and telling Ian the truth of what and why they were there would cause him the same pain she felt. "That was the first indication that something was wrong. The spasms and tremors that he couldn't control were another. He's losing himself, Ian, and it's not going to get better. In fact, it's going to get worse. Eventually, Dash won't come back to us. He has dementia. A form of Alzheimer's but a rapid onset type. CJD. It stands for Creutzfeldt-Jakob disease."

He gave her an incredulous look, his forehead pinched painfully tight, one corner of his mouth crooked in disbelief. "You're bullshittin' me."

A puff of air escaped as Skylar closed her eyes. She shook her head, unable to catch an errant tear. "I wish I was, but I'm not."

Ian took a moment to examine her. As she looked into his eyes, he read the truth. "You're really not, are you?"

Skylar swallowed the lump in her throat. Her eyes stung as a fresh supply of tears threatened to breach the red rims. She watched as Ian shifted uncomfortably in his chair and wiped his hands over his face.

"Is he going to die?"

Suddenly Ian's voice sounded like he'd just swallowed broken glass, his tone so torn with emotion, and her heart broke for him.

She nodded. "Months at best."

"Ah, fuck." Ian ran his hand through his hair, dropping his chin as he sniffed back his tears. It took a few moments before he could again look at her. "We'll get him to the best doctors. It doesn't matter what the fuck it costs, we'll just make it happen. I know the other guys will be more than willing to—"

"He isn't going to get better, Ian. I've already had him to Hopkins. His condition has deteriorated rapidly in the time since you've seen him. He has early-onset Alzheimer's. His prognosis is grim."

Ian pushed himself up from the chair, his emotions clearly getting the best of him. Closing his eyes for a moment as if this news was causing physical pain, he paced, then nervously tapped his foot. There was no denying the information had broken something inside of him he didn't know how to fix. After a few minutes, he looked at Skylar, his eyes sad, his mouth downturned. "So, that's why he called you Abbie?"

Skylar nodded.

Ian bit down on his lip, which was now trembling. "Fuck! Fuck! Fuck!" He walked in circles as he spoke. "And I made a joke out of it." His last comment traveled on a repentant breath before he stopped and looked at her.

She felt the hopelessness that washed over him, and she knew at that moment that Ian loved Dash. There was no denying it. The wave crested as she delivered the news but crashed the moment he realized how grave the situation indeed was.

"He has trouble walking or holding a cup, and he mixes together words in conversation that don't go together. He tells me stories about the business, but he isn't talking about music. He speaks at length about real estate and keeping the books. Sometimes, when I use his name, he becomes flippant, demanding I use either his given name or my nickname for him, which I've learned are Isidore or Izzy. When he raises his voice to me, it's in a strict tone, yet shortly after that, he is repentant and tells me that he loves me. He has called me Abbie at least a hundred times, and, when he does, he has no problem articulating he's lost patience with me. Those are the times when he adopts a fatherly tone and addresses me as Abigail."

Ian picked up a box of tissue from the desk, offering

them to her with an outstretched hand. She plucked two from the box, dabbing at her tears and then swiping them under her nose.

"Thank you." She cleared her throat, looking over at Ian with heartbreak in her eyes. "It isn't always like that. Sometimes he's just Dash, exactly as I've always known him. Warm and tender. Thoughtful and kind. He apologizes though I assure him I'm not upset, and I know that none of this is his fault. He knows that his mind will leave me before his heart stops beating. How tragic is that? I can see the rage behind his eyes, the helplessness that he feels for the situation. Then I see the sadness because of a future together that we'll never have. It breaks him, and all I can do is hold him. I don't have the luxury of a lie to tell him that everything will be all right, because we both know it won't be. And then there are times when he is gone, just like that night on the stage. There is an emptiness in his eyes, a vacancy. Dash isn't there, and there's no way I can predict if he'll ever come back."

Her expression drew up in pain as she gave Ian a desperate look. "It terrifies me, you know? I'm afraid to go to sleep because I might miss him when he's lucid. Every time he is, it could be the last time I ever see him. The last time I ever get to talk to *my* Dash." A sob stole her voice, the remnant strained. "It isn't fair. It just isn't fair." She wrapped her arms around her waist in a feeble attempt to console herself.

Ian listened and then sat quietly as she regained her composure. It was the first time she'd seen him act remotely normal.

That's what pain does to a person. No matter physical or emotional, it has a way of sobering the toughest, exposing the truth that lies beneath a veneer. It's cruel. It's painfully honest. Vicious. Revealing. Inhuman. It takes and takes, and as it strips you raw, it covers you with a blanket of grief, tucking your empty heart into a bed of thorns. Pain's exhaustion makes you sleep but never gives you rest. Grief's food loses its flavor; neither savory nor sweet, only bitter, and you wonder if you'll ever survive the rending.

CHAPTER 40

Some time passed, allowing both Sky and Ian to compose themselves. A gentler human being now replaced the maniacal, eccentric man that had pounded on the door demanding entrance. She brushed back loose strands of hair with open hands and rearranged a messy bun atop her head. Running her tongue over her teeth, she scavenged for any moisture that might remain in her cotton-dry mouth. Rolling her shoulders, she adjusted to a different position, pulling her legs up and tucking her feet beneath her. Ian watched her, his pain-filled gaze now appearing tired.

"Do you have any questions for me? I know this is a lot to take in."

Ian nodded, patting her hand. "Just one. Can I see him?"

A tender smile curved her lips. "Sure. Just don't expect anything other than the unexpected. At least," she shrugged, "that's what Dash's doctors tell me."

Ian nodded. Sky pushed out of the chair while Ian waited for her. She looped her arm in his and walked him through the main living room to the bedroom. She stopped at the door.

"His nurse will be in there. Today was a good day for him. I hope it still is. I know the last time you two saw each other, there was some tension. I hope you can find some peace in your visit, Ian," she said, resigned. "There's no way of knowing if there will be another opportunity."

Sky watched as Ian mulled over the words, a resigned nod indicating he understood her meaning. In an unexpected gesture, he hugged her. Her eyes flew open as did her arms, but a moment later, she returned the embrace.

Ian made it brief. It was apparent he was uncomfortable with genuine displays of affection. He straightened his posture and brushed back his messy hair. "Thank you."

Skylar watched as he entered, then closed the door quietly behind him.

* * *

IAN CAME out of the bedroom. It was apparent he was unnerved. His usual, smart-ass attitude had sobered to one of concern. "He's worse than the last time I saw him. Three months ago, his knees were shaking. Two months ago, his hands started. That was when he started forgetting things. Guitar riffs. A part of a song he'd been playing forever. I guess those were signs of the disease."

His expression was a study of pain. Guilt and sorrow had wielded twin swords, and Ian was the latest one in their world that had fallen victim to their blades. "I know you're going to hate me for saying this, but I can't come back after today, Sky. I can't see him again. Not like this."

Ian hesitated for a moment. His initial cocky attitude having entirely changed from the cavalier man she knew. "I know you and I have been like oil and water, but the one thing we have in common is that we both love Dash." He looked at her with pleading eyes. "Get the doctors to do whatever they can, Sky. Maybe it's the medicine they have him on, but he kept calling me Reginald. He was looking right at me and didn't know me. He asked me how things were at the club. Had I quit smoking those nasty cigars. There was a look in his eye, you know? Like he was having fun at my expense. He looked so . . . Dash. At first, I thought he was fooling around, but he wasn't. He called himself Izzy. I kept slipping and calling him Dash. He got pissed. Then I acted like Reginald was my name, and I told him all his friends at the club asked about him. That seemed to make him happy, but there's definitely some weird shit going on in his head."

* * *

Having seen Ian out, Skylar quietly slipped into the bedroom. A warm and tender smile crossed her lips. Dash was peacefully asleep. She tiptoed to the side of the bed where his nurse sat in a chair. She bent down and whispered in the woman's ear. "Why don't you get some sleep? It's been a long day."

The nurse gave Sky an appreciative nod, closing the door quietly upon her exit. Skylar slipped off her shoes and climbed into bed. Dash reached for her, sliding his arm around her as he moved to his side. Sky loved these quiet moments, especially because she knew they wouldn't last.

She stared out at the night sky. There was a beautiful view from the bedroom. The full moon's glow lit up the water. The tide had come in, the water much more flat and serene than a few hours ago. The tiny waves kissed the shoreline; the sound lulling her into a peaceful state. As her husband spooned her, she snuggled closer to him. It was so hard to comprehend how so much had happened in so short a time. Who would have known their love story would come to this, but then, not all love stories have happy endings. She would have to be satisfied with their lot, taking each day as it came, and being thankful for their happy-for-now.

"Are you sleeping?" The rich tone of Dash's voice made her smile. It always did.

"No. I'm so tired I can barely keep my eyes open, but I'm not sleeping."

"There are things I need to tell you. Things I want to say."

Now cozy in her bed and his arms, Sky's eyelids fluttered. She wasn't sure she could stay awake long enough to hear what he had to say. "I'll try to listen, Dash, but I can't promise I won't fall asleep."

Instantly, he stiffened. "Abbie, why do you keep calling me Dash when you know my name? Isidore or Izzy is acceptable. I'm not comfortable with the moniker Dash. The connotation that I rush through anything simply doesn't resonate with me. You know I am a contemplative man in both my business and personal life."

"You're right, Izzy. Why don't you sleep? We can discuss whatever you want later."

Skylar tried to stay awake, but her eyelids fluttered. This day had been long and trying, especially the purging cry she'd had while Ian had visited with Dash. Although she thought herself superhuman, she'd have to remember that sometimes the caregiver needed to care for herself. After a day of balancing Dash, Vince, and then Ian, all she wanted to do was rest.

"Abigail Eisenberg, you mustn't tire yourself like this. I won't have it. That's why we employ household staff. You have a kind heart, my dear, but I forbid you from collapsing because you haven't delegated duties properly. You must remember your status. It won't do if you set a bad example for the children." His body stiffened, his tone clearly superior.

Even in an agitated state, Dash was more composed than most men would be if their wives had called them by someone else's name. She certainly hadn't maintained a level head when he'd done the same to her. Whether he wanted to be called Izzy or Isidore, Dash was still her husband. His care for her the same. Though Alzheimer's had altered his personality and put him in some strange, convoluted frame of mind, he was the love of her life, and, for whatever time they had left, she would make his days as happy as possible.

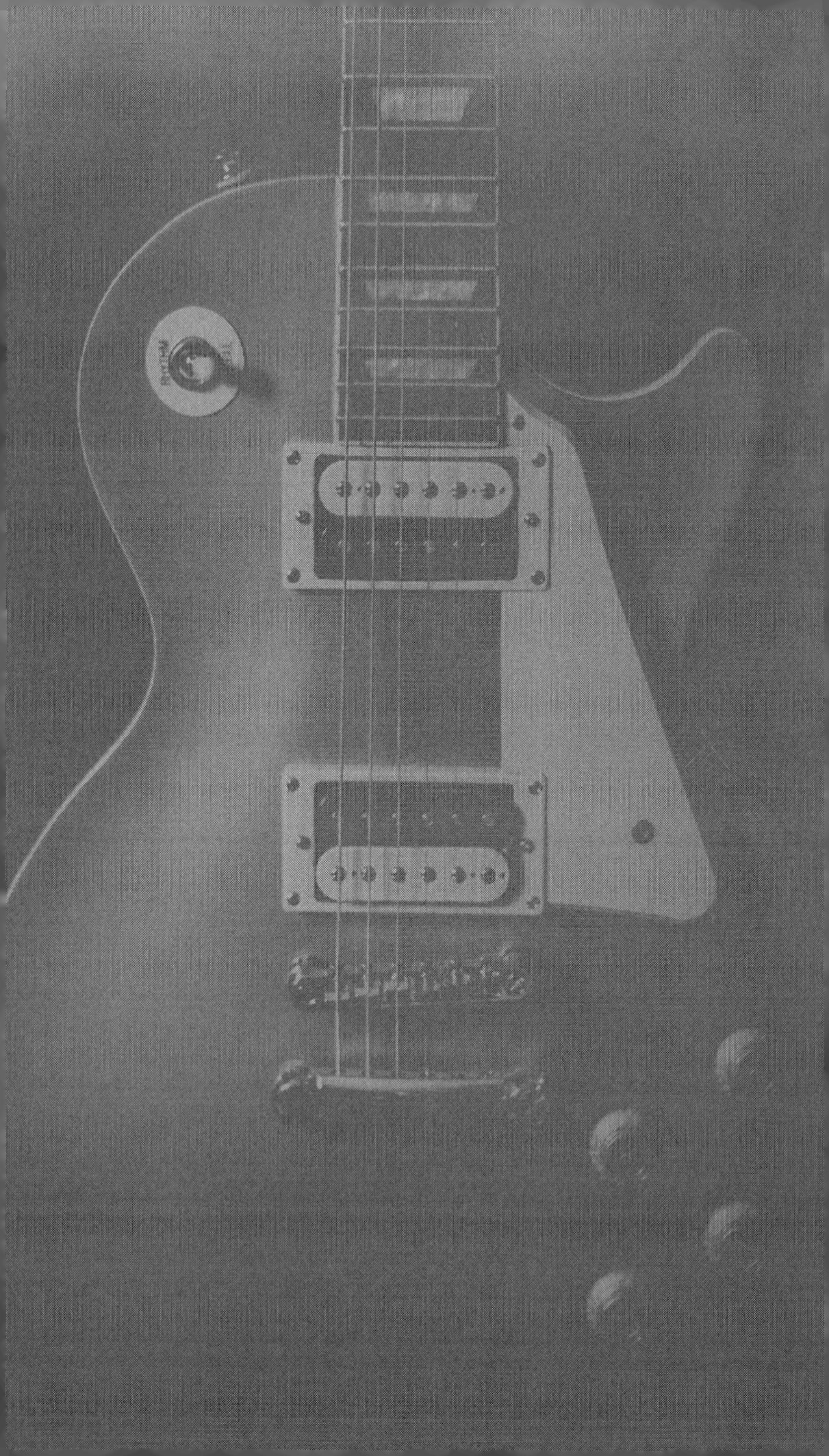

CHAPTER 41

*E*xhausted tears stung her eyes. It wasn't as though she hadn't cried enough of them today, and now that her energy was spent, it seemed they came more easily.

"There, there, my sweet Abbie. There's no need for tears, dearest. I just want you to take care of yourself, my love."

"Yes, Izzy. You're right. You're always right." Skylar flipped onto her other side and hugged him. Immediately she felt him relax. With exhaustion rapidly pulling down the shades on her thoughts, she buried her face into his chest. Her Dash—the rocker who, until a few months ago, jammed to songs by Metallica and Aerosmith—had once again become the prim and proper Izzy. The man who loved her in all the right ways was still inside somewhere. It was so frustrating. So painful. He was disappearing before her eyes, and all she wanted to do was hold him tight. She wanted all the parts of him. To smell his burnt grilled cheese sandwiches. To watch him clean his Harley until it shined before taking her for a ride. To make love with him all through the night and glimpse the sunrise by his side. She didn't know Izzy. All she knew was the man she never thought would come along. He was there, in her arms, but he was devoid of any memories of her. Izzy wanted Abbie. She wanted Dash. It was too much to wrap her head around, but if she closed her eyes, inhaled his scent, touched him, then maybe, just maybe, he would remember how it used to be, and so could she.

He wrapped his arms around her, adjusting them both so that she could hear his heartbeat. "There, there, my love. Our dispute is over. No matter what, Abbie, you'll always be my girl."

Skylar stifled a cry as he gave her a squeeze. The lump in her throat lodged there as he reached for the covers and tucked them around her. The revelation that she might never see, hear, or speak to Dash again shattered her heart. Like a child blowing a dandelion wish, the life she'd pictured scattered on the wind along with a million hopes and dreams.

More tears surfaced, though she thought she'd cried them all. All she could do was sit by and watch as their future disappeared.

"Oh, my goodness, dearest. You must let this go." He gently brushed her cheek with his thumb, the caress so tender she leaned into it. "There's no need to be upset, dear girl. It's nothing."

It was everything.

Skylar slowly nodded. Sleep approached as a welcome friend and, as she lay cradled in her husband's arms, her breaths evened out.

"Abbie, do you remember the dress I purchased for you on my last trip? The blue one? I like that frock. You should wear blue more often."

Sky didn't answer as sleep settled in.

"Oh, my dear girl. You are a tired one, aren't you? You do remember that we're to meet the Fitzgeralds for dinner? They will be our companions tonight. It's sure to be a delightful evening."

"Hmm. I didn't," Sky answered. If she could sneak in a nap as he talked, she was sure she'd be in a better frame of mind. "I'm sorry, Izzy. Why don't you refresh my memory while I rest?"

Laughing heartily, he pressed a kiss to her head. "I most certainly can do that, my dear. You know how I love the propriety of a well-spent evening."

Skylar drifted away as he began, caught up in the rich sound of his voice. As she succumbed to exhaustion, she fell into an unfamiliar place in her dream. Somewhere she'd never been before.

"ABIGAIL, THEY'RE PLAYING OUR SONG." *An outstretched hand appeared before her, and suddenly she wasn't inside their house. When she looked up there stood Dash. The only word she could use to describe him was "dashing." How ironic.*

Dressed in tails, a black bow tie sat perfectly at the hollow of his throat. He was different, yet the same. His eyes were still the warm, chocolaty color that had caught her the first time she'd looked into them.

"Abbie?" An invitation quirked his brow as she hadn't yet taken his hand. As she looked down, she saw she was dressed in a floral gown. The background was soft pink, the other colors scattered throughout with the fresh flowers of spring.

"Izzy?" she questioned.

He nodded, his smile dazzling and oh, so inviting. She was starving for her husband and didn't care that they were in a dream. She was with the one she loved. She took his hand.

The connection weakened her knees. She trembled. Her skin

warmed. With one touch, the world as she knew it spiraled, dizzying her as she traveled toward another time and another place. Heat sparked with a simple touch. Synapses exploded, crackling and sparking as her present persona melded with that of Abigail's. The combination terrified her as she realized that she, Skylar, was Abbie.

How and why that had occurred mystified her, but she didn't care. There she was with her beloved, Izzy—who, by some twist of fate, was, miraculously, Dash.

He led her to the dance floor. Elegant chandeliers hung sparkling from the ceiling as a rainbow of colors dotted the walls, the magical effect of light meeting crystal. A man and woman skated by them as they danced the waltz, he in a tuxedo much like the one Dash was wearing, while the woman, whom Sky presumed to be his wife, wore a dress trimmed with delicate lace. Others joined them on the dance floor, swirling around in her dream, but her attention was only on her husband. Tall and lean, she was well aware of the muscular form hidden beneath his clothes. He smiled, leading her around the dance floor. Her smile equaled his. How could it not? He was there, with her. All else faded away.

"Do you remember this tune, Abbie?" His handsome face beamed. His speech was so clear. He was present. Whatever this was—wherever they were—she suddenly didn't ever want to leave.

"Da da dum, da da dum, da da dum ti dum dum." They danced a waltz, Dash singing the beat as he moved them about the space. But he wasn't Dash; he was Izzy, and she didn't care.

His eyes held a smile, and she was tethered. The love she saw reflected there transcended everything she understood about time and space.

"Is it coming back to you, Abbie? Do you remember me?" His tone was soft and tender.

"Yes." Skylar gazed into his eyes, his pleasure at her response evident.

A relieved smile played on his lips. "I'm so glad. I thought you'd forgotten me." His eyes danced with delight. "There are things that are worth remembering, wouldn't you agree?"

Skylar nearly fell into him as a chill ran up her spine. "Do you know me? Really know me?"

He smiled, the corners of his eyes crinkling with delight. "I do. I could never forget you. I wouldn't exist without the other half of my beating heart."

How was this happening? How could he remember her? She was Skylar, yet she was Abbie. He was Izzy, yet he was Dash. None of it made sense. None of it was real.

Yet it was.

Rational thought seeped into her dreams, and Sky tried to wake herself. Tried to rouse her consciousness to a state that made sense. When she tried to pull away from Izzy in her dream, he refused to let go.

"I know this is hard for you to understand, my sweet girl, but there are some things that stand the test of time. Some braided lives that are so intertwined they are meant to be eternal. The love we shared both then and now knows no bounds. No distance or circumstance can keep us apart. Do you understand that?"

As she abandoned rational thoughts and looked into his eyes, all fear faded away, yet there was a flicker of sadness which flashed within the warm brown color.

"My poor Abbie. I promised you that I would find you, and I'm keeping my word. I only have a little time with you, so I need you to understand what is happening. Sometimes, something magical happens. Two people who were meant to be together will always be. We were before, and I'm sure we will be again, darling. Although the last I saw you, you were terribly afraid. I'm sorry for that. If it had been within my power to save us, to get us both off the ship, I would have done so by love,

grace, and sheer willpower. The tragedy was that you and I weren't finished. Cabin C-26 was never meant to be our final resting place. It was a terrible thing that happened. An unimaginable tragedy. I had planned to surprise you with dinner and a gift when we reached our destination, but it was not meant to be. I was helpless, and you were cold. The waters were so frigid they stole the pink from your cheeks. I watched as the color drained from your lips, but you held my promise in your eyes. They remained as beautiful as a clear sky or a crystal lake. Though I hated knowing we were leaving this earth, I had no doubt our love would survive the passing. And now I've come back to you. I know you are as afraid now as you were then. I want you to know that there is no need. No matter what, we will never be lost to one another. We never were. Please, for me, try to remember."

His words had her spellbound. Like a movie, the scene played in her mind. Suddenly, a wooden door appeared with brass lettering that spelled out C-26. Always the gentleman, Isidore held her hand and turned the handle, opening the door. She didn't know how she knew this, but they had returned from the deck above. A seat in a lifeboat was no longer an option. Suddenly, she knew where she was, and what was before her was tragedy.

The realization made her gasp, but Izzy led her inside. Patting the top of the mattress with his hand, she followed him onto the bed. She could hear music, slow and sad. She shivered as she saw the image clearer. How was it possible that she was seeing herself? It was the two of them—Dash and her—lying side by side.

They were cold.

So cold.

Skylar felt like she was floating above the couple as she drifted in the dreamlike state. Tiny waves splashed against the bed. There were items from a bedside table bobbing atop the water. Sky's gaze traveled the room, and somehow, she knew the circumstance of the couple. Instead of feeling fear, she felt secure.

Was she dead?

She stared at the man, noting the rise and fall of his chest. He, too, wore a heavy coat. Some type of wool, perhaps. When she went to reach out to touch his face, her fingers brushed the woman instead. Suddenly, she was transported, no longer floating but inside the woman's body.

For a fraction of a moment, she felt the woman's pain. Her body was stiff, the frigid temperature registering as it had its impact on fragile muscle and bone. But just as quickly as she'd taken possession inside the woman's skin, she was once again transported, vacating the human shell. It was as if Skylar were present in the moment only to prove its existence.

Strong arms held her tightly, though a moment ago, she could barely feel anything at all. For a third time, her consciousness drifted. This time Dash was Izzy, and he was with her. Together they held hands as they watched the scene below. The woman's hair had loosened from the vintage-style bun she wore. It brushed the collar of her coat. A loud, creaking sound, followed by an earth-shattering crack, split the air, and Skylar jumped.

"Oh, Izzy. I'm scared!"

The man looked at the woman, terror, and adoration mixing in his desperate eyes. Skylar tried to calm herself, looking around in the dream. The door to the cabin flew open as a rush of water joined with what had previously seeped beneath it. It banged against the wall, the force of the sea now showing its might. Anything loose was now adrift in the forceful wave caps.

Sky slammed her eyes shut, squeezing Dash's hand as tightly as her waning strength would allow. The woman screamed.

"Izzy!"

Skylar gasped, feeling the need for air, and then suddenly, she felt at peace. As she looked within her dream, she was no longer on a ship. She was in a large room, surrounded by darkness. A

spotlight startled her. She moved her hand, feeling metal beneath her fingers. It was a number, a designation of some kind. C-26. Her eyes snapped ahead as an image appeared. Another light. Blue this time. Music. A lone guitar. A man with the warmth of the sun in his beautiful brown eyes, strumming softly. A lifetime of love in his expression.
Dash!
Again, she gasped.

Skylar's eyes flew open as she struggled to pull oxygen into her lungs.

"Look at me." Dash's tone was more commanding than her confusion, cutting through her fear. With shaking hands, she freed herself from his arms as confusion swam through her eyes. His eyes met hers, a satisfied smile on his lips.

Skylar trembled. Her voice cracked beneath the weight of possibilities, the memory of living another life tumbling down upon her. "I don't understand." Her voice was a sob.

Dash met her gaze. With shaky hands, she cupped his face, her eyes locked with his as tears streamed down her cheeks.

"Don't you, my dear one?"

Desperately, she pressed her lips to his, the connection a rebranding of souls.

He held her as if the world were ending, and, somehow, Skylar knew that it had.

EPILOGUE

Death claimed Dash.

News vans waited near the private ceremony, journalists waiting patiently to see if they could get her to make a statement. There would be none today. She was without words. An empty shell. In time she would be able to scratch her scars with the keys on her laptop and bleed her heart onto the page. The world needed love stories, no matter how tragic they might be.

Once Skylar spoke to Dash as Izzy the disease ravaged his mind and body. He spent the remainder of his days staring blankly out at the water. She was at peace that she was able to help him realize his dream of having a home by the sea. It was where he held her hand as he took his final breath.

After the reverend had finished with the ceremonial prayers, Skylar stayed behind at the cemetery. She stared at the casket that held what remained of her husband. She knew he wasn't there. No box could contain the essence of a man who was larger than life itself. The man she'd fallen in love with. For whatever remained of her life, this one fact would ring constant: Dash Barrows had made an indelible mark on her soul. Their meeting was the definition of a happy accident. Loving Dash had changed her life, but, then, isn't that the crux of all love stories? How the transforming power of giving away one's soul leaves a remnant of hope when they're gone?

Though she could find many words to describe her love for Dash, there was only one to express her feelings at his passing.

Lost.

Skylar's eyes were nearly swollen shut, the result of too many fallen tears. Her heart begged for this not to be real and she was sure that not a day would pass when she wouldn't think about him. His laugh. His smile. His eyes. How he knitted his brows together when she had an explosive thought for her next book. She would give anything to sit quietly by and listen one more time as he lost himself in a melody. Just one more look at him as his fingers moved on the neck of his guitar. Dash hadn't been the only one to lose himself to his disease; it had claimed her as well.

She dabbed at her eyes and nose with a tissue, aware the concealer she'd applied to cover the red and dark circles was long gone. Mascara and lipstick couldn't hide heartache. Sorrow had a face of its own.

"Sky."

She turned at the sound of her name and met Ian's gaze. Sorrow was also evident in his expression. He looked as bad as she felt. She was happy they'd smoothed out their differences. She had no energy for an argument today. Ian had lost as much as she, perhaps even more. She wasn't weighed down with regret, but she had no doubt Ian was afflicted with that disease. He bore the stripes of too many missed opportunities to be a real friend to Dash. No, she would never suffer his distress, but Ian would be tortured forever.

As he timidly approached her, he reached into his pocket and pulled out a small blue box wrapped with a white silk ribbon. He held it out to her. "This is for you. It's from Dash."

Her gaze dropped to the ground. Specs of crumbled dirt dotted the thick grass. Of course, Dash would have his last word. Alzheimer's might have taken his thoughts and words captive, but it could never take away his ways of expressing his love for her. A comforting hand touched her shoulder.

"Go on. Take it." He placed the box on her lap. "This goes with it." Ian set a small envelope, yellowed and weathered with age, on her lap as well. Skylar picked up the box as a sob shuddered through her. She choked it down, her eyes staying on Ian for only a moment before she tugged at the satin bow.

"After that first concert, Dash couldn't stop talking about you to the boys and me. We'd gone to New York to meet with the lawyers. When we were done, I wanted to go to a bar, but Dash insisted that we go to Tiffany." His voice lowered as his chin dropped, grief delivering another blow to Ian's regrets. "I made fun of him when he dragged me into that damn store, but you know Dash, when he's got his mind set on something..."

Sky rolled the ribbon around two fingers, creating a loop. She sat it off to the side before taking off the lid. She stared at Ian for a moment, uncertain she wanted to share the moment.

"The salesman said that a note came with the gift. I never read it, but Dash seemed to like it. He folded it up and said that he was going to give it to you after you got married. I guess that's why I didn't like you at first. Dash was never the party boy I hoped he would be. I was always trying to get him to hang out with me, but, you know, he was the serious type. Anyway, I found it when I was cleaning out his things from the tour bus. I guess he must have forgotten he'd left it there."

He nervously shuffled his feet, taking a pack of cigarettes from his pocket and lighting one up. He sucked in a long drag, exhaling as he continued. "That was it, Skylar. It never really had anything to do with you. Dash never acted like that for another woman, but for you . . . well, I guess I felt threatened by you. I tried to tell him he was crazy to be so serious about someone he'd just met, but Dash was having none of it. He snapped. Told me to keep my bullshit opinions to myself. Caught me off guard, it did. He'd never done that before, especially because of a chick. I was pissed, and I blamed you for it. I'm ashamed to say I tried to pull you two apart. Clearly, I was wrong."

"Thank you." Her words were barely audible, but Ian heard them. He nodded as a weak smile briefly hooked the corners of his mouth.

He leaned over, placed a light kiss on her cheek, and then stood. "I'll leave you to it then."

She watched as Ian walked back to his car and then turned her eyes once again toward the casket as she opened the box. "What did you do, Dash?" As she removed the velvet box inside, her hands trembled. She opened the hinged lid. Inside was a beautiful pendant. As she took it out, the long chain dangled. She pinched the piece at its neck, the gold chain a brilliant contrast to her black dress. She turned it over.

"To my timeless love."

The inscription was engraved in delicate letters. Using a fingernail, she popped open the piece. One side was a watch. The other held a miniature portrait of a couple. The same couple she'd seen in her dream.

A sob wracked her body as her hand flew to her mouth. She dropped her hand, holding the jewelry on her lap as fresh tears soaked her cheeks. The front bore a starburst design. The tip of each uneven ray held tiny chipped diamonds. It was simply too beautiful for words.

Through her tears, a smile tugged her lips. The thought of Dash wanting to give her something so unique at so early a time in their relationship filled her heart on a day when it was broken.

For the hundredth time today, she wiped her eyes before putting the tissue in her pocket. She turned the envelope over. The paper inside was so old that a crackling sound broke the silence as she carefully unfolded it. When she read the first line, the words stole her breath.

> *"My dearest Abigail,"*
>
> *On this special occasion, I wanted to commemorate the event with a timeless piece for your collection. Inside, you will find a miniature portrait of us taken on the day of our wedding. I don't know if I have ever expressed how smitten I was with you. Even now, though decorum would have me behave otherwise, I am as hopelessly in love with you as I was on that day. I was merely a child when we married, as were you. I am still that boy, madly in love with the woman who has made my life complete. Of course, my darling, that is you.*

I hope that you like this gift. Perhaps this will one day become an heirloom, a symbol of a love well lived. I hope that many years from now, the lucky recipient of this piece will remember us fondly. It is one of a kind, the same as my love for you. For now, I would be honored if you would wear this token of my affection. If ever you find yourself wondering what place you hold in our busy lives, look no further than the end of the chain around your neck, and it will remind you. You are my first thought in the morning and my last thought before I sleep, and even then, my precious wife, you are in my dreams. I loved you then. I love you now. I will love you forever. I promise; no matter where I am, I will always find my way back to you.

Your faithful servant,
And loving husband,
Izzy

The End

* * *

Read on for a *SNEAK PREVIEW* of Ian's story, "**Bone Dust.**"

SNEAK PEEK OF "BONE DUST"

Bone Dust
Rock Hills Book One
By
D.D. Lorenzo

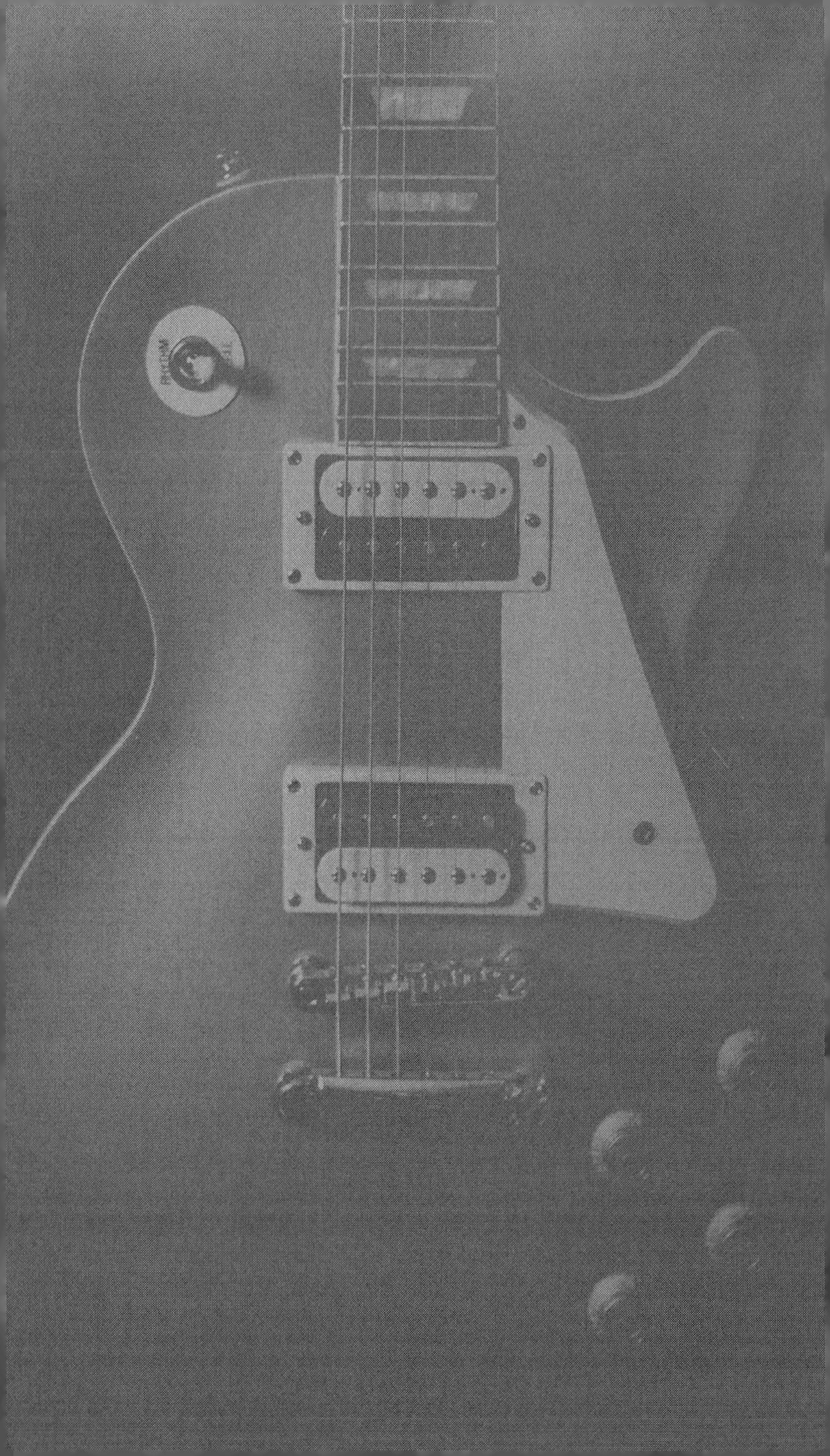

CHAPTER 1

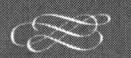

Ian

The bar reeks of old smoke, the smell lingering from a time long ago when a promise of wealth lured men away from their homes and loved ones. The scent has penetrated the ancient hardwood, invading every splinter and mixing with the aromas of desperation, hope, and dreams. Dings and scratches mar the unpolished planks and, given the history of the area, old spurs and boot heels seem the most likely culprits for the divots. This building dates back to the 1800's and, as I take it all in, I can only imagine the goings on here during the Gold Rush days.

Though this area of the country held the most famous promise of fortune hidden within rocks, it wasn't the first place in the US of A that alluded riches to men seeking a better life. Library shelves now hold endless books that chronicle the stories of those prospectors. A few were lucky, but most lost everything including the families they left behind. As I walk over to the bar I'm somehow certain that at least some of the dark and blotchy masses on the floor were bloodstains beneath the soles of my boots. That's what happens when money is your God. It'll expose a man's rotten core as well as the bullets in his gun.

Love of money is the root of all evil.

My momma recited those words to me over and over when my daddy left us to travel. His job required he was gone more than he was home, but Momma said he loved money. His absence meant little to me. I had her and, because I hardly saw Daddy, I barely knew him.

The same scene would play out over and over again. Daddy would leave and Momma would cry herself out. Then she'd take my hand and she and I would go to our secret place. It was really her bed but that's what she called it when we were there with the covers pulled over our heads.

I remember more than most would think seeing I was so young when she died. She was my angel and I got to have her all to myself when my daddy was away. As a child, I feared the boogeyman. My room was a dark and scary place when I was alone but, when I was with Momma, I felt safe. I was her confidante and she talked to me like I was her grown-up friend. She'd tell me she was mad at Daddy for going away, then praise him for doing what was best for our family. Then came the anger. She'd throw things and say she didn't need him anymore. I'd hide under the bed when she did that but once the anger was gone she'd tell me to come out. We'd pray together to keep Daddy safe and then go to the kitchen where Momma would fix us a special tea. We'd drink it out of Mamaw's China cups. It was a special brew, Momma said, one to make us sleep. It tasted like the rock candy she bought me on my birthday, but burned as it made its way from my throat to my belly.

I shake off the memory and take in the pretty woman on the stage. Beneath a lone spotlight, she sits on a high-back barstool, her legs crossed, guitar on her lap, and a lone microphone on a stand. Behind her is a barely visible logo on the wall. It's hidden in the shadow she casts, while that same light showcases glimmering, snowy highlights in the dense curtain of blonde hair that falls around her shoulders.

"How long's she been playing here?" I pitch the question to the busty redhead behind the counter. Her ribbed tank top clings to a set of massive tits, and distorts the image on the front of it. As she comes closer to me, I can make out the design. It's the same logo that's on the stage wall—a sunglass-wearing, cigar-smoking bulldog with a spiked collar, and the enormity of her breasts causes the dog's Aviator glasses to bulge big and round right over perky nipples. It's tight and accentuates her full curves. I look over her shoulder at the wait staff on the floor and catch a glimpse of the other waitresses. I feel the corner of my mouth curl into a smile. Sam Weston is marketing his Mad Dogs Run brand for all it's worth.

"Savannah Grace?" The question quirks the woman's arched and penciled brows. A knowing smile fills her glossy, full lips. "About six or seven months."

"Does she play here every night?" I press.

"Nah. Just a couple of nights a week." She leans in toward me, assuring I see more than a glimpse of ample cleavage as she rests her forearm on the bar top. She looks between me and the stage. "You like her?"

"Do you?" I toss back the question.

"Mister, there ain't nobody who don't. Everybody likes Savannah Grace. She packs in the place when she plays, and a packed house means more tips. We all love that." She straightens up to standing, eyeing a few more customers taking seats at the other end of the bar. "So, what can I get ya?"

"Just a Coke. Tall glass. Lots of ice."

"You got it." She turns away, her ass swaying like a back porch swing as she heads to the other patrons. I turn my attention back to the woman on stage.

Savannah Grace. I don't recall Sam telling me her name, just that he wanted me to come hear her sing. She's good, in my opinion. The song she's singing is slow and easy, just like her tone. It's seductive and has a whispery, breathy quality like Diana Krall or Melody Gardot. What I note most is how she engages the audience and draws them in. They're quiet. Almost reverent. They probably don't notice how much they're into her, but that's something I know well from my days with my band, Boundless Hearts. I could play to a crowd but, where I was as lewd as I could get away with, Savannah Grace croons. Some people lean in toward the stage, while others are so relaxed, they recline back in their seats. She's working them good and that's money in the bank for Sam.

"You want to start a tab, darlin'?" The barmaid flips a coaster on the surface in front of me, then places the glass on top.

"Just take this and keep the change." I reach into the front pocket of my jeans and pull out a twenty-dollar bill.

Her brow shoots up. "Thank you."

"You got a name?"

"Jeri," she answers with a flirty smile.

I'm amused. "Short for Geraldine?"

"Nope. Jerilyn. That's the name my mother calls me, but I'm Jeri to everybody else. What about you?"

"Ian."

"Well, it's nice to meet you, Ian. This your first time at Mad Dogs?"

I nod. "I'm supposed to meet Sam here."

Jeri glances over her shoulder at the clock on the wall. "He should be here anytime now. Let me know if you need anything else." She pauses, leans in a little, and flutters her long, fake lashes. "Anything at all."

"I'll do that."

After Jeri turns her attention elsewhere, I pick up my glass. Sweat beads have rolled to the paper coaster causing it to stick to the bottom of the glass. When I pick it up, the cardboard falls and rattles on the bar top. I pick it up and see, again, Sam marketing the brand. I couldn't read the writing on the wall or Jeri's shirt, but on this I can read the tagline; "Where the Music Kicks Ass and Mad Dogs Run." I grin. This is just like Sam. If he were an animal, he'd be a cigar-smoking bulldog.

I reach into my back pocket for my cell phone and check to see if I might have missed Sam's call. Seeing nothing I return my attention to Savannah Grace.

"You all are familiar with this next song and, when I sing it, I dare you not to think about puppies."

Puppies? Confusion pinches my brows but as soon as Savannah hits the first few notes I grin. She's cute and clever, I'll give her that. Sarah McLachlan's song "Angel" has been used in a television commercial to appeal to bleeding hearts who love animals. The soulful sound entices us to donate to help save neglected animals. A low wave of chuckles carries in the air, telling me the association isn't lost on the audience.

"She's something, ain't she?" The thick, low, rumbling baritone is a deeper volume than I'm used to and is accompanied by a heavy-handed slap on my back. "How you doin', Amigo? Gittin' yer fill of our Savannah Grace?"

I nod. "I am. She's pretty good."

"Damn straight, she's good. She wouldn't be singin' at

my bar if she weren't," he emphatically states. He looks around my shoulder. "I see Jeri took care of getting you something to drink. That's good." His expression turns serious. "You feeling alright bein' here? If you ain't then get on home." Sam's concern is rightfully placed. He's my Alcoholics Anonymous sponsor.

"I'm good."

"Good to hear. I'd never be one to tempt a man, but you ain't had no desire or setbacks, and I'm here if you do."

"You don't have to worry. I'm okay. I haven't wanted a drink since the night of my last concert."

"I'm sure a near-death experience has made many a man think on his vices," he says as he nods.

"I'm not going back, Sam. That night scared the shit out of me."

"Everybody's different but I'm the same as you. I ain't had a drink in over thirty years, and I'm here in this bar near every night." He puts an assuring hand on my shoulder. "I gotta check some things in the back. Listen to Savi and I'll be back in a few minutes."

Savi, huh? Seems she's got a nickname.

As Sam disappears, I tune in to Savannah. She somehow looks familiar, but I'm thinking it's her name and her hair. My momma's name was Susannah, and she had long blond hair as well. Images of my momma drift through my thoughts. She was a good woman and a natural-born storyteller. She regaled in dramatic stories of the devils who chased her and the angels who saved her. Many times we hid under makeshift angel wings so the devil couldn't find her. It wasn't until the night I nearly died that I met my mother's demons and an angel who saved me.

Applause cuts through the memories that wound me like a rusty blade and when Savannah Grace drifts into the next song I fall into the melody. She's pretty. Feminine and dainty in her mannerisms, and I watch as she caresses the neck of the guitar with slender fingers. My shoulders relax as I let her voice guide me into the music's gentle waves. She croons a soft rendition of Aerosmith's "Crazy", and its effect unravels the knot between my shoulder blades. I roll my head side to side and savor a brief memory of my band days. We weren't always rock stars. Once we were just a bunch of high school kids who formed a band, and it took us on the ride of a lifetime.

I go crazy, crazy, crazy for you baby ...

I grin. Steven Tyler never sounded so good. As she sings her song and looks over in my direction my body reacts in the way a man does when looking at a beautiful woman. There's something dangerous here because I know one thing for sure; I'm the devil in human form, and Savannah Grace is as close to an angel as I'll ever get.

About the Author

D.D. Lorenzo is an award-winning author of Women's Fiction and Romantic Suspense novels. She loves a good stiletto strut, a killer cup of coffee, and fresh flowers to balance her obsession with anti-heroes. You can find her most days plotting and planning her character's lives from her beach house on the Delaware shore.

To stay up to date with DD's books, please visit her website at www.ddlorenzo.com and sign-up for her newsletter. Want the inside scoop? Join DD's reader group, DDs Diamonds, at www.facebook.com/groups/ddsdiamonds

Stay connected with D.D.

Website:
www.ddlorenzo.net

- facebook.com/ddlorenzo.author
- twitter.com/ddlorenzobooks
- instagram.com/ddlorenzobooks
- pinterest.com/ddlorenzo
- bookbub.com/authors/d-d-lorenzo
- amazon.com/DD-Lorenzo/e/B00GA5ARJ8
- goodreads.com/D_D_Lorenzo

Other Titles by D.D. Lorenzo

Imperfection Series

No Perfect Man (Book One)

No Perfect Time (Book Two)

No Perfect Couple (Book Three)

No Perfect Secret (Book Four)

No Perfect Woman (Book Five)

Standalones

Indiscretion

Multi-Author Series

Twinkle, Twinkle, Little Star: Fragile Flower to Femme Fatale! (Heels, Rhymes & Nursery Crimes Book 3)

Made in the USA
Columbia, SC
24 May 2024